HIPPY

Anthony Harwood

Published by Anthony Harwood

ISBN: 978-0-9567479-0-7

For Mum and Patrice.

They never stop believing.

A

Home. It was a small two-bedroom flat. Two bedrooms because I had been trying to pick up a flatmate for ages. I was hoping to lighten the economic side of things by getting someone to share the costs. No such luck. All the prospective flatmates either left hurriedly without saying a word or stayed a while before saying, "I'll get back to you," and never calling. The funny thing was I thought I was the one who was supposed to do that.

It was fine, though. I could carry the costs with my new job and a little assistance from my mum whenever I needed it. I guess I have been fortunate in that respect. But on coming home tonight I was glad I lived alone. I was tired, cold, smelling badly and damn well dirty. I needed a shower, a mouth wash and after locking my door behind me I headed straight for the bathroom. No arguing about who gets to use it first or getting the flat mate to vacate the smallest room in the flat. One benefit of living alone, I guess.

It was clean as usual. It wasn't exactly a small room, though it was the smallest. From what I have seen it was actually quite large compared to other apartments. Big shower slash bath with plenty of space to admire yourself in the mirror in the vanity cabinet. Not that I do. I'm not that vain. I at least wait until I get to my bedroom before using the full-length mirror to check out my clothes of choice for the day.

Ok, I must seem obsessed with clothes. In truth, I'm not. I have a bad dress sense, constantly wearing black or white. I don't know the latest fashions and I don't know what colours go with what. I just stuff around by saying or thinking things like that. That's why the black. Yes it is always in style, but it is also easy to throw together a mismatch of black pants and black t-shirt to come out looking half decent.

Anyway, I got home, had a shower and got into my pyjama bottoms and dressing gown. No point getting dressed in anything else because I wasn't exactly planning on going anywhere just yet.

I didn't phone the police. What was I to tell them? 'Hello, Police? I was kidnapped by someone I didn't know. Saved by someone else I didn't know so just called Weedy all the same. And I was held in a warehouse of some kind that I couldn't locate if you gave me all the resources in the world.'

Now that was odd. I had managed to find my way home, but I couldn't remember how or where I had actually come from in the first place. I remember walking down the road to my flat, but that was it. Not even the road before that.

I wish I had found out that guys name. I can't just keep calling him 'Weedy'. Isn't that funny? I can't keep calling Weedy Weedy but I can still think of that other loser as Oaf without the slightest remorse. Bastard. Thinking about it, my head started to throb again.

Oh well. Massaging my temples, I switched on the television. Perhaps it will help me to forget today's happenings. I know, I know. I should be more concerned, traumatised. I should be on the phone to the police or a friend blurting out everything I knew. But really, what would be the point? No one would believe I was kidnapped for no apparent reason and then saved by this short guy who out-manoeuvred a huge ox of a guy who was packing a gun. No point at all. So I'll just watch TV. It's probably more realistic than the day I've had.

Then again, I may be wrong with that assumption. Big Brother was on. Reality television at its worst and most unrealistic. Just a bunch of wannabe actors or people wanting to show how pathetic they really are all shoved into one house to talk about sex, masturbation, sex and who is the real bitch – male or female – that should be voted out next. I sometimes wondered who was more pathetic, the people in the house or those that actually wasted money voting to kick them out. What's more is the incessant need for the networks to wager who will be first to have sex in the house.

I flicked through the channels again and failed to find something else to watch. Re-runs of Friends, All Saints and a number of other depressingly stagnant, poorly written and directed soaps that all tell the same stories with very little in the way of a cohesive, long running storyline. Not to mention lacking any appeal or characters that actually encouraged the audience to sympathise or empathise with them. Sometimes I found I spent more time trying to comprehend the point of having a television than actually watching it.

Thankfully, there was a knock on the door. This was certainly surprising as I rarely get visitors. And with me in my dressing gown. This wasn't good. Ah stuff it.

I got up just as the person at the door knocked again. I was admittedly apprehensive. I couldn't exactly remember how I had been kidnapped the first time. Had they come to my door or grabbed me in the street? Was this them again or was it the saviour formerly known as Weedy? I hadn't actually noticed any signs of a break in when I had come home. But what was really bugging me was the massive gap in my memory. It started somewhere before breakfast, had that little flash in the middle and resumed itself until I found myself on the street. A little like someone had been editing bits out of a movie and replacing it with static.

"Who is it," I called.

"It's Sarah," came the response, "Open up!"

Now Sarah was a good friend of mine. We met each other in the second last year of high school. Neither of us was particularly popular. One chemistry class we sat next to each other and just got to talking. Turned out we had that skill in common and just talked away to each other. She was nice enough though I never expected her to drop around unannounced. She usually phones first.

"I warn you I ain't pretty," I called as I finally got in sight of the door.

"You never are," she laughed and I cringed. I hate being reminded of that. Being reminded I am not particularly good looking. In fact I would most likely be better described as geeky. I suppose that's life though. Throws one bad thing at you after another.

I had thought up a new version of Tom Hanks' character saying in Forest Gump. Life is not box of chocolates but instead: 'Life is like a bowl of cherries. All the rotten ones are hidden beneath the surface.'

I opened the door and from what I could tell, it was Sarah. Her shoulder length, red hair was a real mess. She was also covered in a lot of oil and gunk and smelled as bad as I had earlier. She was still smiling, though. That was a good sign.

"Sarah? What happened?"

She stepped inside my flat and I shut the door, locking it, behind her. She turned and looked at me.

"I had the weirdest day. I mean really weird, weirder than I have ever spent with you in my life."

We both laughed at her little joke. She wasn't in shock. If she was, her laugh wouldn't have been so full.

"Would you like to tell me about it," I started saying and she cut me off.

"Yeah I'd love to."

"I was going to say, after you have a shower."

She looked down at her clothes and sighed, "Fine, I'll have a shower first. But I don't have a change of clothes."

Good point. I looked at her again and then decided, "Well we're about the same size, so you can use some of my gear."

She grimaced, "but I look awful in black."

"I do have some other colours."

She nodded, eyeing me uncertainly before heading towards my bathroom, "Well you get the stuff ready and I'll get cleaned up."

I was already moving toward my bedroom as I replied, "Fine, but don't use all the water."

I heard the bathroom door shut behind me and I made it to my room. While looking through my drawers for some "colourful" clothes for Sarah I decided to get dressed myself. It wouldn't be wise to hang around with her whilst in my p.j's. Not that I actually wore them to bed. It was more of a modesty thing, not walking around my apartment in just my underwear or nothing at all, though I'm sure some guys would kill for that opportunity.

I pulled a second pair of black combat pants out from the corner of the room. They smelled, though only slightly, but I loved wearing them for they could hold anything I wanted to carry. Bus timetables and all manner of other things were currently stuffed down the pockets. I picked up my wallet and keys from the bedside and put them in another pocket. I then pulled on a white t-shirt and a black jumper. It was warm but not warm enough to forget a jumper. Then came my boots. Black also with a ring of tartan around the top.

What I chose for Sarah was much more colourful and bright. I chose a pair of my jeans of which were a little too small for me, a deep blue, long-sleeved shirt and a white, woollen jumper I have never worn. If I remembered correctly, she had her docs with her so she wouldn't need to borrow my shoes as well.

I laid the clothes out on the bed for her and got dressed myself. Shortly after I had settled back down in front of the television, Sarah got out of the bathroom.

"The clothes are on my bed," I called, watching the blur of nonsensical images on the screen.

"Thanks," came a distant reply which was followed by a number of soft thuds as she walked down the hall.

She was a quick dresser for she came into the living room shortly after and looked a lot cleaner. Her hair was slicked back with the water from the shower and this made her pale face stand out more in the room lights. Don't get me wrong. They were bad lights but they certainly helped accentuate some of her better facial features.

She idly wandered around to the couch and sat beside me, lifting her legs up to her chest and wrapping her arms around them. She studied the television for a second and then looked at me, "What's on?"

"Nothing, as usual."

"Thought so," she replied and reached for the remote, which sat on the cluttered coffee table in front of the couch, "Means you won't mind me doing this."

The television went off and my eyes continued to watch the blank screen for a few seconds more, just out of habit I guess. So I looked at her and smiled, "So what made your day so weird and how did you get so dirty?"

She gave a little giggle and began her story, "Well it all began like this..."

I won't bore you with her words but will instead create my own version of what happened to her. I hope that's ok with you.

B

Sarah was walking back to the house she shared with her friends on Maraple Drive, not far from my flat. It was after a night out with her friends and she had a mild hangover. The next morning, this morning, after spending the night at her friend's and finally convincing them she would be fine to walk back home without an escort for protection, she made her way home. It was a nice home actually. The outside was almost as "arty" as the inside. The walls were various colours and the mailbox was a mosaic of tiles, toys and a multitude of other objects I couldn't begin to name. Inside was also multi-coloured but had paintings covering the walls and large, old rugs covering the floor. Sculptures filled the areas not taken up by interestingly designed furniture. I always thought it was over the top but I guess, to each his or her own. I had seen a variety of other places like this but this was the weirdest I had seen by far. So she was walking home. According to her it was rather uneventful, at least until she reached the corner of her street.

There was very little that was actually interesting on that corner. It was a vacant lot with a chicken wire fence around it. Inside was just sand with a variety of ugly shrubs growing over it and the many disused pieces of furniture that had been dumped there.

As she was passing, Sarah said the air in front of her began to sizzle. Sounded weird. She told me that she had to stop because the air around her was getting really hot, as if someone had dumped her in a slowly warming furnace. She didn't even think of running. Perhaps she wasn't totally out of the influence of the alcohol because I knew that was probably what I would have done. So Sarah had hung around to see what was going on.

What happened totally surprised both her and me. She said that the actual air seemed to rip. That the fabric and molecules of air were just torn apart and she could see inside it.

I asked her what she saw. She explained that it was mainly a swirl of colours and then went on to list the twenty odd colours that she believed she saw - puce, mauve, tangerine, and so on. Some artists have a knack for knowing all of the names. It seemed that the colours may have been swirling but they had held a general uniform shape. Not quite being able to make it out, and also still being slightly tipsy, she decided to have a closer look.

All she remembers from that point was an image of a short, weedy little guy who had a bad dress sense.

Now, obviously, this grabbed my attention. I thought back to my mysterious saviour and began to question her for certain details I had made note of myself. I questioned her about his dark, curly, red hair, his puppy brown eyes and even a small scar I had noticed on his forehead. I was amazed at the clarity with which I remembered him, when I couldn't recall paying so much attention to him.

She answered positively to all of my questions and so it seemed, we had both met either the same man or a very identical twin. To finally top off my questioning, I asked if he had an odour to him. She asked me what sort and I promptly gave a brand name of cologne. 'Joop!' The strange thing was she remembered the scent, perhaps a better word for it, and that totally confirmed my suspicions.

"Did you get his name," I asked quickly.

She shrugged, "I did but I can't remember it. That's why it was so weird. I just can't remember anything after I got close to the rip except for him," she stopped and eyed me suspiciously, "Besides, how did you know what he looked like?"

I guessed it was time for me to tell my story. The strange thing was that all I could remember was from the point of waking up to the time I left the car park. Everything else before and after was just a blur. A blur of colour to be exact. This certainly had turned out to be a very weird day.

C

Sitting in a pool of blood with nothing to do. It can really get you down sometimes. But, I just look at the brighter side of things - like, it isn't my blood I'm sitting in. I'm not even sure whose blood it is. Hopefully I'll find out soon enough; once I can get my head back into gear. Then again, do I really want to find out who has been leaking copious amounts of their insides? That thought instantly got me worried about whether it would be my insides that would soon be joining those on the floor.

Things are way too fuzzy at present and I have the worst headache you could wish on someone. Despite that, it is worth trying to look around - to see where I am if nothing else, get my bearings. Still blurry but I can make out enough to be sure it's no place I have ever seen before. It's a huge room. And it smells like – I don't know.

Didn't really notice the smell until I was sitting upright and I managed to remember I actually had a nose to smell through. It smells like... I'm not sure... It's that smell you smell when you dissect an animal, which I only did a couple of times in Biology class. But it's not really a smell - more of a feeling, a sense. It's like you can smell the death of the animal. Dry, almost bitter and it makes me feel sick. And that is exactly how I feel. Sick as all hell with that bugger of a headache.

I'm not totally sure how ears work so I can't exactly say I just heard something. I mean there are vibrations in the air that get directed into your inner ear by your lobes and the like but I was simply confusing and aggravating myself as I began to think about it. Whatever the way I actually heard it, I did, but I really can't understand how I registered it as a clunk or a footfall. It was, in fact, both. Someone was coming. I tried to stand up but my legs were tied. I could see that now as my eyes were slowly clearing up. Four of my senses were slowly coming back, but my skin was dead to the world. I must have fallen asleep on my arms or perhaps the bindings had simply cut the circulation, but everything was numb. It could simply have been my nerves.

"You're awake then?"

"No. I'm a sleep crawler," I nearly vomited. Simply opening my mouth, the fumes made me gag. I would have thought the answer to his question was bloody obvious. But some people have a terrible habit of stating things that their own brain should have registered by now. Perhaps he didn't have a brain. That would be so clichéd.

"Don't get smart with me, boy," the person, male I guess; either that or a very unfortunate woman, was getting closer.

I tried turning around. Do you know how hard that is when your arms and feet are tied? Well as you may guess, my luck being what it was,

I fell on to my stomach and face first into the blood. I was wrong. This blood did smell. It was putrid, old. Add that to the ever present smell of death in the air, "You can get -"

"Watch it!"

I could see his face now. Not too clearly but well enough to tell he was almost twice my age. It wasn't his face that worried me, though. He was a big man. No, big was an understatement. This guy was like three oxen. A baby elephant on two legs.

"Maybe next time I should hit you hard enough to knock some sense into ya. I'm up for another round or two."

So that's why I had a headache. That didn't help my mood any. What I said next was not perhaps the smartest thing, but I was angry and getting worse every second. Soon the blood was going to start boiling, "Ooh big man. Taking on someone like me. From behind as well! Untie me and I'll show you I'm not so easy a target."

The guy laughed but there was a hint of uncertainty in his voice. He was hesitant in speaking again. I don't know if he took me seriously and I seriously hope he didn't. It'd be worse than watching a puppy trying to defend itself against a lion. Well, to some that would be extremely amusing. Right now, however, I was not seeing the funny side to anything.

All the same, he kept coming. I wasn't exactly sure what I was going to do, though. All tied up and no where to go.

"So I'm going to have to escape then?"

"Looks that way, huh?"

"Well could you at least tell me where I am? It'd be ever so helpful."

The guy was right beside me now; he seemed willing to play along. I just wanted to know where I was so I could at least not be completely ignorant when I died. God knows I was bad enough when I was alive. I had no chance of getting out of there, well I did but it would take a miracle. Besides, it's the typical bad guy thing to do, give away either the story, their motive, their location. It's called exposition isn't it?

"Like it's going to be of any help to you. Where you're going, it won't matter."

"Huh?"

And then it happened. My great escape, which I really didn't expect to happen. As I said, the chances of it were virtually nonexistent.

A door crashed open on the other side of the room to where the big guy had made his entrance. I tried straining my head around to see who it was. Both a good idea and one my taste buds totally regretted. A mouthful of stale blood was my reward. That and the chance to get a glimpse of someone I had never seen before in my life. What was going on here?

"Get away from him, you lard arsed butthead!"

"Now there's a guy for words," I mumbled.

"Shut up," I couldn't believe it. They had both said it in complete unison.

As if to re-iterate, the 'lard arsed butthead' as he had been called, spat at me, "Runt," and for good measure followed it up with a good hard kick in my gut.

I automatically curled into a foetal position, wheezing for air. All I could manage was a feeble, "Screw you."

By this time the new guy had started his charge into the room.

What the hell made him so special? I could run like that, faster even. Why hadn't the big oaf of a dork kidnapped this other loser? He was a fairly thin guy, too. Easy to take down.

Oaf was so slow to react he didn't even pull his gun out. Instead he shoved his fist into Weedy's face. Not a good thing if Weedy was supposed to be saving me. He went down like a tonne of bricks, though he was obviously lighter than that 'cos his clothes seemed very baggy on him.

My God. I didn't realise what a bad dress sense either of the men had. Weedy was wearing a pair of jeans, obviously baggy with a navy blue cardigan. Who wears cardigans now days? Oaf was wearing a miss-matched business suit. Green jacket with dark blue trousers and a sick yellow tie. If I was wearing those clothes, I'd most likely die of embarrassment before being killed by anyone. If any of my friends were to see me hanging with these two losers I'd be dead for sure. Who was I kidding? What friends, I joked to myself.

While I was wallowing in my fear of being caught with these two I had barely registered what actually had taken place. It seems that Weedy had gotten up and somehow managed to overpower Oaf through a series of energetic foot attacks. Jackie Chan eat your heart out. He was now sitting on the bigger guy's back holding him in a very painful looking arm lock.

"Bravo," I called half-heartedly. The smell, the headache and the horrible taste in my mouth was all getting to me. If I didn't get out of here soon, my clothes would be a mixture of the blood red, my great black stylising and the sickly colour of Oaf's tie. I could already feel the bile rising in my throat.

"A bit more excitement and appreciation would be nice, you know," Weedy was whining. Made me feel a bit better that did.

"Sorry, but I'm lying here in this… Whatever it is. And I have absolutely no idea what the hell is going on. I need some fresh air or I'm going to puke!"

"I'll have you out of here in a short bit, ok?"

A short bit? How long is that? In a short bit I could be choking on my own vomit. Not a nice picture but a fact none the less.

Weedy had already tied up Oaf and untied me whilst I was complaining. Now he was standing over me, folding up the ropes that had bound me, "Ready to go?"

I got up and nearly fell down again. Balance was off, but it should be fine soon enough, "You think I actually want to stay here? Sure, why not? I could just imagine adding some beautiful decor with a dead cow motif. Don't you think that would look nice?" before I could finish, Weedy had started pulling me to the door through which he had come. For such a short fellow he was quite strong.

When we were outside in the fresh air, he stopped and seemed to check both of us for wounds. It was a tad awkward. Feeling I needed to make conversation I spoke up, "Do you really wear that stuff everyday or is it just on special rescue assignments like this one?"

I could tell from the look on his face that he was offended. He moved away and started looking around for something. I grunted angrily to myself and decided to simply walk away so I didn't come off more of a tosser than I already did. Admittedly I was still in a bit of a daze and wasn't exactly thinking clearly. Not to mention the fact that, despite having been unconscious for whoever knows how long, I was feeling extremely tired, like I had been walking for hours.

"Where are you off to?" he called after me.

I turned around, but kept walking backward. I really wasn't in the mood to talk anymore though. I was quite pissed off with what had transpired but also with myself for not being able to handle it all. I thought I was a stronger person than that.

I managed to call back, "Someone has to call the police."

"Uhh."

"Yeah I know. I don't know where I am but I'm sure I'll find my way to a phone."

I turned away to continue my walk. Maybe it was just me being stupid, maybe it was some sort of disassociation from what had just happened but my attitude was all wrong, "I really appreciate what you did, mate, but I really need to just get home, call the police, get cleaned up and have a think about what the hell happened."

No reply. A quick glance over my shoulder revealed he was gone anyway. Odd. Maybe he was some sort of vigilante, on the run from police but doing good deeds whenever he could. He had just saved my life. I stopped. He had. And what did I do for him? Insult him? What sort of an ungrateful, evil person am I?

I guess I could have at least bought him a drink or something. I don't know. I should have done something. But no. I was a prick.

I started walking. I just had to hope I could find my way home from here.

D

When I had finished retelling my own adventure we began to laugh. We were like two excited school girls, which didn't sit too well with me.

I stood up and asked if Sarah wanted a coffee or tea.

"Tea would be great, thanks."

I headed out of the room to the kitchen. I could still see her and talk to her from there.

"So what do you think about it?" I called.

"I don't really know. I was going to put it down to an hallucination until you piped up."

"And how would you have explained the state of your clothes if it had been an hallucination?"

I could hear her smile, "Oh, I'm sure I could think of something."

Coming back into the room with two mugs of tea, I handed one to Sarah. I had put the standard three sugars and milk in mine to her one and black. She took it gratefully, nursing the warm mug in her hands.

She blew on it for a moment before taking a sip, "Ahh. Now that's a drink to warm up the soul," she sighed and shut her eyes, smelling the aroma of her tea.

Now that was odd. I looked around, looking for an explanation that wasn't there. I was just wondering how her taking a sip of her tea could warm my body as well. I mean, it wasn't hot in the room before she had a drink and even if it was, I shouldn't have felt the extra warmth from her drinking like I just had.

"Yes it certainly does warm things up, doesn't it?"

She looked at me with a look of queer suspicion, "What's that supposed to mean? I was just making a comment."

I looked at her, "No, sorry. I didn't mean it that way at all."

She didn't get it. I didn't know how to explain it because I didn't understand it myself. That was until I saw the light. And that wasn't a figure of speech. From the middle of the lounge, just above the coffee table, a small white light pulsed into existence. It was just suspended in the air. It was soon expelling more than white light. Pinks, greens, reds and blues were shooting out in long thin jets.

Sarah dropped her mug and I took a quick glance at where the contents were spilling out onto my clean carpet. She was going to have to pay for the cleaning bill for sure. But my distraction only lasted a second before my eyes were drawn back to the light. Then I was really pissed off. I had dropped my mug as well. We both began to back away from the, well what else could you call it, the light ball.

It was growing. Quite quickly in fact. You couldn't say it wasn't beautiful. You could actually see inside the ball like it was some kind of looking glass. The lights were swirling around inside, with a number of beams shooting forth into my lounge. . Each time I was hit in the eye by one of the beams, I had a strange feeling that I was inside a tunnel. Like a light tunnel that would take me somewhere if I had the guts to follow. Right now I wasn't sure I had. The guts I mean.

Thoughts flashed through my mind. We should run. What is it? What would happen if we tried to touch it? What would it feel like? Did I really buy my mum some stockings for Christmas and would I see that mysterious man again if I did go through the "rip"?

It was Sarah who finally acted first. She stopped her retreat and reached out to the growing ball that was literally spewing out light. I was going to stop her. I had thrown my hand out to grab her but I was too late. I watched as her body seemed to dissolve, not into nothingness or into a liquid but into light. I mean she was still there but not in a solid state. She was like a holographic projection. She turned and looked at me just before she seemed to break up and was pulled into the ball. It was still growing.

"Bugger you girl!" I yelled and decided that I had nothing to lose. Well of course I did have things to lose, but it was one of those heroic times where you need to convince yourself that you had nothing to lose, even though you had your money, family, apartment and more importantly your family jewels, something I consider very important, still intact.

I looked deep into the ball. There was something in there. The lights seemed to take on a form inside the ball but you couldn't quite see what it was. It was getting to be very hot also. I could feel the sweat break out on my body. It was probably a mixture of nerves and heat. I finally, but very slowly, put out my hand toward the light. I had no idea what to expect and I was scared shitless. Figuratively.

As my hand got nearer the ball, the temperature around my body seemed to drop. Not dramatically, it just wasn't so hot any more. It was a beautiful temperature. The most amazing thing was I could feel a breeze and also what felt like the sun beating down on my neck even though all I had behind me was an old lamp and a wall. The inches that separated my fingers from the ball became mere centimetres, until finally, I touched it.

I can't really explain what happened next. I'll try though. When my finger finally touched the ball, it didn't touch anything yet it touched something. I mean, there was nothing to touch but I could still feel something. It was as if two things were trying to occupy the same space, nothingness and solid matter. A small jolt of energy went through my body, but I remained totally still. I couldn't move. I had been paralysed, be it by fear or the forces at work, I didn't know. Then slowly I could feel my body shifting and being pulled towards the ball. The most disconcerting thing was that it happened gradually, bit by bit until all I could "feel" was my mind. It wasn't something I enjoyed. It scared me half to death. Not the actual experience but being alone with my mind, being able to see what it truly was. I didn't like what I saw.

Another jolt of energy, though I didn't feel it inside of me but rather, it was me and I felt the remnants of Myself being pulled, sucked, even called towards the light. That must sound like some spiritual rubbish but that's what it felt like. Someone, or something was calling out to me and my mind had no choice but to go.

And go I did. I could still see; that's what shocked me, although I had no eyes, I could make out shapes, colours and everything else. Perhaps it was a psychic sight. Corny huh?

But I was travelling, flying even. Flying quickly down a long tunnel. But it wasn't a structured tunnel, more a light tunnel that changed colours every few seconds, swirling with bright flashes of white and red. The flashes soon dissolved then reappeared but this time, with shape. I had never seen such a spectacular light show before. Faces, objects, buildings flashed past my "eyes". The faces all seemed very familiar, distantly familiar, like I had seen them in another life. The buildings and objects also seemed familiar but definitely not like any I had seen in our day and age. Castles, old wooden shacks, swords, shields, daggers and the like sped past me as I headed off down the tunnel.

I was totally captivated by the display, literally and figuratively. I had no idea of how to get out and yet I didn't really want to. It was too beautiful. The flashing colours, the faces, everything seemed almost perfect, like heaven yet it still had evil in it. I could feel it. I also saw it in some of the faces that flashed by me. One in particular was of a man, shadowed deeply by massive scars and sunken features. A smile, yet it had no humour in it. Eyes that dug right into your soul, considering my present form I guess it wouldn't have been hard for that. But the dark brown, almost black, eyes stared at me, followed me as I flew on. Then it would come again. But his wasn't the only face to appear over and over.

Another face was that of Weedy. I enjoyed seeing his face. It was handsome in its own funny way. The dark red hair was cut short yet with all the curls, it was longer than it appeared. His soft brown eyes, also watching me, held an admirable kindness and calmness. His smile was genuine and one of welcome and generosity. I noticed again the scar on his forehead. It was only small but it was part of him. What took my notice was at how much I was trying to get a mental image of him stuck in my head. Every time his face would appear to me again my heart would race and I would wonder, is he real, and did I have a heart at that stage.

It felt like hours but must have only been a few minutes before I felt my "self" begin to slow. The images seemed to fade from around me, only to be replaced by swirls of really weird colours. There were no blues or reds or any of the colours I'd ever seen in my life. It was like a whole new rainbow had been created. Colours I couldn't even give names to danced and swirled around one another, mixing, dividing and at times spewing forth from each other. It looked rather gross actually, sort of like watching someone squeeze the brains out of a fish with their bare hands. No, that's not right. It looked like, well, colour being vomited out of another colour.

You had to be there.

I tried not to look as I passed by, but in doing so I failed to see where I was going. I had no idea where I was and less of an idea what would be at the other end. This didn't particularly faze me. I mean, I was already in an awkward enough position as it was, being without a body and all. Anything had to be better than this.

And then everything stopped. I didn't even realise it for the first few seconds, I just stopped moving. There was none of that pressure you normally associate with braking in a car. It's like it just was. So there I was. Hanging, or perhaps, being inside this light tunnel with no idea what the hell was going to happen next. Then it struck me. This wasn't such a strange phenomenon. This has happened before. Well, not totally the same, but something like it. I could vaguely recall something, but it danced at the edge of my memory, not letting me take hold of it. Obviously, it had something to do with my earlier encounter with Oaf and Wimpy. That much was certain, otherwise this was one hell of a coincidence, having two totally whacked out occurrences in the same day. But I wasn't the only one in this situation.

Sarah! God, I'd almost forgotten about her. She had to be somewhere around here, in this tunnel or perhaps through another of those rips. I tried calling out to her, but that was a waste of non-existent breath. I had no vocal cords, thus no voice. Damn! I couldn't see her. Then again, I couldn't see me either. We just weren't physically there.

But I felt something. A familiar warmth. That could only mean one thing; another rip was about to form. Sure enough, right in front of me, the colours seemed to split. Well, more like the colours seemed to stop crossing over that area, as if someone had stuck their hand into a waterfall, stopping the flow from travelling any further downward. It opened gradually at first, but as the rip grew in size, it seemed to tear itself open faster and faster until it was at least the size of a mini-van.

The funny thing was this rip was the opposite to the one that had appeared in my living room. Instead of letting light and colour out, it seemed to suck it in. To add to the differences, what I could see beyond the rip was not a spectacular tunnel of light as I saw earlier, but a rather grey looking place, a building interior perhaps.

It wasn't long before I felt what I knew was coming. The rip began drawing more than just the colours into it. I could feel my "self" being pulled toward it. Moving slowly, it felt like I was being drawn through a pool of really thick goo. That was, however, until I finally reached the rip. As I started to pass through it, everything began to get really heavy, as if I

18

was being weighed down by a gigantic wet towel. The visual sensation was totally different. All I could do was watch as right before my non-existent eyes, my body began to piece itself back together, layer by layer, molecule by molecule.

When it was all over, I took a deep breath and looked up from my now, finally whole body. (And what a fine body it was now that I had it back) What I saw was rather shocking. I mean it was dirty with dust covering absolutely everything. It was a pigsty. Well, it would have been if there was anything in the room, other than the dust of course.

The funny thing was I couldn't shake this feeling that I had been here before. Something was strangely familiar about the room, yet, totally different. Something was missing. Duh, that was stupid, for obviously everything was missing. Then it hit me. This was the warehouse. This was the slaughter room where I had found myself only a few hours earlier, lying in a pool of blood. But everything was gone. No carcasses, no blood, no smell of death and what's more, quite fortunate I might add, no stupid Oaf looking guy to be saved from.

Actually, was that a good thing? I mean, if I needed to be saved, then maybe Weedy would come along and I'd be able to find out what the heck was going on. That was, if he knew what the deal was with the weird light portals and ridiculous images I keep running into.

There was a loud snap from somewhere in the room. The echo lasted for ages in this massive place. From almost directly above me, a huge light was turned on. It was blinding in its intensity. I blinked a number of times and shaded my eyes by cupping my hand along my brow. It helped a little, but I was far from out of the little spot I'd found myself.

It only took a short while for my eyes to adjust. I had always prided myself on my eyes. They could see well, they were always complimented for their colour and they were just brilliant in every other regard. Even if I do say so myself. But once they had adjusted, I let my eyes roam around the now lit room. Not much had changed; excepting the door at the end of the warehouse was open and in it stood a rather burly-looking figure.

"Hello?"

It was worth a try. Heck, it could have been a complete sociopath for all I knew, but it is always a smart idea to start any conversation on a good note.

The response, when it came, was not what I expected.

"You arsehole, gimme that!"

"I'm sorry?"

"Not you. You shut up!"

Weird. But I didn't think I was in any position to be arguing, "Okey-doke"

"Thank you, you Butt-head."

The figure shook a little and then stepped forward. I couldn't see any details as the light behind it was bright as all heck, causing a silhouette effect.

"You are our... Ooof... I mean, you are my prisoner. Stay right where you are and you won't be hurt."

There were two voices. Both rather high pitched, but I could definitely make out two voices now. This was weird. A schizophrenic castrato with a tendency to argue with himself.

"Leave it alone!"

Gross.

The figure heaved to the side, no longer looking at me but the doorframe.

"Umm," I ventured, "are you okay?"

Okay fine, I'm ever the concerned one. Well, that's not exactly true, but right now I was totally lost to what was going on. Hell, if I could get on this guy's good side, then maybe he wouldn't kill me. That was if he didn't kill himself first.

"See, he's not falling for it. You're a complete arsehole. How could you ruin it like this? The boss is gonna be sooooooo angry with you."

"With me? You're the one ruining it! Get out of my way!"

The figure twitched and spun on its heels, almost falling over in the mean time. Okay. I think I know what's going on. It was just a matter of trying out my theory. I mean, I already knew this was a strange place and this guy's behaviour was telling me it is a lot stranger than I originally thought.

I took a couple of steps toward the door, he didn't seem to notice me, but when I noticed he had stopped squirming, I stopped walking.

"Where do you think you're off to?"

"Well, you seem to be having fun all by yourself, so I thought I would go see if I could find my friend. She seems to have gotten lost."

In actuality, I was quite worried about Sarah. She hadn't shown up and for all I knew, she could have been trapped in that psychedelic roller coaster ride that had dropped me off here. There was also a chance she had landed somewhere else on this 'reality', as I call it. I'm hoping the latter conclusion is the correct one, because I don't especially want to go through the light tunnel again too soon. I'm not sure if my metaphysical stomach could handle it.

"Stay right where you are! I told you already, you're our prisoner."

"My prisoner, you incompetent galoot. It's mine, not ours."

I started heading toward the door, slowly this time. He seemed distracted. As long as he remained so, I would be alright. In all truth, I was getting just as annoyed as the second voice. If this guy or whatever it was didn't hurry up and do whatever it was going to do or get out of my way, then I would soon reach the end of my tether. I mean, it was getting ridiculous.

"Why you little..."

Now this is where I thought it started to get funny. The figure began to shake for a few moments and soon began to teeter on it's toes to the point that it was uncomfortable to think about the strain that he would be feeling; if he felt anything at all. Finally, much to my relief, the figure fell flat on its face.

"Now look what you've done!"

"That was your fault this time!"

"Oh, no. You're the one sitting on the gyro! That is the last time I let your ride shotgun!"

This kind of supported my suspicions. There was only one thing remaining to do. I ran over to the now prone man and frisked him. Not once did I feel a pulse, or warmth to the skin. It was quite horrible to touch, but when I finally found the latch on the man's back, I knew it wasn't a man at all. I snapped open a little panel and looked inside.

What I saw was kind of cute. There were two little men dressed in dark business suits brawling with each other in what looked like a tiny control room. They were standing on what appeared to be a view screen; all I could see on it was the tarmac of the warehouse floor. It took them a while to register my presence, but when they did so, they stopped fighting straight away.

"You are our prisoner," this guy was slightly balding, looking like the older of the two, but he also looked like he wasn't all there. That slightly cross-eyed look that, despite all good intentions and the probably presence of brains, implied some sort of screw was loose.

The other guy lashed out and punched him on the arm, "My prisoner! I told you that!"

I didn't need them to start up again, "Listen to me. I am no one's prisoner, alright? I don't care who you are or what you're doing. All I want to know is where I am and how the heck do I get home?"

There was a stunned silence for a moment as the two men looked at each other.

"Well?"

"Umm," it was the younger one, "You're in One's Domain and we, umm, have no idea how you get home. Can we go now?"

I stood up, "Fine. Sure. Go. Whatever."

Both of the little men began scrambling out of their ruined robot and scuttled across the tarmac, disappearing into the shadows of the warehouse.

And so I was alone again. Annoyed, lost, getting a slight headache and wondering where the hell One's Domain is and if there was a train that would get me back to my suburb. I doubted it.

Outside the warehouse door was not the car park that was there last time I was here. Not that I expected it to be. But what was there instead was creepy enough. All I could see as I looked around was one long tunnel with a bright white light somewhere in the distance. Remind you of something? It certainly sent chills down my spine. I didn't particularly want to go into the light just yet, especially when it meant walking down such a sterile and grey looking corridor. It was almost hospital-like in appearance. Even the floor appeared to be covered in linoleum and there was definitely a bad feel about the place.

But it was the corridor or the warehouse, which would lead me nowhere. So into the light I went.

E

Far from that warehouse. Far from any warehouses, to be exact, was another room. More so a cave than a room. Darkness clung to the walls as iron to a magnet. Where shadows did not reach, there was smoke and steam. The only light was a dull red wash that seemed to ebb out of every surface. Spires of twisted, blackened stalagmites reached up from the uneven, scaly ground. Their partners, the stalactites, threatened to drop from the dark ceiling at any moment. Despite the heat, the steam, the depths and enormity of the cave, there was silence. This was Hell in some people's eyes. What lived there was worse than the devil himself.

This was home to someone; something. This was where it lived, where it slept, where it ruled all that was its and that meant everything. It allowed only one other to be in here. That was Grekon, this other. He was weak. He did its bidding only to be rewarded with compliments and life. Cheap pay but perhaps it was more out of fear that Grekon stayed. It liked fear. It was a friend. Never had it felt it to be an enemy for it was always there to help. Fear gave it power over the myriad of minions, those helpless creatures in its domain. It did not care for these minions, there was no need to. But they cared for it. If they did not, they would be shown how little their lives were cared for. That is how fear became its ally.

On this day, it sat alone in what may be considered its home. The steam warmed it, made it sweat. The putrid stench that emanated from its bodily secretions were more pungent than the sulphurous odours that hissed and twirled from every crack in the floor and walls.

But there was something. Something out of place in its domain and this was not liked; or accepted. Someone was there. Someone that had invaded before and had escaped. Now they were back. Yet, not alone. There was another who had also been here before. And yet another, one that had been here longer. One who belonged here; belonged to it. This creature had defied it and it was not happy. But the first had escaped its attempts to destroy him. Now it was the second's turn.

It had seen the second. A her. She was not far and it would have her.

It was not used to not getting what it wanted. Those that had defied him and lived could be counted on one clawed hand and even they would be dealt with sooner or later It had no doubt of that, no fear of them. In fact, it had no fear of anything. It had never known fear, only cruel and unwavering confidence.

It snapped its fingers. From nowhere Grekon seemed to appear. It knew differently of course. Grekon came from wherever it called him. He would always come. If he did not, then Grekon would be no more. It liked having such power.

23

Grekon was on his knee in an instant, genuflecting, showing his love for the mighty being. Large glowing eyes, burning green, looked down on this manservant. A gaunt man, nearing his sixties, in Earth years this was heading toward the twilight years, but not to it. It lived for eternity, at least it planned to. Grekon raised his head and looked at the being before him, refusing to meet his dark eyes. Grekon knew that all that lived there was insanity and that none should ever dare look there, lest they be turned mad. He had seen it happen before and knew it was bound to happen again, but not to him. Not ever.

When it spoke, it was more than just words. There was a depth, a weight behind every letter that would swoop down on you, crushing you, forcing you to succumb to its ultimate will. It took a great man or woman to defy it and Grekon was not such a man. He cowered as he was spoken to.

"Someone is close. I desire them here. Bring them."

"Who, Master?"

"A woman. There," A massive finger, or claw, pointed toward a crystalline pool barely two metres away. It did not steam as all other natural waters would in such heat. It lay still, but far from stagnant. Grekon looked toward the water and found himself looking into what appeared to be another room. Through the murky surface he could make out a woman, young, barely twenty. Attractive with fiery red hair and a look of stubborn consternation on her pretty face. There was attitude in this woman. But it too would succumb to It's will if so desired.

"If it is what you wish, Master, then it is what you shall have. Allow me some time to apprehend this woman. She will be yours within the day.

"Sixteen hours. You bring her here then."

Grekon bowed his head in reverence, "As you wish."

And he was gone. There was only silence left.

F

The corridor was long, I'll give it that. Nothing had changed since I had started walking. Not a change in decor, not a door in sight. I was quickly losing my patience. It was like I was stuck in the middle of a really boring maze that you could never get out of. I mean, this corridor lacked any of the exciting twists and turns one would find in a maze and that made it all the more tedious. I love mazes and thinking about this long boring corridor as a maze is starting to make me lose my fascination. Nothing to be done, I guess, except keep walking.

That was what I was thinking when I finally saw something. In the distance, silhouetted by the light, the source of which I still could not find. Something was standing right in the middle of the corridor only a couple of meters away. My heart began beating faster. I mean this was exciting. There was actually something in this corridor other than me! Wow. I picked up my pace and ran toward this thing. I didn't care if it was dangerous. I just wanted to see what the heck it was. You could imagine how disappointed I was to discover it was only a chair.

A rather ugly looking chair at that. Blue plastic, like you find in most Australian primary schools. Dreadful things. Uncomfortable, squeaky and so short that it you sat on it, you would be wearing your knees as earmuffs. This was an exact copy of those nightmarish little chairs. I let out a small laugh; it was all I could do to stop myself running, screaming back down the corridor.

No, seriously, I bent over to have a closer look. I was very careful when I did this. I wanted to make sure nobody got the jump on me so I kept my eye out for any strange looking figures, of which there were none.

For all the looking and searching I did, I could find absolutely nothing wrong with the chair. So why the hell had it just been dumped in the middle of this dreadful corridor? I knew it wouldn't be of any use to me. I certainly wasn't going to try carrying it. All I wanted to do was find Sarah and get the hell out of this place. But the way things were heading I found that conclusion being harder to achieve with every passing second.

Well, there was no point me hanging around here all day, so I started off down the corridor again. I swear to you, this corridor is the most boring, stupidest, most inconvenient rooms I have ever encountered in my life, and yet I don't think you could really say that about any room.

Another five minutes passed and I saw something. Another silhouette. The light was brighter, making it harder to make it out, but as I drew closer I finally realised what it was. That bastard of a blue plastic chair again. What was the deal with this thing? You can't tell me that someone would just have left it there to keep unsuspecting idiots, not that I'm an idiot, on their toes.

On closer inspection, however, I realised this chair was unlike the other. On this chair was a piece of paper, sticky-taped to the back.

It read, "Sit on me".

Talk about Alice in Wonderland. This would have to be a joke. I vaguely remembered what happened to Alice when she followed the instructions on the mysterious drink and cake that she found. And knowing my luck if I was to start growing, my clothes probably wouldn't and I'd be stark naked for the rest of the day, or week, or however long I was going to be stuck in this place. That wasn't for me. So I kept walking.

And surprise, surprise what do you think happened? That blasted chair appeared ahead of me again! What was I going to have to do to get rid of the damn thing? But this time I seriously had to think about it. The note had been changed.

"Sit down if you want to live".

Hmm. Is this a good thing? I think not. What could I do? I mean, this could be a ruse to get me to sit down which, in turn, may be a very bad thing, then again, it may truthfully be a warning and a guide to help me in which case, and to not sit down would be a very stupid thing to do indeed. And if I ended up dying because I don't listen to the warning, well wouldn't I be a rightful dickhead. So I made a quick decision.

The chair was just as uncomfortable as I remembered the ones in my school being, more so that I was at least twice the height I was when I used to have to sit in the blasted thing. But at least I would be safe, I hope. As I said, I hope. I certainly wasn't prepared for what happened next. The chair bolted straight up from the ground. I grabbed onto the sides of the thing as I felt myself being propelled toward the ceiling. I remember thinking I had definitely made the wrong choice. I closed my eyes in anticipation of being squashed against the roof, counting down in my head to the point of impact, which never came. I got down to negative twenty-five when I realised I had passed straight through the ceiling and was still flying higher into whatever it was I was flying into. I couldn't feel anything, excepting a cold rush of air as I sped ever upward.

I chanced to open my eyes and I still can't decide whether that was a good thing or not. It was beautiful. Lights flashed past me, as if I was in an elevator in the very centre of a gigantic city with all its lights on. Do you know the effect? Just picture a city at night, and then imagine that whooshing past you at two thousand kilometres per hour. Pretty, but as I said, I wasn't sure if it was a good thing. I felt my stomach begin to lurch. It was sickening to see everything move so fast. I've never been one for travelling, always getting carsick and all. This was ten times as bad as any bout of carsickness I'd ever experienced before.

The chair lurched to a sudden, bone shuddering stop. I barely kept my lunch down as I was going up, this instantaneous stop just blew any sense of control I had on my throat. Okay, I won't get to graphic here, but let's just say, I lost my guts. Fortunately projectile vomiting keeps the majority of your clothes pretty clean.

"Oh my God! Look what you did to my dress!"

Uh-oh.

I looked up from my groggy position on the tiny plastic chair.

She was beautiful. Never before had I seen such a gorgeous, perfectly formed woman in my entire life. She seemed to glow with an aura of extreme and absolute beauty. Everything about her drew my attention. It was as if she was the epitome of good looks, and here I was, me, sitting right next to this gorgeous creature. It took a few moments before I realised that her once white, almost shimmering dress and her long, luxurious brown hair were now bespeckled, for lack of a better word, with what used to lie within my stomach. Her face which I could just see as one crafted in heaven and which you would expect to see only a smile of loving warmth held an expression of pure disgust. All at once I felt down right dirty.

"I am so sorry."

"This is what I get for thanks? My God! What kind of a creature are you to do this to the person who just saved your life?" Her bodily movements were becoming quite large and certainly aggressive. Her arms were flailing wildly around her body, she began pacing, no, stomping back and forth looking at what thanks I had unwillingly given her.

"I couldn't help it," I decided to stand up, give me a better grounding, and to make sure she wouldn't send me back down to where I had just come via the same means. I didn't want to go through that sickening experience again.

That's another thing. Why are all the methods of travelling in this place so disorientating and nauseating? It really was beginning to get on my nerves. And now, after causing me to feel so ill in the first place, this woman was yelling at me for something I could not have controlled, no matter how much I tried all because she wanted to save my life. Obviously the price hadn't been worth it. Now how is that supposed to make me feel? I'm as worthless as a simple bath, of which was all she needed to get rid of any of the offending material. But no. She had to take it out on the little pleb who had no idea what the hell was going on in the first place who didn't even realise he needed saving from anything but a long dull corridor which as far as I knew couldn't have caused me any life threatening problems other than to bore me to death.

"You inconsiderate slob! This is one of my nicest dresses and you go and throw up all over it! You disgust me, you filthy, putrid pile of projectile vomit. You big nosed, ugly bag of pathetic shit. You…"

That was going too far! No one insults my nose to my face and gets away with it!

"Back off!" She stopped and glared at me as if I was nothing but a disgusting insect that had just caught her attention, but at least I did have her attention, "Now, who the hell are you and where in God's name am I?"

"And you want me to help you again? What so you can vomit on me again?"

"Shut up! I've had just about enough!"

She closed her mouth.

"Now, again. Who are you and where am I?"

She waited a few moments before answering, perhaps contemplating whether or not to justify my questions with answers.

"Narelle. It's domain."

All right. Not that that made much sense.

"Okay, Narelle," I figured that one was her name, "Who or what is this It?"

She seemed taken aback, shocked that I didn't know who this It was.

"You don't know who it is? Well, you certainly aren't from around here are you?"

"No. I think. No, I know I'm from another dimension, or parallel world or something."

"Ahh. You're one of them. I thought you looked a bit funny."

Her whole demeanour had changed. The anger and disgust had fallen from her eyes and she was now looking at me with a kind of fascination, "I've heard about your kind, but I've never met any of you. There seem to be a few of you around now days, though. What's your name?"

"Scott."

"Funny name too."

I sighed, "You don't know the half of it."

"So what were you doing down there?"

"Where? Oh, you mean that corridor?"

"Corridor? Oh, no, that's the Hall of Inconsequentiality. You don't want to stay there too long. Everyone that's ever gone down there has died of boredom sooner or later."

"No wonder."

"So?"

"So what?"

"So what were you doing down there?"

"Oh. I was teleported to this warehouse at the end of the corridor. I mean, the Hall of Inconsequentiality. Anyways, the only way out of the Warehouse was down that Hall, or so I thought. I've been walking for a fair while now."

"Hmm. Sounds like you were put there on purpose. Not to say that's definite, but just a reading I put into it. I'm good at that, you know. Making different readings to different circumstances. It's a lot of fun, especially when the people involved are totally paranoid."

"Oh, that's nice," great. Another weirdo. Likes toying with people's minds, this one. Sounds like this whole place is full of whackos. Maybe that's why I'm here. I mean, I'm hardly normal. Or at least I don't think I'm very normal. Then again. Who knows, I could be reading too much into my own way of life without actually considering whether or not other people in the world would live like I do. Hmm. In all truth, right now I don't really care. I just wanted to find Sarah and get out, but you already know that. I'll try to refrain from repeating myself, but, hey, who can help it when they are trying to make a point? Question is what point am I trying to make here? That I am getting to the point of being pissed off, or perhaps it's my eagerness to get out of here.

I think I'll shut up now.

"So, where are you off to?"

Her demeanour had become somewhat chirpy. Not that I minded. Heck, having a gorgeous woman like this one liking you can only be a good thing. Or could it?

"Well, I don't quite know. Not knowing where I am exactly really doesn't help me in deciding where I want to be heading. Maybe you could help me."

"Okay. But hold on a second. I need to change."

With that, she snapped her fingers and her body was enveloped in a bright blue light. I watched with awe as her dress changed from the sparkling white number to a nice black, leathery number that gave the distinct impression of someone wanting to go travelling a fair distance. The stiletto-hiking boots finished it off. Now I knew we were in for a long walk.

The light faded and she turned to me, "What do you think?"

I was almost speechless. I did manage a few words though, "Wow. Accentuating. Nice."

She smiled and I swear I could see something sparkle in her eye, "Gee, thanks."

"So, which way do we go?"

"Well, that all depends. What do you want to do?"

"Find a friend of mine and get out of here as soon as possible."

"Fine. Follow me."

Now this was a good thing. Okay, if you're a feminist go to the next paragraph, cause, wow, this leather-clad babe was just too much. She had the perfect swing to her hips and her suit just showed her perfect curvature down to the last. . hmm... last... Damn. There isn't a word. Well, I think you know what I mean. Anyway, it was a glorious sight to behold.

I finally managed to pull my eyes away from that wondrous sight and let them survey my surroundings.

Inside. White walls, candelabras spaced along this new hall I was walking through. When I say hall I mean the big spacious room you find in mansions, not like the corridor I found below. The candelabras sat on an ornately carved stand that I would have craved to have been able to put somewhere in my apartment. Everything here was beautiful. The tapestry that was the carpet was so intricately sewn it was as if I was looking at a length of photographs. In each was a single person. Each person was just as beautiful as Narelle. The ironic thing was that not one of them was blonde. Okay, not all good-looking people are blonde, but to see so many and not a single one being blonde, I just find that really hard to comprehend. But these men and women were all situated in various positions and poses, but usually in an outdoor setting. The sky was blue, the trees and grass green and, when it was present, the water clear as clear could ever be.

Keeping Narelle in my peripheral vision, I kept my eyes on the people in the pictures. Hell, I'm a voyeur. I like watching people, and when they're attractive, all the better.

"Who is this friend of yours that you're looking for? If you don't mind me asking, that is."

"An old school friend. We just got to chatting away one day and we hit it off. We weren't like best of friends or anything, but we were good friends."

"Oh. That sounds really nice. What's their name?"

"Sarah."

"Sarah. It's an okay name I suppose. Is she pretty?"

"Pretty, yes. She's also really funny."

"Funny? She has a funny face?"

"No. I mean in her attitudes and behaviour."

"Oh, that," Narelle didn't seem too concerned with people, other than in their appearance, "What does she look like?"

Now this was hard. I mean, sure it's easy to describe someone you just barely know, but how do you describe someone you've been friends with for ages?

"Well, she has flame red hair. Quite endearing actually, especially when she gets angry. She looks like an absolute monster."

"So she's ugly?" She cut in.

"No. Just a metaphor. She's pretty, as I said. It's just she has these moods sometimes and when she goes off, she goes off. She has very pale skin, despite a couple of freckles here and there over her little nose. We used to tease her about them, but you get past that. Isn't it funny how people do that?"

"Yeah, whatever," there was a short silence. I didn't have much to say to that. Finally she spoke again, "Is she fat?"

"No, definitely not. Actually…" Then I stopped. Not just talking, but walking as well. There on the ground, right in front of me was Weedy. It was a profile shot, a close up so it was lucky I recognised him. But it was definitely him. Not a bad picture either, "Who is that?"

Narelle stopped and turned back. She came over to me and looked down at where I was pointing.

"Oh, that's Bobbie. He hates that name, but we call him that anyway. He prefers Bob. God knows why, it's so vulgar. He's a funny one. Gangly body, awkward proportions and all. But he has a sweet face, and that hair of his. Everyone loves his hair. Shame about his taste in clothes."

"Tell me about it."

"What?"

I looked up at her. She was looking at me already, a bit confused.

"I've met him before."

"You know Bobbie?"

"If that's his name. Yeah, he saved my neck just this afternoon."

"Really? That's not like him. Then again, what is? So how long have you been here?"

"Not too long."

"Since this afternoon?"

"No. This is the second time I've been here as far as I can tell."

She took a step back. She was afraid of something. I could tell not only from looking at her but from her tone of voice when she next spoke, "You're Him, aren't you?"

Now that lost me, "What?"

"You're Him," She started pacing again, "I should have known. God, I'm such an idiot! You're here because of One! Because of Bobbie, too."

"What are you talking about?"

She was looking very anxious, "I shouldn't be talking to you. Shouldn't even be in the same district as you," She stopped pacing and looked at me, "Sorry. I have to go. I can't be here, not with you."

No. I couldn't let her go. She was the only help I had. She knew where to go and everything.

"Narelle! Please, stay. I need your help."

Her eyes said it all, "I'm sorry, Scott. You're on your own from here on. I can't help you," then she added, "It's been fun. Good luck."

Then she was no longer there.

"Well, That's just brilliant!"

This was getting beyond a joke and I was totally pissed off. I was lost, getting hungry and more than a little peeved. I had just lost my only other friend I had met in this place and was still lost as to anything regarding this hellhole.

"Damn it!"

"Not here, thank you."

"Sorry. What?"

I spun around, but there was no one there.

"No damning of anything in this place. It just isn't good sportsmanship. I mean, I don't mind you doing it, but it just isn't good for publicity."

"Who are you?"

"It's me."

"Who?"

"Me!"

I decided to try another tactic, "Where are you?"

"Here."

This was getting me no where, "Where exactly?"

"Why don't you try looking up? No one ever looks up. Makes us feel really lonely, that does."

What did I have to lose?

"That's better. Now, it's good to see a face once in a while."

I couldn't believe it. Right above me was the ugliest painting I had ever seen and right in the middle of a dark and dingy landscape of gnarled trees and grey skies was a little green frog. And it was talking to me. A talking painting of a frog. Now I was definitely losing my mind.

"Nice weather we've been having, don't you think?"

"Um, yeah, sure," what else was I supposed to say?

The frog was surprised, "You really like it do you?"

"I don't see what's wrong with it."

The frog's expression took an abrupt change at that point. It was down right scary. One minute it was one of cheerful hospitality. It was possible that this was the frog the princess kissed. But ever so quickly and so drastically it was as if his face melted and reformed. What replaced that sweet smile was something horrible, evil looking. His eyes were full of dark mirth and his lips had curled up into what could only be read as an evil smirk. His voice had also taken on a more sinister tone.

"Well. Good," the way it said that last word, drawing it out it a croaky, spine chilling way. It certainly had an effect on my nerves. Think Emperor Palpatine in Return of the Jedi using the same word.

The painting began to shake. The frame and everything depicted in the actual picture looked like it had been hit by an earthquake that shot right off the Richter scale. I took a few steps backward. It looked as though it was going to fall. No other painting could have stayed on a wall, let alone a ceiling with that much force shaking it. But it didn't fall. One end of the painting, the bottom end, lowered itself to the ground as if the whole thing was set on massive hinges. It blocked off any chance of passing, leaving me with only one way to go. Back. But I couldn't go back. If this was the way Narelle was taking me to find Sarah, I had to go this way.

Hell, it was only a painting, what could it… I stopped myself in mid thought. This was not only a painting and this world was nothing like my own. How could I know how things worked in the place?

Took me long enough to realise that didn't it?

But what would I do if I were to turn back? I'd be losing my only lead in finding Sarah. Damn it!

32

I shouted it, "Damn it!"

"I told you not to say that!"

The frog was freaky. It had changed dramatically. Not only its facial expression, but its actual body shape and size. It had grown considerably to about half my size and was still growing. It had also begun to feel surer of its hind legs and had taken up a bipedal stance. Sharp spines had begun growing down a ridge that had formed on its now grey green coloured back. This thing was down right evil.

I began to edge my way backward.

The frog-thing stretched out what had become rather powerful looking arms, but they were no longer restrained by the painting's dimensions. Its hand actually reached out of the painting and I knew exactly what would happen next. It took a step forward, placing its powerfully built leg onto the carpet. I did not want to see any more.

I turned and begun bolting back down the hall.

The frog called out to me, "You ain't going anywhere, Human."

Oh, yeah? That's what it thought. I was a pretty good runner and I trusted my legs enough to keep me ahead of the horror that had now emerged fully from the painting.

It wasn't until I felt what must have been one hundred and fifty kilos of frog land on my back that I realised I was sadly mistaken. How could I have even thought I could outrun a giant frog? Especially in this crazy world.

"Now your time is up. One is angry with you and he wants you to suffer!"

No matter how much I struggled, I couldn't get the damn thing off my back. I couldn't see much of it other than its slimy hands that had pinned down my shoulders, but I could certainly smell it. The strange thing was it wasn't the swampy smell I expected. It still smelt of oils and paints, as if it was still the painting.

"You're not taking me anywhere," yeah, that would scare it. Me, the big man, completely incapacitated telling him what to do. I seem to have a tendency to do that. But what else could I do?

Not much at that stage. I felt something whack the back of my head and found myself swimming into darkness.

G

Sitting in a pool of blood with noth… Hang on. I've been here before. Okay, things were different, but I was beginning to see the ironic side to my predicament. Things either go in a straight line or jump off into a circle. I mean, I found myself back at the warehouse originally. Then there were the two hallways I was walking along. Now I find myself in another pool of blood. I know it is blood because I can see quite clearly now. I guess the main difference is I'm not in the warehouse any more, Toto. Sorry dumb joke with very bad timing. I'm not tied up either.

I was actually sitting with my back against a cold, damp stone wall. The only light came from high on a large wooden door. There was a constant dripping in the background, but luckily I was able to block that out.

From what I could tell I was locked in a cell four metres by four metres. No bed, no chair. Just me, the blood and the dull wash of light that seemed to ooze in. I took my time in standing up. I didn't know how long I'd been out, and I knew going slowly would be the best way to avoid a head spin.

The walls were made of large stone, covered in dark moss and dark crevices where the water must have been eating away for decades, if not centuries. The smell in the air was horrific. Must coalesced with rot and that smell of death again.

A shiver raced down my spine. This is definitely not the place I want to end up dying. It certainly wasn't a place I ever expected to find myself in either, but this whole trip was something of a new experience and a time for a lot of firsts to occur. Not a comforting thought. I could only hope Sarah wasn't in a similar predicament and was still somewhat clean. Hell, they were my clothes she was wearing.

"Swing low, sweet chariot, coming for to carry me home."

Such a cool song, so appropriate. I couldn't help myself from singing that one line. I do try to keep in good humour even at the best of times, even if it meant being a complete tosser to do so. Unfortunately the song didn't have much of an affect on my nerves.

In all truth I was damn near shitting myself. God, it was dark, I was soaked through with someone else's blood and I had no way of getting out of here. At least, that's what I thought. I had no real idea if that were true or not. I hadn't tried the door. Maybe these stones and mortar were so rotten through I could dig myself out. Yeah, maybe in a million years or so. But it's worth a try isn't it?

What? Only to escape and be confronted by some other whacked out, psychotic monster of some ungodly fashioning and be killed in a more torturous, painful way than to die here of starvation or whatever else they had in mind for me.

Then again, who was to say that what they had in mind for me wasn't worse than what I had just pictured?

I hate my brain. Too many inconsistencies and so many times I've found myself at a crossroads and never been able to decide which way to go. Then, inevitably, I would end up making the choice at the last moment only to realise it was the wrong one, just because I hadn't taken the time to think it through. All I would end up doing is weighing up the possibilities in my head, most of which have little basis in fact, not that I knew much about the factuality of this place, and then see the evil side of every direction and just sit in the one place, thinking it to be the best option until I'm forced onward. That way I'm left so far behind everyone else I don't seem to fit into anything or in with anyone and I wind up worse of than I was before, but even more so alone, and just as depressed. Great! Now is just the perfect time to start analysing my life and what I've made of myself so far. Aargh!

I was already standing so I know how I did it, but I don't know where the actual impulse came from for what happened next.

My right foot lashed out at the door, the rest of my body twisting to the side. Now this must sound like some kind of pathetic martial arts manoeuvre, but it did happen. Well, this is how I think it happened. As I said, it happened without much thought.

I felt the underside of my foot smack into what I thought may have been the lock on the door, but once it hit, it didn't stop moving. I heard a thunderous cracking sound and almost panicked, thinking I had just snapped my leg in two, but all that milk my Mum had given me as a kid paid off. In a glass I mean.

My leg had totally smashed the lock. The door sprung open and I kept moving sideways. If I didn't act quickly I would find myself in the sideways splits position. Not a good thought, considering I was only able to do the front ways ones, and only then just barely.

I prepared my body to roll side ways, which turned out to hurt even more when I hit the ground. My whole body shuddered with the impact as my left shoulder hit the ground, fortunately my head missed making contact. I brought my legs together and spun my body round into a sitting position. And there I stayed for a few moments, rubbing my now tender shoulder. For all the pain, I think the end result was worth it.

I looked out into the corridor and then slowly managed to get to my feet again. There was nothing out there but a large flaming torch on the wall opposite my door. I could either go right or left.

Now here was another of my dilemmas.

Ah what the hell. Take a chance. I started off down the way to my left. All along the way, I noted the walls were gradually drying, not so affected by the water, which also began to dissipate. The ground also seemed to be sloping upward somewhat.

In other circumstances, this place would be perfect to visit for a tourist attraction.

Like a scared child, I kept my arms up in the boxing ready position, just in case. Who knows what could be lurking further on? I'm not too afraid to admit I was somewhat apprehensive as to where I was heading. I'm sure you would be too, if only you were in this situation and not me. Now wouldn't that be nice.

Just dreams again. I have to keep my mind on the facts and realities of the matter.

So, here I was, in a long dark corridor that was slowly taking me upward and onward to god knows where, trying as hard as I could to look like a trained ninja, though I only studied two years of Tae Kwon Do. But I did manage to come first in all but one of my tournaments and only then because the guy I was fighting was twice my weight and about two feet taller. Evil looking nitwit, he was.

"One wants him dead. He asked me to do it personally."

I froze in my tracks. Someone was coming.

"I'm the one who caught him. It should be my honour."

And the blasted frog thing too. I was in deep trouble.

They were still some distance away; I couldn't even see them yet. But they were coming straight for me and I had no where to go.

"Oh, if you really want to, then, please, be my guest."

"Why, thank you. I really appreciate that. Are you sure that One won't mind?"

"Heavens, no. I was only fibbing about him telling me to do it personally. It was actually Grekon who told me. He sees nobody but Grekon these days."

"True, true. That man needs more light."

"Which? Grekon or One?"

"Both."

The two on-comers started laughing. I could make out a pair of rather hefty looking shadows far in the distance. I was not looking forward to meeting the frog thing again. My only choice was to go backward, down to the cells. But it could be a dead end, and once they see my door broken then they're bound to send out a search party.

This is so frustrating! But, exciting at the same time, I have to admit. Okay, fine. Back we go.

I started slowly at first, trying not to make too much noise. But as I got further away, I quickened my pace. Bad idea.

I reached a rather clumsy fast walk, not to mention a slick bit of moss that covered the stone I was trying to traverse. At least I hoped it was moss. My foot disappeared from underneath me and I went sailing into the air, feet first. This was going to hurt when I landed.

And that was just it. The way of this world. I didn't land. I was literally hurtling down the corridor. I watched in amazement as my cell door seemed to fly past me, knowing full well that it was me doing the flying. This was truly an uncanny experience. Seconds passed, and they soon grew into minutes and I was still racing through the air. I didn't dare move a muscle, in case it sent me off on a totally new trajectory, say into the wall.

This was starting to get ridiculous. This just wasn't possible. Besides, I can't afford to keep flying all night, I have to find Sarah.

I dared myself to look down. It took a while, but I managed. The ground was still there, but it was getting further away. It was still travelling on that downward angle, where as I seemed to be heading on a more horizontal axis. That meant...

I looked up and I realised my worries were justified. The ceiling was getting closer and closer to my head. It was already only a foot away, but any minute now I would have a huge graze where my head used to be. Not good. Not good at all.

Slowly, I pulled on the sleeves of my jumper and gradually worked them down over my hands. Once I had done this, I lifted my hands to the ceilings, palms up. Maybe this would help slow me down, or perhaps lower me to the ground.

The material over my hand jerked as it made contact with the stone. I pushed upward and pushed my body down. No effect. I was still getting closer. It was as if I was on some sort of invisible conveyer belt that was working against my every strain to push me away from the roof.

This was the end for me. At least it could be. Maybe I was floating on something. Maybe there was something below me holding me up. I tried to wriggle my body, roll it, do anything, keeping my hands firmly pressed against the ceiling. No matter where I moved, nothing changed. I was still getting higher, or at least the roof was getting lower. Bugger! This was getting way beyond a joke.

I felt my heart pumping faster. My palms and my jumper sleeves had become a mixture of sweat and slime. I was very close to panicking.

And then there was no more ceiling.

It didn't just vanish. I saw the end of it flash by me. All I could see now was darkness above me. I was out of danger. I let out a sigh of relief and found myself meeting a wall face on.

Well the truth of it was that my legs actually struck the wall first. The rest of my body acted like a catapult and swung up, ramming my nose and the rest of my face into a very gooey and thankfully soft and soggy-type stone wall. The breath was knocked out of me as were any thoughts I may have had. It didn't exactly hurt, but it was a shock. I guess that's why I didn't even think about grabbing onto something.

I began to peel backwards off the wall until I was falling again, back first. I tried to grab for the wall, but it was too late. It wouldn't be too far a fall. Maybe eight feet.

Eight feet? God! That was going to hurt! But when I actually landed, it wasn't onto the stone I had expected. I was completely immersed in the cold, murky water that had taken up residence at this end of the dungeon corridor, as only I could imagine it was called. One long corridor was like any other, but in each of my cases, they were a lot more trouble than they were worth.

After a few moments of struggling to get upright, I found a foot hold on the ground beneath the surface of the water, and made a much uncoordinated effort at standing. It worked, luckily and I found myself thigh deep in the liquid.

I couldn't see much. There was light coming from somewhere, I wasn't quite sure where, but it seemed to illuminate the whole place.

Looking around, I found that 'place' was a good word for it. It was no longer the corridor I was in before. But it wasn't exactly a room either. The walls were covered in slime, so was my face for that matter. I quickly wiped it off and tried to flick it from my hands. But as I did so, I couldn't help noticing how bright it looked.

I took a closer look. The slime seemed to be glowing. Letting off its own light. Very fortunate for me, and not to mention, nice of nature to have created this kind of stuff. Otherwise I'd be stuck in a totally pitch black place.

But I wasn't and I shouldn't be thinking of what could have been. What I had to concentrate on now was getting out of here, as if there had been anything else on my mind since arriving in this alternate dimension or whatever it is.

I examined the slime-covered walls a little more closely. I was surrounded on all sides, not including the nutty corridor I had just flown down, not that I want to chance going back there for the frog thing and his companion.

It looked as though my only way out was up. The stone should be easy enough to break, to make handholds, to climb up. Then again, what happens when the walls start to dry up as I get higher? I'd be stuffed if I got caught up there with no where to go.

I kicked around the water as I threw around my limited options. But something began to strike me as being wrong. Something was out of place and I couldn't quite put my finger on it. A noise, perhaps.

I listened. There was something. Water. It seemed to be splashing somewhere, but very distant sounding. Like a waterfall. I let my eyes roam but there was no sign of anything like a waterfall. Not even a trickle.

I looked down at the flowing water as it swirled around me legs. That's it! The water was flowing. It was moving somewhere. Therefore it had to be coming from somewhere and, I hoped, going somewhere. It must go somewhere, if it didn't, the room would be flooding already. But the actual water level hadn't seemed to have changed since my arrival. So, there must be a grill or grating or something along one of these walls, something to let me out.

I bent over slightly and let my hands roam over the slime covered walls below the water line. It was funny, the slime still stuck under the water. I expected it to have come off with the flow of the water. Powerful stuff.

I hadn't found anything along the wall opposite the corridor entrance so I moved around to the next one. I was about halfway along when my hand found a rather large gap in the stone work. From the pull of the water, I could tell this was where the water was disappearing to. The sounds of the waterfall were also much more distinct here. It had to be just on the other side of the wall.

Using my leg, I tried to find out how big the actual hole was. Lucky for me, it seemed to be large enough to be able to fit my scrawny little frame through.

Preparing myself, I took a deep breath and jumped down into the water.

Okay, I know I was already in the water, but I'm not really comfortable with water, and when it's dirty I just can't stand the stuff. So, the only way I could really go under was to force myself, which meant jumping. So I did.

When I was under, I kept my eyes closed. My hands felt out in front of me, but they didn't have to do much work. I felt the tug of the current pull my body toward the gap and let it take me, making sure I would enter head first rather than sideways. I felt things float by me as I swam through the water, kicking with my feet in a frog like fashion and feeling the walls to make sure I was heading in the right direction with my hands.

My breath was beginning to run out. I was starting to blow bubbles in the water. Surely it couldn't be that much further. I heard the waterfall as if it were in the next room. Seconds went by and still there was no end to the water. I felt myself starting to panic. Being claustrophobic to a small degree and hating water in the first place, this predicament probably amounts to something worse than staying in that cell. I was beginning to feel the walls close around me. I know that they weren't, at least I hope they weren't. But everything was getting tighter. My chest was pounding now. The breath almost totally out. My kicking had become more excited and wild. That's not to say I was going anywhere faster, it just got to be very erratic, perhaps slowing me down. I really wasn't in the mood for caring. I just wanted to get to that waterfall. It had to be somewhere. Somewhere close by. If it wasn't I was going to lose it. My breath, my calm, my life! This was hell on earth, or where ever the Hell I am.

39

My breath was gone. It had run out. I was screwed. My legs stopped kicking so much as flailing in the water. I started crawling along the walls with my hands clawing at them and with every grasp having a piece of stone and slime coming off in them. Everything was so tight. So close. So threatening. So dark. I was going to die here. I'm going to die here! Get me out of here!

My head broke surface. I could only tell by the lack of watery sensation around it. I still had my eyes squeezed shut. But I wasn't going to take that moment for granted. I opened my nose and mouth and let the air rush in. It was air! I was going to live!

The roar of the waterfall was clear in my ears. It was so loud. It must have been a huge fall.

Oh no! A huge fall. I really hadn't thought this whole thing through at all. My eyes shot open just in time to see the bottom of the body of water I was about to fall into. It was metres away! If it's not one thing, it's another. I can't dive for Christ's sake!

No matter. I shoved my arms forward into a diving position mid air and felt myself start to descend head first toward the water below.

It didn't take long before I felt the impact. Hardly a perfect dive, but it had gotten me safely and painlessly out of my predicament. I found myself bobbing to the surface of the water and I shook my head, clearing the water from my hair, and in turn, clearing the hair from my eyes.

My hair has always been a problem. Mum always says I should get it cut. I always disagree, or if I do finally decide to get it cut, I always leave the fringe. Not always a good thing, like now. It always falls into my eyes at the most inopportune moments, especially when wet. Mind you, I guess everyone's does that. So what am I complaining about? Nothing right now. I was alive and I had to be happy for that.

Continuing my side doggy-paddle, I managed to get away from the spray of the waterfall and make my way to the edge of a large lake. A fresh cool breeze was blowing now.

I was finally outside. It was quite nice actually. On the far banks, I could see a line of large trees. The sky above was bright blue with only the odd pure white cloud breaking that gorgeous colour. Far in the distance I could see a large mountain range. The highest of the peaks were covered in snow. Everything was beautiful. Even the lake, further from the outlet of whatever it was the gunky crap was coming from and from where I had just emerged, was crystal clear.

It could hardly be eco-friendly. Either somebody should get onto the repair men to fix that hole, stopping that polluting leak from destroying this lovely landscape, or that is a purpose built sewage disposal. Neither of the theories had much appeal, especially considering I had just swum through it all. But it definitely wouldn't be doing the water into which it was flowing much good.

Then again, everything was beautiful. And that outlet must have been decades if not centuries old considering the decay and all. So maybe it isn't so bad on the environment after all. No, logically that can't be right.

Well, something wasn't right. No, correct that. Nothing is right about this place. Nothing has any consistency. Nothing flowed properly with the nature of things and the logic of the way I live back in the real world. This place just wasn't real. It couldn't be. I mean, moving paintings? Tiny men controlling robots? Blue chairs flying through the sky? It's all a load of crock! Where is it all coming from and who the heck is creating it?

"Need a hand?"

I looked up. The voice was familiar, and when I saw the face I almost screamed with joy. Not that I'm a screamer or anything.

It was Bob. Or Weedy as I used to know him. He was sitting on a rock ledge just over the outlet I had swum from. In his hand was a piece of rope he had extended toward me.

"Thanks," It was all I could say. I was still slightly out of breath from my ordeal and a little self-conscious after the way I had treated him the last time.

He didn't seem to care, "You certainly have a knack for showing up in the weirdest of places."

"Tell me about it," I grabbed onto the rope and he pulled me over to a rocky bank, just beside the outlet. I wearily pulled myself up, with a little help from Weedy.

When I was up and out of the water, I sat with my back against the wall, breathing heavily, "I wouldn't recommend that ride to anyone."

He laughed, making the rest of the journey down from his ledge to meet me, "I'll take your word for it."

I looked him over. He had changed. Clothes I mean. He was dressed in what would definitely be called my style. Black. Black jeans, Black t-shirt, tight against his not too badly muscled chest. Funny really. In the cardigan I could have sworn he had no body beneath it. Now, seeing him close up, he had quite a good build, albeit slim. His face was speckled with water from the spray of the waterfall.

"So what brings you to this lovely lake?" I had to find out what this coincidental meeting was about, if indeed it was coincidental.

He sighed and looked out over the horizon.

"I saw Narelle. Well, actually, she found me and couldn't keep her mouth shut."

We both laughed at that. I didn't know her well, but it was the sort of impression I had about her. A real gossip queen.

"She told me you were here. Well, not here specifically, but here as in back in this domain."

Which brings me to my next point, "What domain? Who is this It or One everyone is talking about?"

He looked at me. In his eyes there was a weariness, as if this It fellow was draining him of something, energy, hope, I don't know. Just something.

"He now owns this place. It's all his. But it comes at a price. To us. We, the people of this domain, have been made his slaves. We do his dirty work. If ever there is a visitor, we're sent to torture them. If ever someone disobeys the slightest of orders, they are hunted down and killed. Like me. I am targeted by his main guard elite. He absolutely loathes me. But he hasn't got me yet, and I am planning to never let him. But, basically, he is a tyrant. Working the people to the bone for his own wealth and prosperity."

Very eloquently put, "What about a revolution or something?"

"No one has the strength to go against him. Not with his force of will. He is a very powerful monster and we just can't do it."

"Not even together?"

Bob shook his head, "It would be pointless. Getting enough support from those strong enough to stand against his guards let alone him is nigh on impossible. Besides, he would crush us with his will. I've seen it done in person. I was just lucky to have escaped. Now I'm living in constant fear of being caught. They search for me every day and night. Sometimes they get close, other times they seem not to even be there. But I know they are and I have to keep being as careful as I can," he looked away, "It's getting to the point that I'm growing so tired of it all. I don't want to live my life on the run. It's not what I saw myself doing. It's not what anyone should be doing. People should be free. Free to live as they please, within reason of course. But free of the oppression that my people face, without the ability to have fun or any semblance of a happy life."

I didn't even consider this sort of thing to be happening. Here I was stating that this place couldn't be real, and yet the people of this unreal world are facing very real problems that are faced on my own world. What kind of an arsehole am I? And who the hell am I to be able to turn around and say what is real and what isn't? Geez, I'm a prick!

H

Sarah had no idea where she was or how she got there. It wasn't the first time she had found herself in that same predicament since her arrival on this freaky world. After the initial shock of the funny tunnel she had arrived through and finding herself stuck in a warehouse very similar to the computer room she had found herself in only hours before.

It was amazing how quickly her recollection of her last visit had come back to her. No sooner had she stepped into the warehouse than the whole blur of confusing and totally weird memories came swarming in. She recalled that her first visit had brought her to a large room, very much like a warehouse, but lined along the floor was a series of desks with computer terminals on them. At each terminal had been a fuzzy little mouse. They didn't do anything except run through their tiny treadmills.

When she had left the tunnel this time, it was exactly the same room. But this time the floor was covered in blood and it smelled just like a slaughterhouse, which, in fact, was what it was as she found out when that funny looking man had turned on the lights.

It reminded her very much of Scott's story. The warehouse he had found himself in and met those two guys. She had to admit, it did look like a scuffle had taken place, but there was no sign of those two others Scott had mentioned.

As for where she was now, looking around didn't help her a bit. The room was large. But it wasn't what you would call a room. More of a hall, or cavern. The floor was covered with thick plush carpets. Sarah could swear that the very carpet was glowing a dull red. The walls remained bare for the most part, but looked very rocky. Smooth, but somehow naturally formed, like a cave. They were also black as black could ever be. The ceiling she just couldn't see. It seemed to extend forever above her, disappearing into darkness.

There was no source of light, but everything had a reddish hue to it. That's why she was almost certain it was the floor giving off the light. Nothing else seemed capable of doing it.

As far as she could tell she was very much alone. The strange part, well parts, was that she had arrived here in a blink of an eye. Just appeared from that dreadful little corridor she had been walking down for about twenty minutes. The other part was that it wasn't a holding cell of any sort. How did she know? There was an exit. Just a large, smooth and very symmetrical hole in one of the walls.

She had to give the designer their due. It was a very nice looking place, another thing that led her to believe it wasn't a cell. But if it wasn't a cell, what was it? She had encountered two other ugly things that had

43

tried to capture her but were miserably unsuccessful. She had originally thought her transportation here was one of their stupid ideas. But it just seemed too nice for such a couple of losers, unless, of course, they stuffed up again.

It wasn't her concern. All she wanted to do was find Scott and get back home. The place was nice enough to visit, but she certainly wouldn't want to stay here. She would go mad. Anyone who lived here would have to be totally mad with all the inconsistencies and weirdness.

No matter. She started toward the exit. But just as she got within two feet of it, someone appeared around the corner. An elderly guy, drawn face, sad looking. She jolted to a stop out of both fright and courtesy. If the guy wanted in, he could have right of way, it didn't bother her.

The man stopped also. But he wasn't shocked by her presence, or their near collision.

He nodded his head slightly, "Welcome. The master will see you shortly. But until then wishes that you abide here until such a time as desired."

Okay, he talked funny, "Sorry. I've got to be somewhere."

A sly little smile crept across the man's face, "Oh, I doubt that."

"What do you mean by that? And what's it to you anyway?"

"It matters not. You are here. My job is done. The master will see you soon. Farewell."

He began to turn, but Sarah wasn't quite finished. She was very much a feminist and wanted to be treated as equal as any man. She didn't think that this guy had just given her that courtesy and she was not happy. Pissed off would probably be a better word for it.

"Excuse me! I don't have time to play your stupid little games. I have someone to find and some place to be. As far as I'm concerned your little 'master' can go screw himself, at least until both he and you learn some manners and some common decency where it comes to your people skills. As far as I can see, you both seem to be lacking."

The man was still for a moment. Then Sarah heard what sounded like a chuckle. This man was chuckling at her.

"How dare you!"

The man turned to look at her. There was a fire in his eyes that had not been there before. This man was evil, "Oh I dare very much. You have no power here. The One and I will treat you as we deem fit. We don't concern ourselves with your petty thoughts and feelings," As he spoke, he seemed to be getting taller, larger. Physically he hadn't changed, yet his presence was looming over her, "You are nothing! You will do as you're told!"

She cleared her throat and nodded, unable to speak.

The menace totally disappeared from the man, "Good. Glad you see it my way."

He turned and left her standing, frozen to the spot.

I

My clothes had started to dry in the sun, not to mention the help from the warm rock I was sitting on. Bob had tucked his rope on his hip and we both sat, legs dangled over the ledge, me admiring the view, him listening to my story of what had happened since my arrival.

Once I had finished, he nodded and looked back at the outlet I had been spewed from.

"Not unusual."

That's all he had to say. Not unusual? Hmm. He must lead a very exciting life. There was a brief silence between us, until I spoke, "Sorry."

He looked at me, puzzled, "What for?"

"Being such an idiot last time we met. I had no idea what was going on. I was a bit shaken by the whole thing."

Another silence. He broke it this time.

"Your world sounds nice. Not so much happening. No need to keep a look out for One's men. It didn't used to be like this. It once used to be peaceful."

I looked around at the horizon. It seemed very peaceful here, I told him so.

"Oh, yeah, there are a few places that seem not to have been affected so badly by it. But he's still here. Just look at the waterfall. All that muck."

I knew about that muck, but I had a look anyway.

"It's his doing. It's a miracle this place has remained the same. But it's probably only a matter of time before he gets to it. He's like that, you know."

"And there's nothing that can be done?"

He shook his head, "If there is, I haven't found it, yet."

"Exactly! Yet! Not yet. You will one day. I'm sure of it."

He looked at me for a moment and then burst out laughing.

"What?"

"You're one to talk. You've been so pessimistic since I've known you. Now you decide to take the positive approach."

"Just trying to help."

He looked down at the water. His mood had turned rather melancholy, "I know. I appreciate that, but, I don't know. Things are just getting out of hand."

I started to get up. This guy needed motivation and I was going to give it to him, "Well sitting on your arse here isn't going help one little bit. We have to get moving, looking. For one I have to find Sarah. For another, you have to find a way to overcome this demon that's causing so much trouble in your world."

He grabbed my elbow.

"Hey, let go."

"Sit down," he hissed.

"I'm just…"

"Sit down," there was something in his voice that made me obey him. It wasn't that he was trying to be authoritarian. There was something wrong. I looked over at him. His eyes were alert. His whole body was taut, like I could hit him with an axe and he would shatter into a billion pieces. Not that I ever would. Bob was way too nice for that. I shook the idea out of my head. But that didn't help the situation any.

Bob was seriously looking concerned.

"What is it," I whispered.

"They're here."

"Who?"

"Your two friends from the dungeon."

What? Damn. They'd come after me. We should have run. Idiot!

"Where are they?"

He pointed to the bank on the other side of the lake. I had to strain to see, but when I did, I could just make out two figures moving through the bushes just by the shore. The Frog thing was big. At least I had thought so, but his companion was huge! If those two things found us, we'd be dead meat.

Mmmm. Meat. That reminds me, I'm getting hungry. Later.

I looked around again, looking at my more immediate surroundings more closely. It wasn't until my eyes fell across the waterfall that an idea came to mind.

There is always a gap below the falls where people hide from scavengers, monsters or whatever else is coming after them. At least in the movies there is. Who's to say it wouldn't be the case here. And even if it weren't, the physical state of the rock would surely allow us to make one in a matter of moments if we concentrated on clawing it out.

It was worth a look.

I nudged Bob slightly and he looked at me out of the corner of his eye.

"The waterfall. Follow me. Slowly," I whispered it and he nodded, not totally understanding what I was getting at.

I moved ever so slowly, lowering myself back into the water. I didn't make one splash, I was proud. But I was annoyed that my clothes were getting wet again. Bob followed closely behind.

Pushing off from the rocks, I swam slowly toward the falls and finally swam beneath them.

Behind the wall of water and whatever else was sloshing down, I found I was right. There was a little nook in which we could hide. It was quite deep actually, but you wouldn't have been able to tell if you didn't get close enough or look hard enough. It was like a mirage, a fake wall.

Bob bobbed to the surface beside me. He was covered in muck. His hair, his face, everything. It was just like the muck I had found on the walls in that dungeon. There was a difference, however, in the fact that this stuff wasn't glowing. It just made him look like a swamp monster. I knew that I had exactly the same stuff covering me. It wasn't that it was sticky or anything. I could just feel it there, like mud. Not an unpleasant feeling. But when I looked at Bob, well, it was just so funny. Fortunately, I stopped myself from laughing, which wasn't hard under the circumstances, and indicated the gap to Bob.

"Great!" he whispered, patting me on the shoulder.

We both eased ourselves onto the rock that was the floor to the alcove like thing. Once there we moved as far back as we could. I could still see the waterfalls and the noise was deafening, but if it kept us safe, it was worth it.

Our only problem was that we couldn't see our assailants. How were we supposed to know if they had left or not? I guess all we could do was wait. But if we stayed too long, we were bound to catch pneumonia. It was freezing. The walls were damp; the water was still spraying on us. It was really bad conditions, but it was all we had.

It wasn't until I saw something moving in the water below the falls that I began to get worried. There was something big swimming around out there, probably looking, and scouting for us.

Of course! What an idiot I was. Gee, I've been saying that a lot lately.

The frog thing! He could obviously swim, better than either of us. I'd probably just condemned us by trapping us with water. If the Frog looked out of the water, he would see us for sure.

I held my breath subconsciously. I was scared. I squashed against the wall as tightly as I could, hoping it would make me invisible. I couldn't see what Bob was doing. He was behind me, but I could feel him and his body heat. He was like me, hardly breathing. He probably knew of the danger.

Shut up! Of course he knew of the danger! He's not a total witless imbecile!

It was then that I saw two large eyes pop out of the water. The Frog had finally broken the surface and was looking for us.

We were dead.

The eyes made a small circle in the water as if surveying the surroundings. It then blinked, slowly and rather sickly it looked, not that it was sickly, but that it was rather grotesque to watch.

The eyes began to rise. Soon his head was out of the water. He was still looking around, as if he hadn't seen us. He must be toying with us. If he was, I was far from amused. But even if he had, I couldn't be totally sure that he might not have actually seen us. So I didn't move. Not one inch. Nor did Bob as far as I could tell.

The frog's eyes seemed to roll around in their sockets, searching, watching everything. But he still didn't acknowledge our presence. This was ridiculous. I almost believed he hadn't seen us when he started to swim toward our little nook.

He was getting closer, slowly as if to retain some sense of stealth. Why? Had he seen us or not?!

"He is not here, my dear fellow. He must have run deeper into the woods like a chicken without a head. He will not get far. He is confused, alone. He will be easy prey."

It was the frog's companion. It sounded like he was standing just above us, on the ledge perhaps. He had to yell to get over the roar of the falls, but we could still make out his every word.

"Ok," the frog didn't sound too enthusiastic about leaving, but he dove back under the water and I watched as his form moved out from under the waterfall.

I was both offended by the other guy's words as well as glad. They thought I was alone. That I was afraid. But their association of me and a headless chicken was down right rude.

I read way too much into someone's opinion. An opinion of someone I don't like for god's sake. Geez. I need to loosen up a bit.

It was a few moments before I felt Bob moving beside me. I decided it was time to do the same. I allowed myself to start breathing normally again. What a relief that was. I looked over at Bob and was surprised he had disappeared.

"Bob?"

I almost jumped when two white floating eyes seemed to appear out of nowhere and look at me. They disappeared for a moment and came back into existence.

"What happened to you?"

The eyes tilted mid air. Their alignment was perfect, however.

"What are you talking about?"

It was amazing. His mouth had pulled the Cheshire Cat routine. Everything was so Alice in Wonderland. First there was nothing. Okay this isn't anything religious or scientific, just an observation. Then his mouth was there. At least his teeth and tongue were and then they vanished again.

"You're like invisible."

"Nah, it's just the mud. How else do you think the Burjon couldn't see us?"

"Burjon?"

"That thing out there. I think they've gone. Let's go."

As he moved to stand between myself and the waterfall, I realised what he said was right. He was covered entirely in that muddy stuff. It made him practically invisible against the black background of the cave.

48

I looked down at my legs. I was completely covered in the same gunk. We had both been camouflaged against the wall. Was that great luck or what?

I guess I had to count myself lucky that the Burjon hadn't seen my eyes staring at him. I would have been dead if he had. But that's another time line.

Bob jumped into the water. I followed suit. Coming to the surface again, I noticed he was heading back to the same ledge as we had sat before. What could I do but follow him. I did so, pulling myself out of the water. He was standing, so I did too.

Some of the muck had been washed of him, but there were still patches of mud over his clothes and skin. I had to presume I was in the same condition.

"Won't be a tick," he said to me. With that he did exactly as Narelle had done when I had thrown up on her dress. Only this time, he came out with a nice pair of black, close fitting, straight leg corduroy pants and another tight fitting black t-shirt. But this shirt was ribbed in such a way as it looked like it was some sort of armour, padded or something. I don't know for sure, but it looked cool. Over that he wore a forest green button up shirt that he left unbuttoned on the front. Cool clothes. I made a mental note to never insult a guy on his clothes without checking his whole wardrobe first. That done I began to feel really jealous.

I mean, here I was, standing by a lake covered in mud and totally drenched clothes. I envied this guy and whatever powers he had.

He must have noticed I looked uncomfortable because he said, "Need a change of clothes?"

"Yeah, know where I can get some?"

He stood thinking for a moment and finally said, "Here, take mine."

With that, he snapped his fingers and my clothes vanished. In their place was what he had just been wearing. The shirt was baggier on me, which made me feel a little self conscious, but the rest of it was just about right. But Bob wasn't without. He was now wearing a nice pair of purple velvet trousers that looked brilliant. With that was a purplish floral type button up shirt which, in itself, was tight so he had no need for an undershirt like I was now wearing. He, again, looked good.

"What's with your powers?"

"Don't even bother trying to over rate them. They're crap."

"How so?"

"It's all appearance based. We can't do any real magic. All we can do is change clothes and appearance or whatever else to do with looks. My race is totally vain. I can't stand it. Some of them, like Narelle, don't worry too much about what they look like, but others are so avid about their appearance it really pisses me off. That's why I stay away from them most of the time. Doesn't mean I can escape my heritage though."

I still couldn't see a negative side to his powers. Why was he complaining, "Still sounds like a cool power to have."

"If you're so self indulgent and arrogant, yeah. But, that's not for me."

Oops. He must think I'm vain if I can't see that. Oh well, what can I do? It's part of me. That's who I am, though I don't really think I'm that vain at all. But to each his or her own and if he thinks me vain, so be it.

I hope he doesn't, though.

"Anyway, we should get a move on. They may come back," he may be right. They could come back and I might be somewhat vain, but I don't show it that much do I? I guess I do with all this clothes crap. Hey, can I help it if I like good clothes? I just wish I could wear them all.

See!! I'm not vain. Can't you only be vain if you think you're great? What does vain mean anyway? Damn. I should have listened to my grandmother. I should carry a dictionary so I can look up the meaning of words. Ah well, I should know what vain means anyway.

See!!! I'm not vain. I can keep finding flaws in my nature!

Shut up!!!

God I'm full of it sometimes!

I have to get a move on if I am to find Sarah and get home. That reminds me. What time is it?

I looked at my watch. Oh my God. It was two thirty in the morning. We have been here for over six hours!

Strange thing is I'm not tired. Probably comes from being knocked out so much. But I heard that being knocked out doesn't affect your body clock. Then again, it must do, look at coma patients and stuff. They'd have to readjust to the time when they wake up again.

I do feel sorry for people in that situation. Not only because of the body clock situation, but they miss so much without even knowing it. What's worse is the family and friends that also have to endure it. It's so sad. But I guess there are many different reasons for it and one day, the doctors will find new ways to get people to come out of those deep sleeps.

We can only hope.

Well, now I'm on a negative note. Hmm.

"Let's go," it was all I could say.

J

We followed the rock ledge around until we came to the shore of the lake. From here I could get a good look at the dungeon walls. What I saw was breath taking. I hadn't just come out of a dungeon. What I had been escaping from was a gorgeous looking castle. It must have reached up for miles.

In truth it looked to be about sixty stories high, but that was huge. The grey stone walls were smooth and curving creating a picturesque image of something I only imagined I would see in a movie or my dreams. The spires seemed to twist around one another, but never touched the central spire that was the thickest and tallest of them all. On the very top of that tower was what appeared to be a high set of battlements. I could just make out a number of shapes moving around on top. I wasn't sure if they would be able to see us or not, but if they could, it would probably take them hours to get anyone to come after us.

That sort of made the architecture of the castle totally illogical, but as with all things of this world, I found myself thinking, what's new?

"Who lives there?"

"That is Its home. He lives somewhere inside there. That is why you were brought here. He was wanting you dead and he doesn't trust anyone to do his important dirty work."

"But those two guys were arguing that they were going to kill me."

"Firstly, how do you know it was you they were talking about?"

"Well," I was going to have to think about this one, "The Burjon said he had found me and he wanted the honour to be his."

"It could have been any of the other prisoners down there. They may have chanced across your broken door and then sent out the alarm. And secondly, it was Grekon who had told them to kill who ever it was they were going to kill. That basically means that whomever they were going to kill was not important enough for One to deal with personally. But both yourself and your friend are far too important to be wiped out by those incompetent twits, he wouldn't dare risk it."

"Why? Why are we so important?"

"You're visitors. You aren't his people. He has no real control over you. Sure he can do things to you. Burn you, cut off your arms and legs. Physical things. But nothing mental. He can't control your minds and that scares him."

And I was supposed to be comforted by that fact? Physical harm seems a lot worse than the mental kind at this point in time, "Still sounds like he can do a fair amount of damage."

"In this world, the physical means very little to what is really going on inside the mind of an individual. What you see, a lot of it is just illusion. I thought you would have realised that by now."

He was joking right, "You're joking right?"

He bent over and picked up a stone, "Why would I be? This whole place is an illusion. There aren't really any mountains over there. It's a wall. It's the boundary of the castle. The outside wall. Beyond that is wasteland. Past that wall there are only a few minor spots where they are closed off, creating a range of different, usually deadly environments that he can torment his people with. You've been to some of them already."

"The warehouses?"

"Yes! Those were only two of the thousands of places he has set up out there."

"So what's with the rock?"

He looked at the stone in his hand. Then he looked a little embarrassed, "I thought I was going to have to prove to you that the mountains were only an illusion. Sorry."

I shrugged, "You can still show me if you want."

He nodded and pulled his arm back. He had a rather powerful throw. I watched the rock fly through the sky for a fair distance before it finally hit the sky. Literally. It hit what appeared to be a clear patch of blue, but what was obviously a wall and bounced right off it. It was a fair distance away still, but it gave me an idea of how big this place really was.

"So how did I get here from the warehouse?"

"Narelle told me about the corridor you were walking down."

"Oh the Inconsequentiality one?"

"That's the one. That's one of three similar tunnels. They totally circumnavigate the globe. You can walk forever but you won't really be going anywhere. Anyway, it just so happened Narelle brought you out of it while you were in the boundaries of this city. From then on in, you've been inside this place."

"Well, finally I am getting an idea of what is really going on here."

"It's not hard once you learn the details, is it?"

"But do you have any idea how I get home?"

He shook his head but didn't say a word.

He probably didn't even know how I got here in the first place. Well, I couldn't say he hadn't been a big help. For one that would be totally rude. Secondly, he had saved my life before and three, at least now I knew what the situation was. It's better than being totally in the dark. The only question remaining was what to do now. Well, okay there was also that of where do we go. But with one I'm sure would come the other.

"So what do we do now?"

He looked at me and shrugged, "I don't know. I don't know how to get you home, I don't know who would. I'm sorry."

"Hey, no, that's fine," I lied, "I was talking about what to do to keep away from the goons and to find Sarah."

"Oh. Um. Well, I haven't heard anything about her. Are you sure she's here?"

Good point, "Umm. No. But if I'm here, wouldn't she be?"

"Well even if she was, she could be anywhere."

This guy's tone had turned totally pessimistic.

"Well it can't hurt to look. Surely the bad guys would have gone after her. If they want me so badly, they would sure as hell want her."

"Good point."

"If there was only a way to find out if those guys knew anything or not."

Bob looked at me. His eyes were wide.

"I have an idea."

"Great! What is it?"

"Come with me. We have to go into the city."

Now that was just suicide. His pessimistic side had probably just gotten a total hold on him.

"Are you out of your mind? If we go in there they'll get us."

"Yeah, but we'll have a better way of knowing if Sarah is here or not. Besides, where else can we go?"

"True."

I didn't really mind going back into the city. I just wanted to be sure he had a justifiable reason for doing so. Hell, a few monster things couldn't scare me. Yeah, and you already know I lie through my teeth sometimes. So what?

We followed the shoreline and headed away from the lake. I lost sight of the castle every so often as we started moving through the trees but I had a vague idea of which way we were heading and how close we were getting.

It took us around half an hour to finally reach the gates of the city and once there, I don't know how I can describe it. It was just incredible. They were huge. Everything in this place seemed to be totally out of proportion. Rather than the same dull grey wall I had seen as we had walked around to the gates, the actual wall rose up to form a sort of battlement on top. Below this was a set of two large wooden doors. Each was carved with intricate designs. The weird thing, and there always was in this place, was the fact that every time I blinked, the designs would change. Not totally every time, but back and forth. One moment what I saw was leaves and trees, a beautiful design. But when I blinked, it was horrible. There were faces on that door, screaming, in agonising pain. It made my gut churn every time I looked at it. Thankfully, my attention was turned elsewhere only moments after the doors came into line of sight.

In front of the doors, or gates or hell passages or whatever they were, was a giant man. He was hardly a giant as he would have been only eight-foot tall. A giant would be over twenty-foot tall. No, this man was just very tall.

He wore a form of medieval armour. The majority of the covering looked to be made of silver chain, though of course it wasn't true silver, it was clearly polished often. The various plates that covered the chain mail were something else. It looked to be gold or bronze, but, once again, it wasn't what it appeared to be. There was another quality to it. I can't say what it was, not that I was a metallurgist or whatever it is that studies rocks. The plates were fashioned into rather cool looking designs. The breastplate of this man looked like a huge wolf's head. Its teeth were bared and the look in its eyes was one of pure evil. Oh, I could tell this because we decided to approach the guy. Or should I say, Bob decided to approach.

He had turned his attention our way, as if to look us over. When he spoke, his voice was as deep as the Grand Canyon; unfortunately it was not as beautiful. It was a rather chilling experience to listen to him, "What?"

Okay, good question. I decided to throw it back at him, "What?"

Bob nudged me with his elbow, a signal to keep my mouth shut.

"We wish to gain entry to the city."

"And what were you doing outside the city?"

Bob's demeanour totally changed at that point. He took a couple of steps toward the big guy in the cool armour and stopped legs apart and crossed his arms. I have no idea what he was trying to do, but the stance he had adopted looked as though he was trying to put himself above the guard.

"Giving you a reason to have a job."

The guard changed his stance also. He leant back against the doors, crossing both his arms and his right foot over his left. It looked as if he was totally bored with Bob. Strange.

"If it weren't for people like you I wouldn't need this job, I could be an accountant."

Bob yawned and brought his hand up to his eyes, rubbing them as if he were tired.

"Only an accountant? You don't seem to have high aspirations. Maybe you're better suited for this job."

The guard turned his body to the side, leaning against the wall with his elbow. His hand supported his head. He gave us both a quick look over and then turned his attention to the nails on his other hand.

Now that was pure and simple vanity.

"This job passes my time adequately. It also gives me some financial stability. One such as yourself couldn't understand that, being a wanderer and all."

A wanderer? Ahh, he must have gotten that impression with us being outside the city.

Bob strode over to stand just beside the big guy and copied his position. This time, he looked directly at the guy. It was like a chess game. Each person taking on a different stance. Strong move, that one.

"It surely lacks a lot of the excitement I encounter in my kind of work. I'm surprised you receive payment at all with the amount of work you do."

The big guy didn't move. Instead, he smiled. It was a huge smile, friendly and full of humour. It's amazing how much a smile can change a face. He had gone from being a sour, beef of a man to a large cuddly bear type figure.

"Not bad, Bob. Not bad at all. We both need a lot of work, though."

Bob stood on his own two feet and smiled also, "Yes, but it's been a long time."

"Too long."

Okay. I get it. Bob knows this guy. That was just a traditional banter between the two. I still don't understand why the hell he didn't just say, "Hi," and get it over with. I was beginning to wonder where the actual conversation was heading. I mean, it is quite possible that it was some kind of password thing or just a way of gaining entry. It could also have been a ploy of Bob's to get us inside. It sounds kind of stupid to think it was just a little banter between friends. Then again, it's good to see that Bob still has a few good friends of his own. I mean that in the sense that with everything he has experienced because of this it guy, he still has friends he can joke with.

Certainly beneficial in keeping him away from suicide, not that he'd even be thinking about that. It was good to see him happy, none the less.

"So what brings you here?"

"My friend and I," he indicated me, "Need to get inside. We've got some important business to attend to."

"Hmm. Important business. It wouldn't have anything to do with you know who?"

A sly little smile crossed Bob's face, "Maybe, maybe not."

The big guy knocked on the door once. It started to swing open rather slowly, "Just take care of yourself."

At least I knew this guy was on our side.

Bob indicated for me to follow. As I passed the big guy I nodded my head in greeting. He copied my movement.

"Thanks," It was all I could say.

"Good luck."

We walked into the city and I could hardly believe my eyes. It was incredible! Everything was so dingy, dirty. I couldn't understand how anyone could survive in such squalor.

As if reading my mind, Bob spoke to me, "Don't worry. Their homes are kept a lot cleaner. They just don't have time to keep the rest of the city clean, what with the so called jobs It gives to them."

So their homes were clean, their sanctuaries. I could understand that. My bedroom was always my sanctuary when I lived with my folks. I could always go in there and veg-out. Here, it seemed to be the only place they could get away from the dirty and depressing world It had created for them. Even then I wasn't totally sure how far or deeply he affected the lives of these people. Looking at their faces, they were far from happy. Even the children, not one smile could I see. They sat on the curbs of the cobbled streets and looked so glum. It was a horrible visage.

The ironic thing was that my sanctuary, or my bedroom as I call it, was completely the opposite. A mess. Clothes strewn everywhere, maybe the odd chocolate bar wrapper, piles of paper and books. I find that mess comforting. Then again the streets at home are generally clean. I guess it is a sense of reverse psychology.

I looked down the main street of the city. As far as I could tell, it led straight to the castle, which stood out like a gigantic glowing gem in a pile of refuse. Horses and carts were being walked, ridden or driven down this street, the people clung mainly to footpaths, carrying various bundles, going about their business, afraid to even look at one another let alone speak. As they walked past me, I couldn't help feeling sorry for each and every one of them.

Such depression, such gloom. I was amazed they hadn't tried to revolt against this horrible state of being. Then I was reminded of this It's power over them. They had no choice from the sounds of it. They had to live this way, regardless of what they wanted.

And then my mind was set.

This could not go on. These people shouldn't have to suffer for another's well being or wealth. These people needed liberation and freedom. It wasn't hard to come to that conclusion. But when it came to the idea of what I could do to help them, well, my mind decided to go blank. I had no idea what I could do. In some ways I was just as helpless as they were, but of course I was much more fortunate. I could leave this place some how and return to my own world, a more tolerant and equal world, though there is still plenty of corruption, bias and conflict, but hey, it wasn't a part of our everyday life as this was. Then again, there are thousands of people on my planet living in these conditions, this hard life that I wouldn't even dare try to imagine myself living. I wouldn't last an hour.

God. These people need help and I am willing to do all I can to give it to them.

With that in mind, I set my posture and started to stride toward the castle.

Well, I tried to. Bob grabbed my shoulder and yanked me backwards.

"Where do you think you're going?"

I pointed at the castle, "There."

"Fine. But if you're going to walk like that down the middle of the road, you've got Buckley's chance of reaching it alive. There are guards everywhere. If they spot you doing that, you're dead."

Good point. I told him so.

"Okay, so what do we do?"

He indicated the sidewalk, "Stick to the paths, look down at your feet and don't ever look up. Ever."

Sounded easy. In practice however, it is a lot harder. I hadn't walked more than five meters when I nearly bumped into a lamp post. I couldn't see where I was going, where anyone else was or anything. It was very disconcerting, not to mention the fact that it gave me a horrible sense of being totally vulnerable. If anyone decided to jump me they'd have no problem at all. I wouldn't see them coming and I'd be such an easy target.

I felt my body begin to tense slightly, instinctively of course. I felt Bob's elbow in my side.

"Loosen up."

"I can't. I hate this."

"Get used to it. These people have."

"Hmm," I groaned.

Only minutes later I bumped into one of the passing people. It was only a shoulder bump, "Sorry."

The other person didn't say a word. Ooh, I couldn't stand living in a place like this. Fine, they weren't too polite, but it wasn't their choosing. I continued for only a brief moment when I felt a hand on my shoulder. But it didn't stop right there. It forcefully flung me to my left, turning me around as I did so. I knew this one was not Bob. My back hit a wall and I slid down it to land heavily on my butt. I managed to keep my head down, but that didn't stop my eyes from wandering. I saw the ugliest pair of feet I have ever seen in my life.

Corns, blisters, cuts, calluses, scars, warts, everything you could think of as gross covered these feet and they were so dirty. The long, over-grown nails were black from gathering grit. Hair covered a large portion of the upper side and I didn't want to know what lay underneath.

I watched these feet as they came toward me. I could see Bob's feet in my peripheral vision but they were slowly disappearing into the crowd. But there was no crowd. That was the funny thing. No one had stopped to watch. They just continued to walk. Obviously Bob had chosen to do the same thing.

Sure enough, these ugly feet were coming straight toward me. I was hoping that they were just idly walking around, but no, not with my luck.

I started to rise to my feet, keeping my head down the whole time, but I never made it on my own. The same hand I had felt on my shoulder earlier grasped onto the front of my shirt. I didn't even want to think where that hand had been, but there was very little I could do about it without causing a real problem, not that I didn't have one already. It pulled me away from the wall until I could feel and smell the horrible breath of whatever it was that was holding me. I didn't struggle. I let it treat me like a rag doll.

"Did I say you stand?"

Its voice was gruff, what I would imagine an Ogre's voice to sound like. Its accent was harsh, guttural even as if his grasp on English was very limited but he had another tongue he could speak in.

I didn't say a word. I didn't know what I should do. Should I speak when I'm spoken to, was the question rhetorical or should I remain like a total useless fool and let it do to me what it saw fit?

I could see its chin now. It was covered in stubble, the hair thick and wiry. The kind of strands that when you tried to shave would tear your face up before letting go of it. But the skin I could see underneath the hair was a very dark tanned colour. Wrinkled and tough looking, like a hide. More of the same hair on its chin was hanging down over its shoulders, long and unkempt and black as charcoal.

It grunted at me. Again, I could smell it as well as feel it. Maybe one thing I could help this world with was toothpaste. They damn well needed it.

"You funny looker. You come with me."

Uh-oh. I was getting in deeper even though I wasn't doing anything. And funny looking? What was that supposed to mean? Was he saying I'm ugly? Or good looking, which in his standards I really don't want to think about it. But why the hell does everything come down to looks? It's always looks. What someone looks like has a huge impact on people, and obviously monsters and the way I looked was definitely helping my situation any. Now this creature was taking advantage of my appearance! My appearance, for God's sake! I had no say over my face and this bloody creature was discriminating against me because of the strangeness that is my face! This was pissing me right off.

I could feel my blood start to boil. I was really mad at that. I hate when people or things make appearance an issue. It shouldn't have to be and because I'm not the greatest looking people should know that I would make a deal of it! God, what ugly person doesn't? I don't give into that crap of beauty is in the Eye of the Beholder or it's not what's on the outside that matters. It's all bullshit. And the worst thing about all this, as I said before, is that we can't define what we look like! I hated this creature, not because of its looks, though I guess I was very judgemental and discriminating myself on that account…

Bugger! Now I'm a hypocrite.

"Aaaaaaaah."

Ooops. I didn't mean to let that out.

I was pushed away from the creature and lifted off my feet.

"You say something?"

"Yes," I'd blown it already, may as well finish the job. I looked up at the thing that was holding me. Yes, it was quite hideous but with my hypocrisy in mind I didn't let that phase me so much. It was time to not be so judgemental of everything, "I said, Aaaaaaaah. I didn't mean to but I did, is that okay?"

The creature was obviously confused. I could see it in its big green eyes, "I guess so."

That was not the response I was expecting.

"The others don't speak, but you do. You funnier than I thought."

"Would you mind putting me down?"

It laughed a rather demented little laugh, "Nup."

"Thank you," but I didn't move. This creature had said he would put me down but hadn't. All he had done was adopt a stupid little smile that seemed to light up his whole face. It was like he was playing some kind of game, "Well?"

He laughed again, "I said I don't mind. Don't mean I will."

Great, he was playing a game. I thought for a moment for the right kind of wording to get him to do what I wanted, "Will you put me down now, please?"

He thought about it a moment and nodded, doing as I had asked. Once my feet were on the ground, he let go of me. I straightened my clothes and looked back at him. He was regarding me with a rather innocent looking tilt of his head.

"Thank you."

"Welcome," I looked into his eyes. They were almost totally devoid of anything. Well, that wasn't true. There was a spark of something in there. An inner smile. Yes, that's what it was. This creature was smiling on the inside, as well as the out. He definitely wasn't all there, but he was there as a young child is.

I extended my hand to him, "Hi, my name is Scott."

He regarded my hand for a moment then took it in his own grimy hand, "Hi, my name is Tom."

"Hello, Tom. What do you do here?"

"Nothing. What do you do here?"

You had to admit, beyond his rather grotesque exterior, Tom was rather endearing. His nose was squashed and piggish, his large bushy eyebrows sat on large bone ridges that overshadowed his bright green eyes. His tough skin gave him a slight appearance of a brown elephant or something with a similar texture. And his ears. They were rather large, but they looked more like satellite dishes than ears. It was his eyelashes that stood out the most. Most girls I know would have killed for lashes like those Tom had.

I wasn't sure how to answer his question, though. I still wasn't sure if he was 'controlled' by It or not. Everything he sees may be sent straight back to it for all I know. Then again, he could be harmless.

"I'm here to help everyone."

"Help?"

"To make them happy again, to make them talk to each other as I am to you."

"Ooh," he nodded enthusiastically, "Good."

"Made a new friend I see," it was Bob. He had found his way back.

"Yes, I thought I'd lost one there for a moment," I said to him. I know the tone of my voice said what I was implying.

He merely smiled at me, "Nah, I'd never leave you alone in this place. I was just trying to look inconspicuous so I'd be able to initiate a surprise attack."

"Yeah, okay."

Tom was looking between the two of us, "Who is he?"

"He's a friend of mine, Tom. His name is Bob."

"Bob?"

"Bob."

"Okay, Bob."

"Say, Tom, do you think you could help us?"

The big child-like creature smiled at Bob, "Yes."

"Do you know of any way we can get into the castle?"

Tom let out a little laugh, "Yes."

"Could you show us?"

Tom was nearly ecstatic, "Yes!"

I knew what he was laughing at. He was playing his game again. It was like he enjoyed getting the people all hopeful only to dash their spirits by telling them everything they had asked was totally pointless unless you know how to word it the correct way. Smart kid, but annoying too.

"Tom," he turned to look at me, his eyes were glowing with joy, "Will you show us the way you know into the castle when we ask you to?"

He stopped for a moment and nodded at me, "Yup!"

"Will it take long to get there?"

"Nup."

"What do you say, Bob? Shall we go now or wait till nightfall?"

"I suggest we go now. If we leave it too long, who knows what will happen to your friend."

He was right, "Tom, please show us your way into the castle."

We followed Tom down the main street. So much for not drawing attention to ourselves. He was jumping and leaping all over the place. Bob and I had adopted the same posturing as we had before, but Tom was too excited to walk properly. At least he wasn't singing. I wasn't sure if I wanted to hear that kind of noise.

We were getting closer to the castle, but along the way, I had begun seeing what looked to be patrol units. Three men in each group, they carried these funny looking weapons. I wasn't sure if they were supposed to be fired, swung, thrown or what. But either way I didn't want to get into a fight with these blokes. They were rather serious looking and I'm sure they would be just as serious in a fight to the point of being glad to die for it. I was no where near that serious about fighting, thus I didn't even want to look at these guys much in case I drew their attention.

Okay, so I held my head up a bit more than before, that's how I could see the patrols. I wasn't in the mood to walk into people or light poles. I just wanted to reach the castle in the quickest and safest way.

Fortunately it wasn't a very long walk to the castle. It wasn't too much longer before I could see the gates that led into the courtyard within the outer castle walls. But here, the streets were rather cluttered. There were hundreds of people, selling, buying, and working. It was like a market place. That would make it easier for us to hide in the crowd, but it would also make it harder to spot any patrols if ever they came by.

I noticed that the people here held their heads a little higher, almost to the point of looking normal, but still stooped and they still refused to look at one another. I took the risk and lifted my head more. Bob was doing the same but we remained silent.

Following Tom wasn't going to be a problem. He was clearing a path in the people, not always peacefully either. In some cases, he knocked people to the ground, or almost flattened them. I can only guess it was sort of the way he had knocked me over earlier as I saw he was grabbing onto people's shoulders to push himself upward into the sky. The only problem was that in following Tom, we could draw attention to ourselves. I mean, who in this city would even dare follow such a large creature, so blatantly, especially if they could see what he was doing to the people he was passing.

There wasn't much we could do about it really, so we continued on our way. We followed him around the street until he led us into a small alleyway. From the looks of it, it was a dark and dingy place. The walls were covered in grime and the floor was wet and puddled. Rubbish lay strewn everywhere as if this alley was the meeting point of every little piece of discarded rubbish in the city. We waited a few moments after he had moved into the alley before we walked in, otherwise we would look far too conspicuous. He was almost to the other end when we got half way, but he stopped. He looked back at us and pointed at a set of garbage bins that sat against the wall.

"There it is. That's the way."

Okay. Sure. A couple of bins? Hmm.

"How do you mean, Tom?"

"In there. Go through there."

"What's in there, Tom?"

We had reached him by this point. Looking at the bins, there was absolutely nothing extraordinary about them. They could hardly be a gateway into the city. Then again, anything is possible.

"The castle. It's in there," he looked around for a moment, "I gotta go. Hope you find the castle. Bye!"

He turned to leave, "You have to go? Why?"

Tom turned back and pointed down the end of the alley, "They're coming."

I looked to where he was pointing. He was right. They were coming. A patrol of those serious looking men had stopped at the other end of the alley and were looking toward us. They weren't moving, just waiting.

I knew it was best for Tom to go, "Thanks Tom. You've been a great help."

"Bye, Scott. Bye, Bob."

With that, he disappeared out of the alley.

Bob, who had remained silent the whole time, stayed that way. He was eyeing the bins with a slight consternation.

"What is it?"

"I don't want to get inside a bin."

"If it's the only way in."

"There has to be another way."

I looked back at the patrol. They had started moving. Only slowly, but they had their weapons ready.

"I don't care, Bob. The patrol is coming and I don't think we have time to find out."

K

I grabbed the lid off a bin and looked inside. Nothing but rubbish. I put the lid back on and tried another.

Wow. Inside was a glowing ball of light. Just like the one I had seen appear in my living room. It had to be another transporter thingy to get us inside.

"Halt!"

It was one of the patrol men.

"Bob, get inside."

"I don't want to."

I was a bit more forceful this time, "Get inside!"

He looked at me, then the patrol. They had started to jog toward us now. I think that set his mind. He put one leg inside and promptly dematerialised before my eyes. Just as Sarah had back in my apartment.

Something whizzed by me. I looked at the patrol. One of the men's weapons was glowing. I could tell he had just fired by the smoke that was rising from it. Another of the men had raised his weapon toward me and was preparing to fire. I saw a small flash of light and my arms rose to my head to protect it, not that it would do any good. Or so I thought. I heard a clang and something hit my arm, but by no means was it as painful as I thought it would be. When I opened my eyes again, I realised why. The trashcan lid I was holding had ricocheted the projectile, knocking the can back to hit my arm. I had saved myself without even thinking about it. But I didn't want to risk that again. I Frisbee threw the lid toward the oncoming men, striking one of them in the gut. He doubled over, but I didn't want to hang around to see how he was feeling. I reached into the bin and tried to grasp the light. Sure enough, I couldn't touch it, but the effects of my proximity to it were rather drastic.

It was different this time. No tunnel of light. It was just a case of, one moment I was in the alley; the next I was doing a balancing act on my hand in some dark cavern I could only presume was inside the castle.

My arm gave way beneath me and I fell in a heap on the hard ground. I should be getting used to that by now.

"Effective," it was Bob. He was standing not too far away.

I quickly jumped to my feet, "We better get going. They'll be coming after us in a second."

He pointed to a dark tunnel, "This way."

I only managed to catch a glimpse of the rest of the room before we headed into the tunnel. All I could see was that it seemed to be a junction. Lots of tunnels meeting in the one spot. I just hoped Bob knew where he was going.

Not soon after we had rounded a corner did I hear a muffled zap followed by another, and another. There was a series of mumbled words. The patrol had arrived. There was a clumping of loud footsteps that echoed throughout the tunnel and I didn't have the faintest idea whether they had come down our tunnel or another.

I didn't really care; I just kept running after Bob. We were sure to end up somewhere sooner or later. And once we find out just where that was, well, we'd have to cross that bridge when we come to it.

My legs were starting to ache by the time I thought we were really lost. Shows how much I was paying attention. We passed a number of forks, junctions and crossroads and I had totally forgotten which way we had come. But as far as I was concerned, the patrol didn't seem to be anywhere near us.

"Bob?"

"What?"

"Can we stop for a second?"

"Why?"

"My legs are dead."

He slowed to a walk and fell in beside me, "You're not very fit are you?"

"I haven't needed to be until now."

"You should do some exercise."

"Don't start."

"What?"

"I don't need someone on this world lecturing me about keeping healthy and fit."

He shrugged, "Whatever you say."

I looked around. It was like any other tunnel we had been running down, "Where are we?"

"From the looks of it, we're on sub-level three corridor forty seven."

"Very precise."

"I used to live here."

That got me, "Really?"

"Yes, now, if I'm right, around the next corner should be the escalators."

Sure enough, we turned the next corner and found four sets of escalators. One coming up, one going up, one going down and one coming down. It sort of looked like what you'd find in a department store. But it was rather ridiculous to look at. These shiny, mechanical, mobile stairs in the centre of a dark, rocky cave. Well, I wouldn't let it get to me. I was starting to take things as I saw them. There was no point questioning the logic or reality behind everything on this world. Then again, where was the power supply? They had electricity? Why not? They had what seemed to be laser weapons. But what about the horses and carts I saw in the city. Everything but the patrol men appeared to be

64

something out of the seventeenth century. The buildings all seemed Elizabethan in style, not that I was a historian or an architect. But they had modern day escalators in a medieval castle? Hmm. Okay. Whatever.

I moved over to the escalators. Looking both up and down, I could see that they continued up in a series of escalators for a number of levels as well as down into further sub-levels.

"Which way?"

I didn't hear Bob's reply. Something hit me on my arm and sent me flying to the ground. It had been hard and didn't tickle very much either. I crawled backward on my hands and feet like an upside down crab looking for my assailant.

There were two of them. They appeared to be men and not one of the more unusual inhabitants of this dimension. I couldn't be sure though as they were covered in dark red robes. They carried long staffs. One had attacked Bob, who was in a similar situation to myself, on the floor. The other was standing about three meters from me with its staff held in both hands.

"You have violated Its domain. You are to be punished accordingly."

"Which means?"

"Death."

She, as it sounded very much like a woman, said it so matter-of-factly. It was scary.

I scrambled to my feet. My arm was still sore, but it was worth defending myself. I took up my Tae Kwon Do ready position and waited for the onslaught, or whatever was to come.

She swung the stick at my head, but I ducked it, fortunately. Unfortunately, however, she followed it through with her foot, which caught me on my upper right arm on my way back up. It was sore before, but now it really hurt. So, it was my turn to retaliate. I attempted a jumping front kick and only managed to knock her on her shoulder as she dodged to the side.

I quickly jumped out of reach as she tried to swing her staff at me again. That thing was going to prove annoying, but if I could recall all my Tae Kwon Do stuff, I may just be able to make it a little more even.

I decided to try an old ploy of mine. Not my low stance ploy that made me look like a monkey, because that would leave my legs way too vulnerable for her staff to hit. By this I meant I would spread my legs wide and squat right down, but keep my weight moving constantly around my feet so I was constantly moving. I was thinking of my 'eternal side kick' ploy. This too required me to keep moving but most of the action was focussed on one foot.

I waited for her to move in a little closer and then struck out with a sidekick. But once I had hit her in the gut, I kept my leg up and lashed out again and again and again. The second missed, but the third got her on her hand that was holding her pole. She didn't drop it, though, but that was okay. At least I was hitting her. I tapped my foot on the ground and lifted it again into a ready position so I could lash out at any moment.

I saw her start to swing the pole before she tried to lash out at me again. It looked as though I had hurt her hand with my boot. Good. So, I used my kick again. I knocked the pole as it was coming at me. It sent a jar up my leg, but nothing painful as I struck it, but my kick sent it flying out of her hand. It clattered against the escalators for a couple of seconds before coming to rest, but I wasn't too interested in that. This woman was still dangerous if she wanted to be. And of course why wouldn't she want to? How stupid would I be to think she wouldn't?

She adapted to the loss of her weapon pretty quickly by charging at me. Not a good idea.

Any of my old sparring partners would have warned her against that. I always kept them at bay with my sidekicks, as I planned to on this occasion. As it happened, it worked perfectly. The ferocious scream she was letting out as she raced at me was cut short, quite sickeningly actually, by my foot catching her square in the stomach. It would have winded her if nothing else. But the way she fell backwards and onto the floor, it didn't look like she would be getting up too soon.

I raced over to her, turned her onto her front and grabbed her arm, putting it into a lock that would keep her down for the count, at least until I let go.

Bob, when I had a look, wasn't doing so well. It seemed he hadn't learnt to dodge from the last time I saw him fight. He was looking a little sore and was still taking hits from his opponent. Not good.

I reached into my gal's robes and found her belt. Rope, thank goodness. I love these traditional garbs, they always come in handy and they look good, too.

It didn't take me long to tie her up like a pig. You know. Hands and feet in the one big knot. Once done, though, I raced over to help Bob.

His attacker saw me coming and stepped back so she could see the two of us. Her head, at least the hood of the robe, was looking back and forth at us, sizing us up. Even with Bob injured, She didn't seem too sure of herself.

My ego got a bit carried away here, however. I mean, I had just taken one of these girls out with my own special move. Hell, why wouldn't it work a second time? Maybe because she was a little better trained than I was.

I lifted my leg to strike her with a sidekick. The next thing I knew I was on the floor. It appears, and felt like she had somehow latched onto my leg with her pole. In doing so, she used all her weight and strength to lever my leg higher than I intended, launching me into the air and falling backward onto my buttocks. Pure physics. Fortunately all that was done was a bruising to my backside and my ego. Then again, I should have known my tactics rarely work twice. At least not in reality.

Okay, okay. So this isn't my reality. And not much of this place is actually real. What does that prove? Only that I'm not as good a fighter as I thought. Shut up. I have more important things to worry about.

She came at me with her pole, ready to impale me with it, but as I began to roll aside, I saw Bob grab onto the stick with both hands and swing it like a hammer, you know like in the Olympics. Anyway, she definitely was not ready. She went flying past me and disappeared out of my line of sight, so I looked to where she had gone. I was lucky, because I managed to look in time to see her go face first into one of the cavern walls. It was hilarious. It had to have hurt. When she hit the wall, there was a loud thud. She collapsed to the floor and didn't get up again. Two down, none to go.

We made quick work of tying the second attacker up. She was still unconscious as we did so, so we decided to try the other one.

We rolled her onto her side so we could get a look at her face. It was a shame really that she was a bad girl. She was rather attractive, but hey, not all baddies are uglies.

"Where can we find It?"

It was a simple question that only I could have thought of. Okay, that's a lie, anyone would have thought of it, but, heck, my ego was still bruised so I have to give myself some credit.

"Go to Hell!"

It was Bob's turn, "Maybe if you looked outside once in a while, you'll see that that's what One has made of this place!"

"That's of no concern to me."

My turn, "Well it wouldn't be if you can live inside this castle your whole life and never get in touch with reality and the people that have to live in it."

"Your point?"

Bitch! I didn't say it but it was seething at the tip of my tongue.

"Tell us where we can find him!"

"Go hang yourself."

"Oh, get off your high horse and talk to us," I actually had another word in mind other than 'high horse', but I didn't want to be too sexist, crude or rude.

"Only to die for betrayal?"

"Did you ever think that you may die now as you have failed your duties?"

This got her. She looked rather uncertain for a moment before speaking again, slowly and a little more agreeable, "Level thirty eight. The end of corridor One Oh Two."

"Of course, the king's old chambers."

"And what happened to the king?" I asked Bob.

He was quiet for a moment. Something about his answer catching in his throat. Maybe he was just a royalist at heart, "It killed him while he usurped the throne."

"Hmm," I turned my attention back to the girl, "We could untie you. That way you could escape. But you may also try to be stupid and attack us."

"I would not."

I looked over at Bob. He was looking at me. We both had the same thought in mind. Liar, "How can we trust you?"

"I give you my word."

Bob considered this for a moment and nodded, "I believe you, then. They almost always stick to their word."

Well, if he said so. I pulled the rope clear of her hands and feet and backed away, as did Bob, toward the escalators. She rubbed her wrists and ankles, but made no move to stand.

"You can free your friend and try and make the most of your lives. Hopefully, if things work our way, you won't have to be on the run for long."

She nodded.

"Let's go."

Bob and I started toward the up escalator. I almost faltered in my step when I heard her speak again, "Good luck."

I looked over to her as we started our ascension, "Thanks. We'll need it."

L

We continued up the escalators until we reached the ground floor. I knew it was the ground floor as there was a large neon sign hanging from the ceiling stating as much. It was here that that our ascension stopped. It was also here that the whole architecture changed. It was grandiose and beautiful. Amazing could have been another word used to describe it. Everything was huge and wonderful. It was like stepping into an old Victorian castle with all the furniture, paintings and ornaments in place. The rugs were clean and massive. The chairs and tables polished and spotless. The gigantic paintings that adorned the walls were dust free and their frames in perfect condition, though I avoided getting too close, especially after my last encounter with a painting. Wood panelling lined the walls, a deep brown, also spotless and varnished.

A man-size fireplace sat in the middle of the hall we were in. The windows opposite filled the entire wall. The only things out of place here were the escalators and the neon sign. In light of the beauty of this place, I could easily ignore them and continue looking around.

It very much reminded me of a castle come museum in Goslar, Germany I went to see a couple of years ago. I didn't go to Germany solely to see this castle in Goslar. I simply happened to be passing through and noticed the building. Not that I didn't notice all the buildings. Germany has some very interesting towns. Each has a different style, history and atmosphere. This place, however, was perfectly kept. Looking out the windows, I could see a high wall in the distance, what I guessed to be the outer castle wall, and beyond that would be the city. The people who languished here wouldn't have to bother themselves with the sufferings of the people out there. Arseholes.

There were two ways out of this room, besides climbing the chimney and breaking out of the windows. Two large double doors lay on either end of the room. It was going to be hard to decide which to chose, but with Bob here, it would be okay. He seemed to know this place pretty well.

"Which way?"

"Those doors. But, be careful. Who knows what's on the other side of them."

Obviously not as well as I hoped, but, hey, he was just being careful.

We moved toward the doors, both of us tense, both ready to jump behind a piece of furniture at the slightest sound. But none came. We made it to the door and I was dazzled by the beautiful door handles. Solid gold. They must have been. Each curved and wound around itself like a mass of vines. And their size, I could wrap both hands around each one. I found that I had to when I tried to open the door.

When I had unlatched it, I pushed it slightly ajar to peer into the next room. It was pitch black.

Not a single light, nor window. Nothing. But there was a sound. It was, well, different. It sounded very much like we were standing in the middle of a forest late at night. The crickets chirped and there were numerous other animalistic sounds. It was really weird to be inside of a beautiful building like this and yet hearing the noises of a forest. Could be a CD. The worst thing about it was the fact that I wasn't sure if, indeed, this new room wasn't actually the forest it sounded like.

I pulled the door to and looked at Bob. The noise abruptly stopped once the door closed. Sound proofed so even if someone was on the other side, we wouldn't have noticed.

"What is that room?"

"The aviary."

"Birds?"

"Amongst other things," he was rather non-plussed by the whole thing, "I used to call it the zoo when I was younger. That was until I actually found the zoo room, otherwise known as the Wilderness."

Now that was a room I didn't want to go into. It sounded a bit too hazardous. But this one seemed okay.

"Shall we?"

Bob nodded and I pushed the door open.

When I took my first step into the room, I knew I was no longer walking on the wooden boards that covered the floor in the other room. It was squishy and gross. But I could endure that.

Bob shut the door behind us and I felt him take my elbow, as if to guide me. I winced slightly at the pain in my arm, but he knew what he was doing, so I could put up with it, at least until we got out of here.

Something croaked next to me and I jumped. A frog. I couldn't see it, but it probably was. That didn't settle my nerves any. I mean, what if it was that creature that had jumped me from the painting earlier. Maybe he could see in the dark. Then again, I never heard it croak before.

Then again, it could have croaked to cover some other noise he was making, like drawing a pistol or prowling up behind us, he stepped on a twig. I don't know. It could have been anything, anyone. I didn't like this place. I liked it even less when I shouldered a tree. It swayed a little as a result. I could feel it as I grabbed it to steady myself. I could also hear the rustling in the leaves. We moved on, but the rustling didn't cease.

A few seconds passed and I knew it should have subsided by now.

"What did you do?"

It was Bob, whispering very quietly I could barely make out what he said.

I tried to be just as quiet when I said, "I hit a tree, that's all."

I don't think it quite came out that way, but Bob seemed to have gotten the message.

"Oh bugger."

"What?"

"You've woken them up."

"What up?"

"The birds."

I knew by the way he said it; it was not a good thing. Of course it wouldn't be. Nothing good happens in this place. Heck, everything so far has been one long slide down hill and now something else had gone wrong. Was it just me or was everything just a coincidence? Everything was happening to me. That may sound egocentric, but, hey, I don't want this crap to happen, and yet it does.

Everything is happening It's like a really bad movie. Something is always happening to the lead guy. One bad guy after another. One hard predicament to get out of after another. It was exactly the same. Now I find those movies annoying enough as it is, but now, in my life, it was just down right pissing me off. Couldn't it be an easy trip to find Sarah? Why must everything go wrong? Karma? I don't think I've been that bad a person to deserve all this to fall on me at the same time.

Here I was, standing in the middle of a pitch-black room and I've supposedly woken something up. I don't know what they are, but they don't sound too friendly by Bob's indication. What else could go wrong?

"We best get out of here then, I suppose?"

"We best do more than that. Stay low and move as quickly as you can."

"Fine by me."

I stooped over and the thought of hitting a tree head on was a bit daunting, but, it was better than being attacked by these 'Birds' I guess.

Bob was moving faster than I was. I was too nervous about tripping over something or hitting something, but he was pulling away from me. I could tell because his hand was pulling harder on my elbow. Problem was that he wasn't holding my elbow any more. He was pulling on my shirtsleeve.

"Slow down," I hissed.

"I don't think that's a good idea."

"Why not?"

"Take a quick look over your shoulder."

"Its pitch black. I won't see anything," I argued.

"Fine, don't look. Probably best that you don't."

Now that spurred on my curiosity. So, of course, I took a quick peek.

Oh my God! I don't know how to explain what I saw. I guess I could say that there were four sets of eyes chasing after us. Like when I saw Bob covered in the mud. Pitch blackness with these eight eyes floating, well these were bobbing, through the air. But these weren't just any eyes. They were angled awkwardly and every so often one of each pair would disappear so I could see one of the eyes directly. Like when a bird turns its head to regard you. These were birds alright. But their eyes were glowing a horrid green and each one was bigger than my head. These things were huge!

Well, my peek became a bit more of a bewildered stare as I was paying more attention to these 'Birds' than to where I was going, not that I could see anything. But I finally looked back when I felt the pull on my sleeve take a totally different direction.

My arm was jerked quickly and painfully downward. I heard Bob call out and the pull on my sleeve disappeared. He must have tripped over something. I stopped, but the next thing I heard was Bob yelling something.

"Run."

He was screaming it. But it didn't stop. He kept screaming, but I never heard him land. His scream was getting further away. He was falling. Falling further than just onto the ground. A pit or something. He had fallen into a pit. What the heck was I supposed to do? I couldn't leave him here, could I? God, no!

But I couldn't hang around either. These 'Birds' were too damn close.

I made up my mind. I dropped to the floor, flattened myself out. Maybe they couldn't see us. My reasoning behind this? Well, if they sleep at night, then maybe they couldn't see at night. So, their eyes glowed. So what? Lot's of things glow. That slime in the dungeons. Lot's of things. I thought it best I take my chance with the ground than running for a door I probably would never be able to find in this light.

Then again, maybe it was this light for a reason. Maybe it was because they hated the light. Maybe I had made the wrong decision.

Too late now. I was lying on the ground with these four things bobbing toward me.

I ignored them for now and tried to feel to my right for the pit in which Bob had fallen. His scream had disappeared, only its echo remained. But that was every bit as disconcerting. The pit must still be there. That was a relief. It may have covered over or something, like a trap door. I managed to find the edge of it. Smooth as a baby's backside. As far as I could reach down the hole, I couldn't find a ledge or a stone out of place. He would have had no chance to have saved himself. That left me thinking about what would happen once he reached the bottom.

Oh, God. He could be killed. I cringed at the thought.

A slight whoosh-whoosh-whoosh sound brought me back from my morbid thoughts to my morbid reality. The 'Birds' were right above me. I looked up but I couldn't see anything. No eyes, no anything. But just as quickly as the whooshing had started, it stopped. Silent fliers, I thought. Either that or they have landed. But I didn't hear them earlier while I had been running, so my first guess was more likely.

So how had they been tracking us? The sound of us running? Had to have been. Then… oh bugger me blue and paint me green. They would have lost our trail. I was no longer running. No more noise, thus, well if they used logic, they would realise that we had stopped. And hearing the scream, they may come back to this position and start searching around for us. I had to be quick.

But I didn't have any options open to me. I could take the plunge down the pit and possibly be killed or continue on my journey, chancing the 'Birds' find me and eat me.

My best choice was the latter, or that's what I figured.

I waited a few moments. No sound. I was ready. I jumped to my feet and started running toward the direction we had been going earlier. Hopefully Bob was right, that we were heading in the right direction. I pushed myself forward. If I ran into anything, I'm sure it would be knocked over by the force of my running. Either that or I'd be knocked senseless.

As it happened, I didn't hit anything. But I did almost trip and skid when I noticed a pair of big glowing eyes appear in front of me. I was running too fast on soggy ground to even risk slowing down. I would hit the 'Bird' head on. So, where was the most vulnerable part of a bird? As far as I knew, the legs.

Idea! I already had my body pretty much sitting further forward than my legs as I ran. The only thing I would need was to spring or jump forward and down. I did so.

I felt my hands hit the ground first. It was good that it was soggy, otherwise it may have hurt. But as the rest of me landed, I watched as the eyes disappeared over me. Something snapped by my leg as I sped underneath the 'Bird'. I could only guess it had tried to bite at me, guessing where I was by sound. Thank God it had missed. I kept sliding, but I was losing momentum. If I didn't pick up speed, I would be bird meat.

Hang on, I thought birds ate birdseed. Carnivorous birds? Give me a break! No probably just territorial.

Before I found myself slowing to a stop, I felt myself hitting something. Something hard. Something flat. A wall? I wasn't sure. I jumped to my feet, nearly slipping over and losing my balance because of the soggy ground and the darkness, which makes it hard as hell to find which way is up or down. I felt the wall in front of me. Not just a wall. A door. I had reached the door. I could feel the same engravings as I had seen on the other door we had come through only minutes before.

But where was the handle? I was feeling erratically around the door for the handle. But couldn't find it.

Looking over my shoulder, I could see the 'Bird' was after me again. Its eyes were bobbing ever closer.

My hand ran over the wood. The smooth wood. Totally smooth. Other than the engravings and all, there was nothing that I could feel. No handle! I was trapped inside. I moved my hand to the left a little more and found myself hitting the doorframe.

Idiot! I was looking for it on the wrong bloody side. I swung my hands over to the right and felt my knuckles rap against the gold handle. I was guessing it was gold as the other one was. I let out a little yelp of pain but made more of an effort to open the door. It was hard, like the last one, but I used every ounce of energy and strength I had in my tiny body.

The 'Bird' had to be drawing close. Almost right on me. I was going to be screwed in a second or two.

Finally, the door swung open and I fell through the doorway onto nice soft carpet. Safe. I was safe.

But the door was still open! I spun onto my back and saw the eyes. They were almost right on me. I reached to the side with my leg and tried to swing the door closed. Just as it was half way there, the 'Bird' rammed into it, sending both the door and my leg flying aside. I spun on my backside, twisting my pants as I did so. Carpet isn't exactly the best thing to spin on.

Something hissed behind me. I rolled forward, away from the door, landing facing the wrong way still. I turned around and tried jumping to my feet again, but fell over. I was not having a good day. I was able, however, to catch sight of the 'Bird'.

Again, like everything else in this place, it was huge. About eight foot tall. The worst thing though, was that it looked exactly like a giant Australian magpie. And I hate, I mean loath magpies. They are evil looking creatures. Their black and white feathers add a sense of military camouflaging and insensitivity. They swoop when unprovoked and when provoked and they could be dangerous and very painful if they made contact. Its beak was razor sharp so I was counting my lucky stars that it had missed me when I had gone flying under it. The only good thing about magpies was that I had heard they were one of only a couple of birds that could learn how to speak. Like a cockatoo.

It walked on its rather thick stubs called legs. The monstrously huge wings were retracted as it was not flying, and couldn't be for lack of air space, but that didn't mean it couldn't be deadly. I pushed myself up onto my hands and knees and started crawling away, pushing myself up into a run as I went.

This room was similarly furnished to the first room, though the floor was carpeted. There were tables, chairs, sofas, lamps and all manner of objects I could have hidden under or used as a weapon, but my mind was in disarray. I didn't know what to do.

I did know, however, that my first priority was to get the door closed either with or without letting this Magpie in. If I didn't, its friends would surely come through as well.

I heard a thumping behind me. Heavy, yet light considering the size of the actual bird. It was chasing me and I had to find some cover before it got too close.

I grabbed onto the end of a sofa and swung myself around it, running on a tangent to the way I was heading before. If I could circle around it I should be able to shut the door, no problem.

Bad idea. The 'Bird' also changed direction and was running straight for the sofa. When it got close enough, it let out its wings slightly and flapped itself up. When it landed again, it was standing on the sofa's back.

Bad idea again, but not on my behalf. The sofa, like all sofas, was already back heavy as people with children may know from experience. Not having anything to counter weight it, the sofa began to tip backwards. The bird let out a screech as it toppled over. It managed to flap its wings and land safely, however. Meaning I was right back where I had started. It was on the other side of the couch and I had no way of getting back to the door to get it shut.

"Go away!"

It regarded me with a side on glance. Its eyes were so sinister. Horrible creature.

I began to back away from the sofa slowly. I had to find something to ward it off. I bumped into a table and reached my hand around to search for anything that could come in handy. Unfortunately, the only thing I found was a large lamp, electric to boot. The lamp's black cord disappeared off the edge of the table and under the chair that the table sat beside. Oh well. I yanked at the cord and got a proper grip on the lamp. It was rather heavy. I had no idea what it was made of. I didn't care as long as it would hurt if I had to throw it.

The magpie was still getting closer. It had jumped over the sofa and was stalking me. Yeah, right. More like playing with me.

I felt my way around the table and continued moving back, holding the lamp in a rather menacing position. Or as menacing as someone of my stature competing with a giant magpie could get.

When I finally came in contact with the wall on the other side of the room, I nearly started to cack myself. I was trapped. I tried to press myself further into the wall, hoping I would be able to sink through it, or become part of it like a drop of water does in the sea. To disappear out of consequence to this bird. But it wasn't to be.

The bird was getting too close and I had nothing but the lamp to defend me.

Not true! I had the cord. It was a rather long one. About three meters. And the heavy plug at the end would cause considerable painage if it came into contact with anything. I took hold of the cord about two metres of the way down and started swinging it in front of me forming a shield of sorts. It was good because I could still keep a good view on the

'Bird' as it hesitated. It wasn't sure what the cord was so it didn't want to risk coming too close just yet.

I moved sideways along the wall, keeping an eye out for any blocking objects. Thank god there were none. There was, however, a door. Not a double door as had been the case earlier. But a single door. Small, unassuming, if that's the right word to describe it. And the handle wasn't gold from what I could tell.

Something blurred at the edge of my vision. I turned my head slightly to look back at the magpie. But it wasn't the bird that had caused the blur. It was even further around. I turned my head more and saw it. Another 'Bird' had jumped against the wall, not literally, but it had closed me in on that side. Great. I should have been paying attention to the other birds. It was too late to think about closing the first set of doors.

I looked past the first Magpie and saw the other two birds rushing through the doors.

"Welcome to the new and improved aviary," I thought to myself, "With all the comforts of home."

One of the other birds was getting closer, quickly. It was moving a lot faster than the other. Once over the sofa, it changed its heading toward my newly found door. My only exit.

I could see it coming before it happened. They were going to box me in.

The reason I saw it before it happened though, was because I wasn't about to let it happen.

There was no way they were going to get my door. That was my only way out. I started moving faster, more like jogging toward my door. It was going to be close. I wasn't going to risk running because I would probably stop swinging the cord or I would trip over it.

It was looking more promising as I moved. I was going to get there first, but, it was still moving at a considerable speed. If it wasn't careful, it was going to collide with me. I know who would come out second best in that confrontation.

I finally made the door. I pushed myself back into the alcove made by the door frame and prepared to dodge the on-coming beak. It was coming in fast. But it seemed to realise that I had made the door. It started to slow itself slightly, but kept on moving. This was going to hurt if I wasn't able to dodge it. Only seconds passed but I started to cringe. I was quite shocked, really, when I heard a loud "Clunk" and a squawk. The bird had run straight into my shield. The cord swung wildly in my hand and was coming back at me after bouncing off the magpie's head. I ducked quickly as it hit the door and swung down.

The magpie had retreated to the side, but the other three were coming at me now. The cord was no longer protecting me.

I started to swing it again and they stopped, unsure of what to do.

I let off some slack and slid the lamp down between my body and the door to the ground. That way, I had a spare hand to open the door, only enough that I could edge my way through. I slid in through that gap, dropped the cord and slammed the door shut. Easy as that. I'd like to see them get out of there now.

"Well, well, well. What 'ave we 'ere?"

M

Someone was behind me. An English policeman? Sounded like it. But I wasn't going to bet on it.

"House maid," I thought it was worth a try.

"You don't look like a maid. Turn around and let me get a look at you."

I followed his order, very slowly mind you, so I wouldn't be shocked if it turned out to be some grotesque creature. You can imagine how I felt when I saw Narelle dressed in the blue uniform and large hat of the English Policeman She was impersonating. I could scarce believe my eyes. She must have been a damn good impressionist.

"Well, you're a sight for sore eyes," I meant it too. She was always a beauty to behold and so what, my eyes weren't sore, but the rest of me was.

"Thank you," She said it rather modestly. It was almost laughable. This woman couldn't be seriously modest if she tried. Well, that could be a harsh judgement, but I don't feel I am too far off the mark, "What in the world have you been up to?"

She sounded rather disgusted, yet again. Then I realised, my clothes must be in one heck of a state. I regarded myself and my dirty clothes. The front of me was covered in muddy stuff and my button up shirt was torn a bit on the sleeve. I had a rip where my breast pocket used to be, it must have caught on something as I slid. The T-shirt underneath was untucked and dishevelled. It had a small number of rips and tears and was no longer black. The mud covered both it and some of my skin as it had been revealed to the dirt. I must have reeked and the sweat must be unbearable, not that I could smell myself. I was hot before, when I was fighting those women, now, I was breathing deeply and run haggard. Too much excitement for an otherwise dull life.

Okay, so that's not entirely true. I've had some exciting moments in my life, but, hey, nothing like this.

"Just a few run ins with the local fauna, nothing serious."

She smiled at me, "Just wait a moment."

She clicked her fingers and I felt a peculiar buzzing sensation over my body. When next I looked down, everything was back to the way it was before. And my mind was allowed to wonder back over past events. The women, the 'Birds', Bob. Bob!

"Bob!"

"What about him?"

I swallowed before I spoke next, "He's... He's gone."

She didn't seem to understand, "Gone where?"

"There was a pit in the aviary. He fell down it. I couldn't save him."

I looked down at my boots in shame. Not just as an affect, but because I was feeling it. God, I wish there was something I could have done to help him, but there was nothing. Nothing at all.

Narelle made a little noise.

I looked up at her to see her stifling a smile. I couldn't believe it. She was smiling. No, laughing. That was a laugh she had made.

"What? What the hell is so funny?"

And she lost it. She made one of those bursts of laughter. You know when you're holding it in and you just can't contain it any longer. One of those. She let out some saliva onto my shirts as well, which sort of made up, but only by the minutest of fractions for my vomiting over her.

"What is so damn funny?"

She settled a little before answering, "You."

"What?"

"You have no idea, do you?"

"What about?"

"Us! You think Bob's dead! That's so funny!"

"Why?"

"Just because he fell? Don't be absurd."

She had totally lost me.

"You've seen me disappear into thin air right?"

I had, "Yes."

"It isn't hard, you know. He would have done that and gone to safety."

That was totally inconsistent with everything that had happened so far. If he could disappear or teleport like that, then why the hell hadn't he done that to get us inside? Why hadn't he attacked One that way or something? It just didn't fit.

"So he isn't dead?"

"No, of course not!"

"Then where is he?"

"I'd say he'd be at home resting. It does take a lot out of us to do it you know."

There's an excuse, I guess.

"Could you teleport more than yourself?"

She looked at me strangely, "No. Why in the world would we do that?"

"Oh, I don't know. Maybe so we could lead a successful assault without being killed!"

"Oh, to make things easier?"

"Yeah, something like that."

"Nope."

Nope? Simple as that?

"Why not?"

"It takes a lot out of us, as I told you. If we tried doing that, we would never materialise again. It would be suicide for us and whoever we tried doing it with."

Point taken. I nodded to show that I understood.

"Anyway, I just came to tell you that the next room is going to be a real doozey. Bob thought I should warn you."

"When will he be back?"

She shrugged, "I don't know. It takes a while, different for each of us and depending on the circumstances."

"Well, won't you stay?"

She shook her head, "I told you before. If One knew I was talking to you, I'd be dead."

I didn't want to put her life at risk if I didn't need to, "Well, thanks for coming along. You better go then."

"Okay," she bent over and gave me a kiss on my cheek, "Good luck, Cutey."

With that, she was gone. It left me wondering. This doozey of a next room? What was it? How much further did I have to go and Cutey? Where the devil did that come from?

I didn't have time to dwell on that. Then again, I could probably dwell on it while I walked.

I wasn't in a room any more. It was another hallway. Only short. There was a door at the other end. A very ominous looking door. It just stood there, like any other door, but the warning Narelle had given me was playing with my mind and my perception of things. To me, this door was foreboding, evil incarnate, just dreadful to even think about. But, of course, I had to. Or did I?

I tried very hard to clear my mind as I approached that door. With every step I emptied my mind of all the horrible possibilities I was imagining lay beyond that wooden portal of doom. Ooops. Let that thought slip.

Make everything peaceful. Quiet my mind and my thoughts. "In with anger out with love," something I remembered from an Absolutely Fabulous episode.

It's amazing how the mind wanders when you try to clear it. No matter how much you try to wipe it completely clean, something always manages to slip in. Be it relevant to the current situation or something way off in the insane world of your private thoughts to even something you were trying to remember over a year ago. I attribute that to the natural order of things.

As far as I am concerned, nothing can be empty or devoid of everything. Something must occupy as much space as possible. This is the excuse I gave when I was living at home to have a messy room.

Don't understand? Well, look at gas. It expands to take up as much space as possible. You let off a little helium and it doesn't hang around in one clump now does it? No. It spreads out into the atmosphere until it is no longer noticeable and its affects have no effect because the concentration is so small.

I believe everything follows this principal. Clothes, for example. You wear them. You take them off and somehow, God knows how, they manage to find their way to every corner of your room. Like paper as well. You stack it somewhere and by some freak chance you're bound to find it covering your desk or your floor in a short period of time.

Well, I think thoughts follow the same pattern. They can't help it. It's natural law. Your mind, like the floor of your room just can not stay completely clean or devoid of rubbish, not that all thoughts are rubbish.

See what I mean? Just take this whole train of thought. It came flowing in just as I was trying to wipe my mind. Great, huh? Now I find myself facing a door that could very well open to reveal my own death and destiny and I'm thinking about dirty clothes and helium gas. How stupid could you be?

Ah, well. Nothing to be done. I took hold of the door knob and twisted it.

I started opening the door slowly at first, millimetre by millimetre. But then I thought what the hell? The slower I am at opening the door, the longer I put off my inevitable death.

Shows how pessimistic I can be when I don't want to be, doesn't it?

I pushed the door wide-open and stood legs apart and feeling rather brave to face what may come at me. I was rather shocked to see that I was faced by whom appeared to be myself.

I blinked. I let my eyes wander and so did I, my copy that is. But we weren't alone. There, in front of and all around me and him, or, rather, me was another hundred Me's. I was everywhere. No matter where I turned my head, there I was. Or parts of me at least.

Mirrors. Every surface in this room was covered by mirrors. The ground, the ceiling and the walls. But this was no four walled room. This was no long annoying corridor either. This was a literal mirror maze.

"Cool!"

I couldn't help myself. I couldn't say anything else. I mean, since I was a young kid I dreamed of a chance to either be stuck in a gigantic maze or to be lost in a room full of mirrors so large I would probably die before finding my way out again. This was like a wet dream to me. The whole notion that this room was full of mirrors sent shivers up my spine. This was going to be hell fun!

I stepped into the room and tried to make out which way to go. I couldn't tell which way was a wall or not. Each piece of mirror was the height of the room, but they were only about three feet wide. So where there was a join between mirrors, it looked as though it was a way to go, but in actuality it was a mirror reflecting the actual way to go which could quite possibly have been right behind me. Really cool!

I ran my hands over the mirror in front of me. Cold to touch and very smooth. I kept my hand on it and started moving to my left. A friend of mine told me always to stay to your left when you're in a maze. I didn't like the idea initially as it sort of ruins the fun in mazes, but in this case it was a very real possibility that I would die before I got out of here. So the faster I moved and the more 'cheats' I used, the quicker I would get out of here.

I was feeling my way along when the wall disappeared in front of me. I pushed forward through the air until I found another mirror. Once I had, I looked around. I could still see the door in many of the mirrors, but I was no longer sure if it was really the door or just a reflection.

Following along the mirror, I clung to the left wall. Watching for any new exits and trying not to get disorientated or scared out of my wits when I saw my own reflection moving in another mirror. I had to remind myself, "It's just me."

Even then I was still rather nervous. I picked up my pace a little, but not too much. The mirrors on the floor would prove to be slippery if I moved too quickly.

The mirrors turned sharply to the left and seemed to back track on itself, running totally parallel to the way I had just come.

It was funny. Even though I could see, I felt my eyes going numb. They were really wide and relaxed, not numb as in not working. It was as if, with my hands doing the seeing, my eyes shut themselves off to allow me to concentrate on where I was going. In this kind of environment they would be totally useless anyway.

The mirrors eased slightly around and then turned sharply again. I followed them around. It took a bit long to do so, however. When I finally found the corridor out again, I realised it was a total dead end. That was okay. Just meant that either I had missed a turn off on the other side or my initial path was wrong.

I liked these sorts of challenges. I followed the mirrors still until I felt it disappear from touch. Okay, another path. I walked straight ahead this time, at least until my hands found another solid surface.

Stopping for a moment, I looked at my reflection. There was me. Then there was the back of me. Then there was me again and so on. My eyes had gone a really deep blue. They always change colour, I find. From deep blue to stormy grey. Usually when I am enjoying myself or am really pissed off, my eyes stay deep blue, attractive in their own way. The number of times people have asked me if I wear coloured contacts is amazing. But when I'm in a non-plussed mood, my eyes are grey and bland. I guess they'd been very blue all day with everything that has been happening.

Narelle had done a good job cleaning my clothes. Everything was repaired and fresh. I had to admit, even though I was far from attractive, I didn't look too bad in the get up I was wearing. She had also managed to do my hair in some new way that wasn't all together different to how I normally comb it. Trimmed a little and neatened. Didn't look too bad. Not bad at all.

Now there is vanity for you.

Well, enough gloating. I'd have plenty of opportunities to look at myself in the maze.

"Ti-i-i-ime is on my side…"

I don't know why that song came to mind. I don't know the singer, the title or even the words. Again, I just sing the chorus over and over. It's not really a true statement of fact. Time was by no means on my side. But it was a catchy song. It reminded me of that movie with Denzel Washington. "Fallen".

Weird movie. Not your most typical of mystery come thrillers. But I liked it. It opens your mind to new theories and beliefs. To think that such a demon exists that can be passed on from body to body by touch. It was a shame, however, they didn't do the opposite as well. You know, like a good version of the demon. I sometimes feel the same about "Touched by an Angel". Why don't they show one episode or start a new series with a bad angel, or one of the Devil's advocates. In doing so, they could show how the human spirit can win out over the evil influences of the Devil. It could prove that humans have the strength to look after themselves. And if they want to keep it all preachy, then they could use Mankind's faith as the excuse to keep people being swayed by the devil. And like in some of the normal episodes, they could sort of fail and be swayed by the Devil. It could be a totally new look at the nature of man. It could be quite cool.

Then again, the whole notion of being influenced by the devil might be a little too harsh for young kids. So, put it on late at night. If the parents don't want them watching it, then don't let them. Use a little discipline. Not necessarily the physical kind, but just have the sense of discipline in mind. They're going to need to learn it sooner or later in their lives anyway and the sooner the better.

Another thing I think it would be cool to see would be an "Aliens" and "Terminator" on the "Titanic". Three James Cameron movies tied into one. It would be excellent. Just think. Ripley and the Aliens get transported back in time as does a terminator who is coming after John Connor's great grandfather or something. Guns get fired, causing the rip in the hull, rather than the iceberg and the rest of the movie is about Rose and Jack escaping the aliens, helping John's great grandfather destroy the Terminator and then eventually escaping the ship as the aliens and the terminator go down with it. Ripley, Rose and the Great Grandfather survive and each sets about living a normal life on earth of that era, except for Rose who goes and does what she promised Jack she would.

Anyway, that's just my idea and it would probably be really stupid, but it does put together some really good movies. Though I think "Alien 3" was the best of the four. It was so much more personal and insightful into the character of Ripley and for her to have the guts to kill herself to save mankind that has treated her so badly; it shows one heck of a spirit and will in the one woman.

I admire both the character and Sigourney Weaver. She is one hell of a person. A brilliant actor and a powerful minded woman. Not to mention damn attractive. I know I said Narelle was my idea of the ideal woman earlier, but, hell, Sigourney beats her hands down in every aspect. She is the epitome of woman. I have a great deal of respect for her.

See what I mean about thoughts wandering? Well, I'm not exactly trying to clear my mind at present, just keep it occupied so I don't get agitated by the mirrors. I've been in this room for a while and I haven't really gotten anywhere, not that I could really tell if I had.

I could see nothing but myself in the mirrors. No more door, no indication of another one. I was lost and no matter how fun I thought it was, I was not really in the mood for this right now. I know once I get out of here, or if I do, I will regret not making the most of it, but I have other more important things to do and I can't really waste my time here. I had to find Sarah. That thought was right there in my mind. I knew I had to do it and I really wanted to do it soon so I could go home and forget all about this place.

Now why on Earth would I want to do that? Thinking about it, I don't think I would want to forget about this place. It's been exciting. Some of it fun. Some insightful. No. I don't think I would want to forget about this place. Besides, how many other people in the world can say they were transported into another dimension and had to survive giant frogs and birds, mini men and long corridors. Come to think of it, I don't think anyone would have the guts to admit it even if they had. It's so ludicrous. No one would believe them even if it were true.

Well, I wasn't home yet. I should try and keep my mind on my objective.

"Are we having fun yet?" the voice came from nowhere.

N

I froze, my hands still against the mirror. I began to focus on all the surrounding reflections. There was someone else besides me in this maze. That was one of those things… A use of a word that didn't need to be used. I can't remember the term used for it, but I shouldn't have used the words 'besides me', but I did, so what? I wasn't going to start analysing my grammar just now. Although, I just had.

It was a man. Old in appearance. His cheeks seemed to hollow out, his bones were protruding. The dark rings under his eyes made him look either sad or very, very tired. His balding head added to my thoughts that he was old. Not because he was balding because young men go bald too. Nor because he was pure grey, again because lots of people go grey early, but because it was so thin and wiry and having it pulled back into a funny looking pony tail gathered all his wrinkles at the top of his scalp like some failed attempt at a face lift. It would have been a cheap alternative, though, so I'll give him points for trying. He was short and wore a rather cool looking robe made of black velvet with red designs stitched into the front and back. I could only see him in one mirror. That didn't help. Firstly because a mirror maze was already a problem. Secondly, how freak is it that he didn't seem to have a reflection. Or did he was just strategically placed? I had no idea where I was, let alone where he could have been.

I decided to answer him, "Yup! How about you?"

He scowled at me, "Oh, I am just ecstatic."

"Glad to see it," I smiled

The ends of his mouth curved upward slightly into a smile, "One wonders if you are missing your little friend."

That got my attention. Was he talking about Sarah? He had to be.

"A little, why?"

"Have a look," With that, he waved his right hand in front of him and I could no longer see him. The mirror in front of me was no longer a mirror, but rather a window looking in on some dark and evil looking place. It reminded me very much of the sub levels Bob and I had been on earlier. Black walls, cavernous. But there was a reddish light coming out of somewhere. There was no visible light source. Steam rose from various pool-like holes in the ground. I could only guess them as hot water pools or steam baths. But it wasn't that that caught my attention.

In the very middle of the room was a large X. Made entirely of wood. It took up the whole central area. I had no idea how it stayed up, besides its two lower pieces, it had no other means of support. But again, this was not my concern.

For on this X, tied up by wrist and ankle, was Sarah. Her head hung loosely down, her hair was dishevelled and covered her face. Her clothes were also dishevelled and torn; spots of blood were patched here and there over her. It was a horrific sight to see. A good friend strung up, unconscious and bleeding. I was so furious. I felt the anger boiling inside me, growing in intensity as I looked at this visage. How could anyone, anything be so sadistic? So evil? Sarah was such a nice person, She didn't deserve this, didn't deserve any pain. She was always so willing to help others that there was no way on Earth anyone would purposely hurt her, not like this.

"You bastard! Let her go! Let her go, send us home and we'll never bother   you   again."
"I don't believe you have much say in that. We know you had no choice in your coming here. We also know you have no grounds or power to make us do what you ask."

"What has she done to you?" I was getting so angry. He knew it and his smile was getting bigger.

"Nothing," smug little bastard, "But that matters not. One likes the look of her, so she'll be staying right where she is."

I looked at my dear friend strung up like some kind of animal put on display. I wanted so much to be able to help her. To save her from this dreadful fate. That was, however, until I noticed a rather major mistake in their part. I must have been an absolute idiot and completely blind to have missed it in the first place. The truth, however, is that I still wasn't sure if it really was Sarah or not. But there was a rather large chance it wasn't.

This image may not be Sarah. Okay, She may have done something outrageous with her hair in her travels, but I know how much She loves her long red hair. There is no way in hell she would have dyed it green voluntarily. But as I said, it was possible something freaky caused it to happen. But the other option, however, was that this guy was red-green colour blind.

That was it. I had to take my chance. I swung back my leg and kicked at this image in front of me. It was still glass; I could feel it under my hands. Sure enough, when my foot made contact, the mirror shattered. No longer could I see the image of Sarah. All that was left was broken shards of mirror. They fell, tinkling to the floor. And all that stood before me was another mirror as if it led into an adjoining corridor.

The little man let out an evil sounding laugh.

"Oh, you petty little creature. I don't know what you could possibly think you could do here. You may as well leave this place; try to live out your life in the city below. Oh, we promise to leave you alone. If you do the same. We may even let your little friend go."

Then something dawned on me. Something about both this guy and this One character. Oh it was so sweet. I waited until I had calmed down a little before I spoke and when I lifted my head to address this little, little man I had a smile on my own face.

"Why? Why are you so afraid of us? It seems to me that you may not be as 'omnipotent' as you thought you were. Are you so scared of a couple of helpless humans that you have to threaten us, show us forged pictures, trying to scare us into submission?"

His smile disappeared. I had struck a nerve. That was it. It totally confirmed my suspicions, "That's it, isn't it? You can't control us. You can't make us bend to your paltry little will. Can't make us do your dirty work as you have every other person and creature in this world of yours. And that scares you. We scare you because we are free thinkers, and you can't handle that."

I could tell by the look on his face I was right, "Well, I suggest you go back to your little master and tell him he can go shove his false images and his self confidence where the sun don't shine because Sarah and I are here and as long as we are, we're going to make your life a living hell!"

That scared him. Well, actually, it angered him. It was like a fire rising in him. His face turned a shade of red I'd never thought possible on a person. His eyes literally flared with flames. I mean it. Little orange flames flickered around in there.

His voice was harsh, its inflections were so dark and evil they scared the daylight out of me, but I would not let that show. I am an actor and I am a better person than this man. Two things that helped me keep a defiant face as this man flared in anger.

"You dare defy us!"

It was a statement. There was no other way to take my words and he knew I would not be swayed in my stance. I was adamant we would not budge and he was sure as hell adamant we were going to give in or die. I didn't like either option.

"Well, I sure as hell won't be bending over to kiss your arse anytime soon," I said it so casually that I did myself proud. And probably made the situation worse.

"Then die!"

His harsh rasp seemed to get louder as he said that last word. But it didn't just end with the 'e'. It kept going. His mouth stayed open and in it I saw his tongue was no more. It was like inside his eyes. Fire. This man was a 'Pyro'. I didn't know how far that went, but it appeared he was made of fire. What's more, as he kept his mouth open and that dreadful rasp going, the flames inside him got bigger and brighter. All of a sudden they lashed out of his mouth and flew straight at me.

I jumped to the side and bounced into a mirror. I fell backwards against another mirror, but I let it take me as I slid down it onto my backside. The mirror I had hit was shaking, but only for a few moments. After that I watched as it broke free from its adjoining mirrors and begin to fall over. This wouldn't be good. I covered my face with my arms, to shield me from any breaking glass. But I was able to watch the reflection in another mirror. I saw the little old guy with his flaming breath and didn't I feel like a complete fool when I saw that the flame had hit a mirror.

He had aimed straight at me but hit a mirror. He couldn't tell which one was the real me, just as I couldn't tell which was really him. He was restricted just as I was.

There was a crashing noise in front of me. The mirror I had knocked over had fallen against another, shattering them both. When I thought it safe, I uncovered my face and saw that beyond the two shattered mirrors, a whole lot more lay ahead of me, but, hell, at least it was a way out of here. I dove head on, keeping my arms ahead of me and my body bent over. I don't know why. Maybe to keep me more aerodynamic or out of the flames way, not that he probably couldn't aim his flame breath quite proficiently or anything.

When I hit the next mirror in front of me, it too began to fall, but not on its own. One of the adjoining mirrors broke free also and they both began to tumble backward. I kept my balance and moved to the side, against another mirror in the hopes of shielding myself from the breaking glass.

In the mirror opposite I could see my assailant. He looked as though he was about to let loose another burst of fire. I ducked for cover just in case and was quite surprised to feel a burning heat pass right over me. He was in the same corridor as I was in.

"Oh, shit!"

But before he could readjust his aim, his flare burnt out. It seemed he was limited in his abilities. But, he still had these extraordinary powers so I should by no means start testing him now.

The mirrors shattered next to me. It made one hell of a noise. But it was now time to act.

I jumped to the opposite side of the corridor and spun on my heels, allowing me a run up to jump over some of the broken glass. Fortunately I stopped myself from jumping just in time. I was an idiot to even think I could do it. I would have landed and fallen flat on my arse. The ground was far too slippery to even attempt it. I kept running, straight through the broken glass, being very careful as I did so, so I wouldn't fall over. And found myself not coming into contact with another mirror for a few moments.

When I did, however, I turned to my right and felt for another mirror. There was one there.

I decided to try something tricky. I let out a kick, shattering the mirror. I protected my face with my arms. Luckily I wasn't touched by the shattering glass. But once I was sure I had shattered it, pretty hard to be wrong about that, though, don't you think, I started moving backward, not forward. I was hoping that giving the impression I went the other way would help put this guy off my trail. I couldn't see him in any of the mirrors so I may just fool him.

I turned around and started moving off. Still no sign of him, but I had to find the way out of here.

I had no idea which way to go or which way I was actually facing. But I had to do all I could to get out of here. I found myself at the end of a corridor and felt my way around to my right. When I came across another turn to my left, I moved only one frame to the side and let out another kick. The mirror shattered and without waiting I ran through the falling shards. My clothes got covered by them as did my hair, but I was still able to avoid any cuts.

Another bloody mirror corridor and no sign of an exit. I needed to get out of here!

I know that the image he had shown me of Sarah was false. I didn't, however, know if they would be able to capture her or not and do that to her. I had to assume she was in a similar predicament to myself and if I didn't find her soon, she would be in deep trouble.

I decided my best shot was to break as many mirrors as I could until I found my exit. I pushed heavily at the wall of mirrors on my left and right. After doing so, I stepped back into the other corridor and to the side for protection. There was a tremendous crash as they fell. The subsequent twinkling was loud too, but mild in comparison to the following crash. It sounded as though there was some sort of domino effect occurring as there was another crash that followed the last. This was going to be one hell of a mess to clean up.

I heard another five or six mirrors crash until silence finally took over.

"There's no point trying to hide, Infidel. We will find you, sooner or later."

He sounded close. It would be easy to follow the breaking of glass, thus I was hardly doing a good stealth run, but right now I saw it as my only way of getting out of here.

Something moved in a couple of the reflections. It was him. All I had seen was a flash of his black robe, but I was sure he was getting closer. I stepped around my protective barrier and saw what my vandalism had caused. I was standing in a newly created room of mirrors. The ground was cracked and covered with broken shards. I could see a number of ways I could go from here. I could tell by the dispersion of the mirror shards. The unevenness of it all gave me a better idea of how to navigate my way through this little section.

I chose one of the paths open for me and headed for it. Once inside it turned sharply to my right and again to the left. I walked on for a few moments before hitting another mirror and turned right only to be faced with the image of that little old man.

"I told you we would find you."

"You haven't got me yet. You still have to make sure you've got the real me or just some cheap copy."

"There is little difference between you and your copies."

Oh, this guy had a wit. But calling me cheap was hardly going to get me annoyed.

"Why don't you give up now and we may be generous and not kill you."

Yeah, I could see that happening.

I continued to move, trying not to let the images of this guy faze me. The problem was, however, that I wasn't sure whether I was walking straight toward the real him or not. My only choice, that I could see, was to start breaking the glass again. I stopped and turned to my right. Again, there was the image of that ugly little dude. That would make my breaking the glass that much more fun.

I swung back my leg and let out a kick and boy was I surprised when the image began to howl in pain.

It didn't shatter, it didn't even crack. It just picked up its leg and started rubbing its shin.

I had just kicked the real little old guy. What a fluke! That was more fun than I thought it would be. But I couldn't stop now. I reached over and shoved him backwards. With him hoping on one foot it was easy to knock him off balance. He went sprawling backward in a heap of robing, getting tangled up as he slid along the smooth mirrors that were the floor. He slid against a mirror wall and I walked straight toward him. He was easy to see as the real thing now. A bit more three-dimensional than his copies.

I noticed that the fire in his eyes had died a little since I had kicked him. Maybe he had lost concentration and wasn't able to let off any sparks. Who knows?

He was only a weak little dude so it was easy to kick him over onto his front as I had done to the women Bob and I had fought earlier. Once done, I searched through his robes for some rope or a belt. There wasn't one. So, I held him done with one hand and undid my own belt with my other.

It was easier to hog-tie him with my leather belt. The problem was, however, it would probably be easier for him to break out by simply breaking the belt buckle. I didn't have any other choice, though, so I finished belting his feet and hands together and stood back away from him.

"You really are pathetic."

He couldn't turn to look at me, but I could see his face in the mirrors. He was not a happy man.

"You will not succeed outlander. You will die, and your little friend too."

Now where have I heard something like that before?

O

So I didn't have a witty come back. So what? I think "We'll see," has a nice sound to it. Sort of defiant, short and sweet also. Heck, it certainly left him speechless. Either that or he was too busy trying to free himself from my belt.

Fortunately my cord pants were tight enough to keep themselves up. I turned away from the hog-tied guy and started walking casually away. I wasn't going to show any weakness to this man.

That was my mistake.

When I heard him groaning loudly, I knew something was wrong. I didn't associate his need to make noise to use his fire breath with this occasion, so I was taken completely by surprise by what happened next.

Something hit me from behind. Something that wasn't tangible but was very much like a shock wave. I could see it as it passed me. Sort of purplish in colour. But I wasn't interested in looking at it. I was worried about what was happening. All around me mirrors were shattering as they were struck by the shock wave.

When it hit me, I found that the ground was taken from beneath my feet. I was sent flying as if I was thrown through the air. It was very hard to see the mirror as I went flying at it, but I knew it was coming. When I finally made contact, I felt it shatter. My loose clothes kept me from being cut by any of the breaking glass. What's more, the breath was knocked from my body.

Once I had passed through the falling shards of mirror, I kept going, but more on a sloping arc. I was about to hit the floor and it was going to hurt. That was actually wishful thinking.

Instead of hitting the floor, I hit another mirror, shattering it also and as it slowed down my trajectory, I realised I was about to land hands and knees first in a pile of broken glass. I was going to be pulling splinters out of me fingers for weeks, if I was lucky enough not to slice an artery or vein when I landed.

I tucked my arms into my body and my head, to protect them when I landed. But there was little I could do for my knees. If I tucked them in so I would land feet first, I would shatter the ground covering mirrors and probably do myself more damage. It would be best if I let my knees make contact and try and roll with it the best I can.

As I landed, I felt shards of glass slice across and into my legs. I kept that out of my mind and I used my momentum to help me to roll forward over my shoulder, where I felt another few cuts and slices. I winced with pain, letting out a number of whines as I went. Unable to say more from lack of breath. The initial impact on my knees started to register. A dull throbbing took over from the sharp pain. I could only imagine how long I would be limping for, until my knees found their true alignment again.

When I get out of this, I was not going to be in good shape.

I continued to roll over my shoulder, but I stopped; my back on the ground and my legs against another wall. I couldn't help groaning with the pain I felt. My cords had already begun sticking to my knees as blood seeped out of my wounds. My shoulder wasn't as bad, but I was still rather tentative about looking, worrying about large pieces of mirror that may be sticking out of me.

I twisted around, so I was sitting upright and looking back at where the old guy had been. He was still there, but he was no longer tied up.

He was walking in my direction looking rather smug with himself. All I could think was, "You bastard!"

It kept running over and over in my mind, mixing with the pain that my brain had started to register all over my body. My right shoulder and elbow had started to play up again from the impact.

I was hurting and that was no joke.

I tried to stand up, but my legs gave way under me. It looked like it was going to be a hard haul.

So, I pulled the sleeves of my shirt over my hands and began pulling myself through the broken glass along the corridor I had found myself in. It was hard work, with both the glass and the material slipping on the ground. But I managed to move a few inches before head-butting a mirror.

"Get away from me!"

I yelled it at the mirror, not the old guy. It was useless anyway; neither of them would listen to me. It was amazing how quickly this room had gone from being a source of wonder and enjoyment to a curse.

I turned around and inched my way along the other way. I made it past the broken glass and let go of my sleeves, making it easier to drag myself. I noticed the not so small trail of blood I was leaving on the shiny surface behind me.

It would be impossible for me to hide from this guy now, especially with him so close. He hadn't caught up to me yet, which meant he was taking a slow walk, savouring the approach, knowing it would torment me. Damn right it was. I couldn't do anything. I couldn't run away. I couldn't get up and fight. I was totally screwed. And in a few moments I would be totally dead.

My knees were dragging against the floor, so I tried to use my shoes as leverage. I found it helped. The trail stopped along the glass, though my knees were dripping blood every so often. Every time I bent them to use my feet to push me along, sharp pains went searing up my limbs. It was painful going, but it was a hell of a lot faster than just going on my hands.

I looked behind me. He was there, back where I had landed.

"How pathetic you are. Trying to escape still? You'll never make it."

I flipped myself over onto my back so I could get a better look at him, so I wouldn't die by being hit from behind. That wasn't to say I stopped moving. I kept using my hands and feet to crab walk backwards. It hurt like hell, but I was going to show this guy I wasn't a weak and useless pile of ugliness. I was not going to give into him nor his brain demented master. I am me and I am not going to give up or succumb to weakness or idleness or any other form of nesses I could think of. This screwed up faggot was not going to beat me. By faggot I meant pile of sticks, as a reference to his tiny build, not some derogatory term, though in the context of my statement, it is derogatory, so what the heck.

Damn, I wish my mind would stop wondering. This guy had stopped right at the end of this corridor and he was smiling. Smiling an evil little smile. I wanted so much to run over and wipe it off his face. Wishful thinking, but hey, I was still able to do that and that wasn't something he would be able to take away from me as he had all those poor people who slaved under his and this One guy's control! But what did my capacity to think give me now? I was so pissed off with this guy. He was going to beat me no matter what I said or thought and there was nothing that could be done. I couldn't retaliate, I couldn't do anything! I was totally stuffed!

That was until the mirror beside this prick suddenly shattered. Everything seemed to happen in slow motion. I watched as the shards flew out toward him. He moved backwards, but some of the falling shards scratched at his face, causing a number of small cuts. But that wasn't what interested me. Not by a long shot.

A hand shot out from where the mirror used to be and grabbed this little guy by the throat. The arm was covered in a dirty white sleeve. The hand at the end of it was also covered in dirt and what looked to be fresh cuts from breaking the mirror.

The little guy's eyes opened wide in panic as he struggled to breath and as he examined who it was that had just grabbed hold of him. His hands had shot up and taken hold of the arm that was closing off his air supply.

Even I was shocked when the person stepped into the corridor. It was Sarah. Her red hair was matted with gunk of all kinds, but was definitely not green. Thank God I had made the right call earlier. Her clothes, well, my clothes were tattered and torn. She obviously hadn't had the assistance of Bob and Narelle as I had. But what struck me the most was the expression on her face. She was not happy. In fact she was down right pissed off.

I feel an 'Aliens' analogy coming on. Picture Ripley as she comes out in that big loader thingy to fight the queen. That's how pissed off Sarah looked at this moment. Her faced held a scowl so dark and deep I nearly didn't recognise her. Her head was tilted just slightly to the side as she regarded the struggling man in her grasp. It was a patronising position as if she was blaming a very bad little child for doing something he shouldn't have.

She had not had a good day by all appearances and, unlike hiding it as she usually does; she was ready to take it out on someone. Now I felt sorry for the guy in her hands. Even though he was the prick who had hurt me and taunted me so much, I knew Sarah when she had a temper and she was worse than any monster I could even imagine.

For a mediumly built woman, She certainly was strong. With the one hand, she lifted this little guy off the ground and told him in no uncertain terms to-

"Back off and leave us alone!"

Not quite as concise nor as well delivered as "Get away from her, you Bitch!" It did get the message across, though.

With that she shoved the guy against the mirror I had bumped into earlier and punched him square in the face.

Violence was never her strong point and it would have taken a lot to have gotten her to resort to it.

The little guy went limp in her hands. He wasn't dead, just unconscious. She let him drop to the floor.

She turned to look at me.

"Sarah?"

It took a couple of seconds but the scowl seemed to fall from her face. Her eyes lit up with joy and relief and a smile slowly worked its way past the scowl that had taken control of her.

She moved toward me, extending her hands as if offering to help me up.

"Scott, I'm so glad your okay."

I shook my head at her, not taking her hands. She obviously hadn't looked too closely at my legs. Even I could see a number of largish shards of mirror sticking out of them. They didn't go too deeply, but there was a hell of a lot of blood starting to ooze out. My moving of my legs hadn't helped my injuries any, helping the shards to work a little deeper into the wounds and cut me open a little more.

"You'll have to forgive me if I don't get up," I indicated my legs, "I had a little accident."

She seemed to notice what I was talking about because her eyes widened in both sympathy and a form of horror. She didn't like blood at the best of times, I knew that, and this would be rather gross for her.

"Oh, god, I'm sorry."

"Hey, it's not your fault. You paid the prick that did this to me what I was hoping to give to him, so I feel a little better."

She squatted next to my legs to regard them. She didn't know what to do, neither did I. She looked around as if looking for a first aid kit or something, but, of course, that was useless.

"What should we do?"

I shook my head, "You tell me."

"Well, we can't stay here. He's going to wake up soon."

I smiled, "Then give him another of those wonderful left hooks."

She smiled, but didn't laugh. It wasn't a laughing moment. She was obviously concerned about me. I was just happy to see she was alright.

I was about to speak again, tell her I had been looking for her, of all the different things that had happened, but Sarah jumped to her feet and moved back to where the old guy lay. She picked up his feet and pulled him away from the mirror. His head thumped against the ground loudly. She pulled on his legs and dragged him around the space. I realised what she was trying to do was use him as a broom or mop. It was quite successful actually. Once she had finished with him, the ground was free from glass. I was now wondering about the old guy's backside. That brought a smile to my face again. I hope he got stabbed a few times.

Sarah came back over to me.

"Okay. I'm going to take your arms. Try not to move your legs at all. I'm going to drag you out of here. We need to find someone that can help us."

"You'll be hard pressed to do that."

I heard her sigh, but she got up and took hold of my armpits, lifting my arms like handles. Once she had a secure hold, she turned me around and started pulling me back the way she had come.

"You know the way out of here?"

"Yes. It's just through here."

Sure enough, she pulled me through where she had come and in the reflection of the mirrors of this new corridor, I saw the other door out of this room. I was so close. Damn it. If only I hadn't tried being so smug and sure of myself with that little prick, I probably would have been out of here by now or at least still able to walk.

Sarah stopped at the door, opened it and then pulled me through. I couldn't see much of the next room. It was darker than the other rooms, except the aviary of course, and I could only see the door. She closed it behind us and left me sitting while she found a chair to wedge under the handle, making it very hard to open the door. Though if that guy wanted to, he could probably use his powers to get out. That wasn't my concern now, though.

"What happened to you?"

She continued pulling me along a wooden floor as she answered.

"I found myself in a slaughterhouse, sort of like a computer room I was in earlier. Oh, I didn't tell you about that because I couldn't remember it. Sorry."

"That's cool. It sounds similar to what happened to me. Go on anyway."

We moved past various pieces of furniture, "Anyway, I left the slaughterhouse with some help from this really weird looking guy. Anyway, I found myself in this corridor. It just went on and on for ever," sounded familiar, "And then I was somehow teleported into this other room, where I met that tosser in there. He told me I had to stay in that room in the rudest way. When he left, I thought what the heck, he couldn't be so rude and get away with it. So I walked straight out. I got so lost from there, going through really dark and grimy tunnels to this room that was full of these really big spiders. It was horrible," she hesitated as if she was thinking about it, "But fascinating at the same time."

Trust Sarah to see both sides to our predicament. It sounded like she had probably had a worse time than I had. But she was better off than I was.

"Anyway, I found myself in that mirror place and I heard that guy's voice on the other side of that mirror wall. As I said, I wasn't going to let him get away with speaking to me like that and I was definitely in no mood for any more nonsense. I guess being chased by seven horny, perverted dwarfs does that to you."

"You were brilliant in there," I was being very honest. I admired her for what she did, and what she had been through. She was a damn strong woman. It was hard not to see that, nor to respect that.

"Yeah, but now we've got more important things to worry about. Like finding something resembling a hospital or doctor."

She let me down again and I heard her fumbling at the handle.

"What the...?"

"What?"

I tried to turn to see what was wrong, but the strain was too much. I gave up trying and sat back facing the room. It was like the first room. Nicely furnished and everything. But it had lost its appeal to me now. I wanted out of this place and I wanted it now.

"The door. It's locked."

Talking about coincidence, "You're sure?"

"Of course I'm sure," She was getting snappy. I felt ashamed. How stupid a question was that? She must really be feeling the tension now and I wish there was something I could do to help her, but there wasn't. I was a dead weight. Useless, "It wasn't locked a couple of minutes ago. Someone must have been stuffing around."

"How do you mean?"

She came back to squat beside me, lowering her voice, "I mean that all the way here, I was finding rooms full of locked doors. I just find it really coincidental that they just happened to lead me to you. Not that that isn't a good thing, but why on Earth would One want us together?"

She had a damn good point, "Maybe it was someone else."

She looked thoughtful, "Maybe. But maybe not," She stood up again and moved behind me, "We have to get out of here, no matter who is doing it."

"Is that door the only way out?"

I heard her sigh, "Yup. Looks as though we're trapped."

"You said it, little lady," it was him, that little guy. But he wasn't in the room. He sounded different too. Not so high and mighty and formal. Now he sounded down right sinister, like when he had told me to die.

Suddenly, the ground gave way beneath me. I could tell I wasn't alone as I started falling. Sarah had started screaming, and I could see her arms flailing for something to grab onto. Me, I just fell. I could already see there was nothing to grab. It was very much like the pit Bob had fallen down. Smooth edges, but I didn't know how far it went. I didn't scream though. I was too stuffed. I just kept falling and falling, listening to Sarah's scream slowly fade out, letting the darkness of the pit overcome me.

P

When I awoke, I found myself lying in a large bed. The covers had been pulled up to my neck, as if someone had taken the time to tuck me in.

"Sarah?"

"I'm here."

A shadow appeared over the bed and sat down beside me. I winced a little as the bed moved, aggravating my wounds.

"Sorry."

"That's okay. Where are we?"

She looked around, I could just make out her features in the dim light, "I've been here before. Or somewhere like it. It's where I met that old guy."

She was very mellow and there was a slight edge to her voice. Not one of anger, but one of sadness. Like something was being caught in her throat.

I pulled my arm free of my covers and took hold of her hand, "You okay?"

She turned her head away from me, "I just want to get out of here. I want to go home."

I could tell she was near tears. I didn't blame her. If I wasn't feeling so weak, I would have been the same. I felt a little better, more refreshed, but my weakness grew from my pain. I just didn't want to move.

"They looked after your wounds. I don't know why. They've been treating me okay. Left me food, there's some here for you too."

I pulled myself up in the bed and found I could lean back on a headboard.

"Is there any way out?"

She shook her head, "Not this time. They've closed the exit."

I let my head rest on the board for a while. Neither of us moved. We had nothing to do and nowhere to go.

"I guess they'll come for us when they want us," She wasn't sounding very confident any more. Not that I could blame her. But I did know I couldn't sit here any longer and do nothing. I reached for the covers and threw them back. I looked down at my legs. They had torn open my cords to bandage me up. Nice of them, but they totally ruined these really cool pants. I could say that made me mad, but I was already mad. I was mad at the fact I had been so useless. I was madder still at the fact that we were trapped and I was the maddest about everything that had happened to Sarah. I knew I couldn't blame myself and Sarah didn't blame me and that she would probably hate me for thinking her weak as it's sexist, but stuff sexism. I was genuinely concerned about her. She was my friend, one of the few, and I didn't want to lose her. But before that, I didn't want her to suffer. And I was determined not to let that happen.

"What are you doing?"

She stood up, regarding me, "Getting up."

I swung my legs over the side of the bed, let my feet touch the ground for a few moments and then pushed myself up. The pain was bad, but not unbearable. I wasn't sure if it would aggravate my wounds, making me bleed again or what, but if it did, who cares. I may die here anyway.

The rest of the room was rather well lit by the floor. Yes, the floor was glowing. Like everything else inanimate in this world, it was glowing. I accepted that now.

I could see a doorway. It was a set of double doors, big heavy looking wood with bolts stuck through them. It wasn't hard to guess that they were locked. But, hell, it's always worth a try.

I limped over toward the doors, Sarah followed behind me, and I tried the knobs.

"I already tried that," She informed me.

"Great, now I am. Okay, so we've established we're locked in. What happens, though, when we do this?"

With that, I knocked on the door.

A little panel, invisible to us before, swung open in the left-hand door. It was only small enough to see the eyes, nose and mouth of the man that was on the other side.

"What?"

"We wish to see One."

The face turned to the side and I could hear a little mumbling. A moment later it turned back, "Okay."

The panel shut and everything went silent. I looked over at Sarah. She was stunned at what I was doing, but didn't look angry or upset by it.

The silence was broken by the rattling of a key in the lock. The doors soon swung open and who should be standing there, but that old little dude with the cuts on his face. Obviously his doctors hadn't done as good a job on him as me.

"Nice to see you, mind if we see One now?"

I said it just as he opened his mouth to speak. He seemed taken aback by my forwardness, but more so, my politeness. I believed it was time to take a different tack, and if it got us killed, so be it. The other way of waiting around would be more boring and probably leave us dead anyway.

He was about to speak again so I cut in again, "Great. Could you kindly lead the way?"

He scowled at me, but nodded. He indicated to his right and I indicated for Sarah to go through first. She gave me a quizzical look but accepted my invite. This was going to be very interesting.

We walked for a while, going down a long corridor, turning right, entering rooms and more rooms until we came to this great big hall. As we walked, Sarah had noticed my limping. She moved beside me and hoisted me up onto her shoulder,

"Lean on me," was all she said. I wasn't in much of a mood to argue, so I did as she told me.

The hall we found ourselves in looked like it would be the kind of place a king would sit. Perhaps a throne room or something. But One wasn't here.

I let my eyes roam over the black walls, the big pillars, of which I was sure the roof would collapse if they weren't present, and another set of blood red double doors that sat in the centre of the opposite wall.

Okay, one guess for where we would find this One fellow.

Correct!

We followed this old guy across the room, our shoes echoed loudly on the hard glowing floor. I was preparing myself for a confrontation, easing my breathing and calming myself so as to release some pent up tension. Sarah was looking at me as if I was crazy. She may very well be right for the mood I was in right now. I didn't want any nonsense and I was ready to retaliate if any of it came my way.

The old guy stopped once he reached the doors and turned to us. I was now leaning heavily on Sarah. I knew that was cruel on my behalf, but I needed to save as much strength as I could. Besides, my knees were killing me.

He seemed to look us over a couple of times and then turned back to the door. As he did so, I put my weight back onto my own two feet and steadied myself. I was going in under my own steam and not showing any weakness at all. I was not going to look completely useless when I faced this character. And I was not going to behave that way either.

The doors swung open and the old guy disappeared inside. I pulled Sarah's supporting arm from my back and shook my head at her. She nodded as if understanding. She always understands, well almost always, but she does her best. I would so much rather she didn't go in with me, but I knew arguing with her would be pointless, yet again. Although I just said she was understanding, it didn't mean she couldn't be pig-headed too. But can't we all be?

This was different. I didn't know what to expect and I knew it was definitely not going to be safe.

It was dark within, but I could make out the old guy standing just inside, waiting.

I looked over at Sarah and she looked back. Neither of us looked or felt particularly confident or happy, so I smiled at her. I wanted it to be something reassuring, but it felt kind of stupid, foolish even. I was happy, though, when I saw her smile back. I took her hand and we squeezed together. We were about to face something big and terrifying, but we weren't going to do it alone. I was there for her as she was for me and although we could see that, I think we both needed to feel it too.

We stepped at the same time and neither of us even twitched when the two doors closed noisily behind us. We were now trapped. We were totally enclosed in One's domain. We were very nearly his to command.

It was dark. The floor, like in the other rooms was giving off a faint reddish glow. It gave the black walls and ceiling a blood-like hue as it reflected of the smooth glass-like surfaces. That was the funny thing about this black rock. It was always smooth and well cut. Even in here. Weird.

From what I could tell, we were standing on some kind of platform. It extended for about three meters but then dropped suddenly into nothingness. There was, however, one single path that led further into the darkness. It, too, glowed, but not nearly enough to let us see where it led.

This bridge-like thing was only wide enough for a single person to walk across. The old guy had already started making his way across. Sarah started moving ahead, but my feet wouldn't move. She tugged at my hand and looked back at me. But I couldn't look at her. I couldn't take my eyes off this bridge. I just couldn't move.

I don't know if I told you before, but heights scare me to death. This bridge was like the spitting image of the worst nightmare I'd ever had as a child. I would always be forced to cross a really narrow bridge without railings that seemed to go on and on forever. I never tried it standing. I would always crawl across like a baby, fearing to let go of the edges, making sure with every movement I was still steady and safe as I could possibly be on the bridge.

Now I was faced with it, I couldn't do it. I knew I couldn't. It was impossible. Fear had taken hold of my legs and my arms had begun shaking. It was terrible.

Sarah pulled on my arm again but I shook my head, "Please, no."

She came back to stand in front of me, blocking my view of the bridge, "Scott, we have to. There is no other way."

Of course she was right. But I couldn't do it!

"If it makes you feel any safer, I'll go behind you and make sure nothing will happen."

I looked at her now. I knew she was doing her best to comfort me, but it wasn't going to work, "How could you do that? How could you guarantee that nothing happens?"

She looked down at her shoes for a moment and then back into my eyes. A very powerful move on her behalf. In doing that she took my complete attention. I was grabbed in that instant by her brown eyes.

"Scott, I can't and you know that. But this is important. Not only to you and me, but to everyone here. I am sure as hell not going to face him alone and if I can find a way to get back home over there, I am not going to go without you. You will come with me, even if I have to carry you. And if we can do any good here, then that would be worth so much more than turning away now. You know that. You know the only thing we can do now is cross that bridge. Now are you coming with me or not?"

I thought about it, but only for a couple of seconds. I thought about what the worst could be if I crossed that bridge. I thought about what would happen if I didn't. I thought about going home. About Sarah and her safety. I thought about everything in only a couple of seconds. It was the clearest my thinking had been the whole time I had been on this god-forsaken reality. And I knew I had to go.

It was no longer a case of could or couldn't. It was a need, the concept of having to do it. And so I decided.

"You lead."

She gave me a huge smile and wrapped her arms around me gently. When she pulled away, she turned toward the bridge and waited for me to follow.

It took a lot of self control to take my first step onto that bridge. I focused on the rock ahead of where I stepped, where I would put my other foot. I would not let myself think about what lay below. It was easier to imagine that there was no nothing below me, rather that there was just another level of rock, black like the roof. I kept my focus, however, on moving forward. I could see Sarah ahead of me, but I didn't let her movement distract me. That wasn't to say I didn't keep an eye on her in case something went wrong, but she was doing well. But I kept focusing. Step by step I would make it. Step by step across the bridge. One step after the other. I let it run through my mind. "Just one step after another. Just one step after..."

"Scott."

I looked up. It was Sarah. She had a big smile on her face.

"We made it."

I looked down again and blinked. She was right. I was no longer walking on that narrow bridge. I hadn't even noticed that it had widened at least six feet in either direction, nor that the black pit had disappeared from below me. I had made it across. I was safe again. I was...

"Come."

Great. The old guy had to go and ruin it. Fine. We weren't safe. It wasn't over, but I had conquered one of my greatest fears. I wiped at my face and found the back of my hand covered in sweat.

The old guy had started to move off, so Sarah and I followed side by side this time. I noticed that there were holes in the ground that seemed to disappear into nothing, just as the pit we had crossed had. That wasn't too comforting as it began to dawn on me we were still only on one singular little platform, high above nothingness.

I refused to let that get to me, though. I had crossed the bridge, now I could face anything they decided to throw at me.

He rounded a corner, staying in Sarah's line of sight, but not mine, but once I turned the same corner, I realised he had come to a small archway and stopped.

"You will go inside."

"And you," I asked.

"Will stay here."

Okay, fine by me.

I walked past him, knowing Sarah was following closely behind. Once I got close to the archway, however, I had to stop for a moment. It was hot in there. I could feel the heat emanating from inside. There was also a small amount of steam escaping from inside, telling me it was going to be very hot and muggy.

I took a breath and stepped inside and to the side, to allow Sarah to come in.

It was a strange little place. Same black rock, same red glowing floor. But there were little steam baths everywhere. The roof was no longer smooth, but covered in stalactites and the ground was littered with their cousins, the stalagmites Looking up, the air around the tops of the stalactites was swirling with steam, making it impossible to see the real roof of this place. Obviously it was coming from the baths, I was just admiring how cool and atmospheric it looked.

There was a small pathway worn through the 'mites. I took it as our only option from here.

I turned back to the old guy and gave him a quick salute, flashing a cheesy grin as I said, "Thanks for the ride, Pops."

He sneered at me, but I didn't mind. I was hoping not to see him again.

I led the way along the path, keeping my eye out for anyone who may claim to be One or anything that could be just as dangerous. My ears were also alert.

I could hear something. Breathing, I think. It was hard to tell as it was sort of long and drawn it sounded like some kind of weird background noise. Perhaps the seedy beginning to some sicko heavy metal band. Other than that, however, there was nothing.

Something moved ahead of us. I indicated for Sarah to stop. I did so, too.

It was behind a steam bath. I couldn't make it out clearly as the moisture as it rose was forming a cover for it. But it was more than that. Shadows were clinging to every wall, every nook and cranny the light from the ground couldn't reach. This thing behind the steam was virtually invisible, but I knew it was there. I tried to peer deeper, you know, straining my eyes, pretending I have x-ray vision of some sort. I still couldn't see anything. I watched for a few moments.

"What is it?"

"I don't know," was all I could say.

Something moved slowly through the veil of steam. It was long and black, moving slowly and gracefully. Whatever it was looked to be about as thick as a basketball's diameter. But it's length gave the distinct impression of a tail.

"Wait here," I told her. I didn't know what I was going to do, but I started to walk forward.

I made it to within six meters of whatever it was before I got a response.

"Come no closer."

The words were like punches. I felt like it had struck out at me with every syllable. It didn't hurt, but it seemed to wash over me, clinging to me like the slime back at the dungeon. I shook my head and did what I was asked. It wasn't because he asked me to stop, but because I just didn't want to get any closer.

In the darkness, it stirred again. I could see it's sleek, black bulk now. It appeared to be curled into one great big mass, but I couldn't make out any clear details.

"You have invaded that which is mine."

It was a moment before I could compose myself to speak, "I have done no such thing. This place is the people's as much as yours. They seem not to have any complaints to my being here."

The words that came out of my mouth sounded different. They were mine, but they were so formal. I wasn't possessed or anything, but I don't know, they just came out that way.

"They do and think only what I want them to."

I smiled at it, "You do not give them enough credit."

"You insubordinate little creature. You have no idea whom you are talking to, nor any comprehension of that in which you are involving yourself."

"Oh, I think I have an idea. You are just another big dictator that wants absolute power. And with all your wealth and power, you think you deserve the reverence and worship of everyone who is not so fortunate. Does that about sum it up?"

Two large fiery green eyes appeared from within the bulk. It was as if he had only now bothered to open his eyes. In doing so, however, I could make out a little more of his face as the light gleamed off his features.

I couldn't be sure, but it appeared to have a longish snout, smooth in texture as the protrusion I had seen earlier and just as black. The brow ridges above its eyes were strong and thick. There was no sign of hair anywhere, yet it was no reptile I had ever seen. I didn't know what it was.

"So you have been paying attention to what you have seen around you. That, nor your thoughts on the matter are of any consequence to me."

"Then what do you want from us?"

I heard Sarah moving behind me. She had come closer, to either join the conversation or just be present to hear his answer. I wasn't sure which.

Above the breathing, I heard something else. Something deep and resonating. It started as only a noise, mixed with the background breaths, but it steadily grew louder, more distinguishable until it was obvious that this monster was laughing at us.

But why? Why would he laugh? All I did was ask him what he wanted from us.

It took in a deep breath of air and returned to a low chuckle.

"What? What is it you want from us?"

The eyes tilted slightly and blinked. I could make out its pupils now. Wide and black, surrounded by the glowing green. They looked like those pits from earlier, disappearing into complete darkness. I contained a shudder at the thought of how evil this monster could be.

"As I said, you are of no consequence to me, alive. More a hindrance soon to be rectified."

"Rectified?"

It was Sarah.

The creature chuckled again, "Yes. Rectified. Vanquished... destroyed, if you like."

Not on my watch.

"And how do you plan to do that?"

It raised its head and rested it against something. I could only guess it was its hand.

"Easily enough."

"Why don't you return us home," Sarah asked. She still sounded strong, not cracking under his threats.

It paused, sighing a deep sigh as if talking to some naive fellow who hasn't grasped a concept yet.

"You are of more use to us dead. Easier to control. Easier to study."

What did he mean by that? I had to ask, "Study?"

"Yes. Study. I wish to learn how you and your petty acquaintances manage to find your way here from your worlds. I wish to know how I, too, can travel as you, back and forth. And I plan to find out through studying your remains once you and your companion are no longer living."

He didn't know how we got here? He didn't know? My God! Neither did we! I was hoping he would at least be helpful and compromise, sending us home in return for us never to annoy him again. But he didn't even know how we got here in the first place. He was going to be of little or no help to us at all!

I looked at Sarah, she looked just as annoyed as I was at the fact that no one seemed to know how we could get home.

I then realised that that was totally irrelevant now. We had more important things to worry about. Like staying alive to find a way home.

I looked back at the creature that still lay hidden in the shadows.

"You want to learn how we travel across realities? You want to do this why? So you can take over our worlds too? So you can force people to worship you as you have here?"

"Yes."

Just one word. No thought behind it. It knew what it wanted and it was pleased.

I was startled when I saw a flash of white appear beneath its eyes. It grew gradually until it became a full, toothy smile. It was as if his very teeth glowed. I had not seen his teeth as he had spoken earlier. They must have been hidden by the steam and his lips, but now I was wishing I still had not.

They were very much like ours, human, I mean. Most were flat and white, but its two upper canines were huge and sharp as large knives. The lower two were by no means blunt either, but they seemed to be tiny in comparison to those two massive fangs he had.

"You do realise that they don't worship you. They don't respect you, honour you, love you. How can they? They aren't even allowed free thought. They can't think for themselves. They can't truly worship you," I was trying to pull some heart strings here. Play the emotional card either to get him to wise up or get mad and irrational. His response showed me it wasn't going to work.

"So?"

He kept his smile. He was winning and he knew it. We were going to be dead if we didn't do something.

As it happened, we didn't have to do anything.

The room was hot. I knew that, but it was hard not to notice the extra heat as the temperature seemed to rise up another notch. I initially thought it had something to do with some kind of thermostat, that maybe he was going to bake us alive.

But when a little speck of white appeared right in front of me, I knew what was going on. I had seen this before and by god was it a miracle.

A beam of white shot out of that little speck. And it began to sweep wildly around the room. It flashed across the monster in the darkness, allowing me short glimpses of what it looked like. I still couldn't distinguish much, but I could tell by both the look in its eye, the disappearance of its smile and the movement I saw as the light swept over him. He was moving, gathering itself up, and trying to stand. The

106

eyes were wide with both wonder and horror. He must have realised we were about to make our escape.

I looked over at Sarah. She was watching the ball of light as it began to grow.

We were going to make it out of here.

When I looked back, I noticed that the ball had grown quite considerably from the tiny speck it had been before. Everything took on a sort of strobe look. Why? Because those beams of light were still flaying around the room, striking me in the face and the eye. They didn't blind me but I found myself with that familiar sensation of looking down a tunnel of light into something, somewhere else. I still didn't know what it was, but I couldn't let it distract me. I didn't know how long we had to wait before we attempted touching it or going through it or whatever you called it.

"Grekon!"

It was One. He was not happy. But he was doing a good job at getting up and moving that massive bulk of his. The various coloured lights that were being shot out from the ball had lit up his body now and I could see him in his totality. He was massive. At least thirteen feet long. Long for he walked on all fours and that was not counting his tail. It would reach for another nine feet totally stretched from the looks of it, but I wasn't willing to wait around to find out.

"Sarah, go!"

She looked over at me. I could already hear the old guy behind us, scuffling along the ground.

"Go! Now!"

Q

She struck out at the light with her hand and, as earlier in my living room, she lost her solidity and vanished into the ball.

I looked toward One who was making a clumsy attempt at getting over the stalagmites. His tough hide was protecting him from their sharp points, but he was still being hindered in his movement. I could finally make out his face.

I was rather shocked to see it was not as horrible and gruesome as I had imagined it. It was almost dog like, with a long snout and dog-like ears, but its eyes, the lines around them, the other features on its face were so human. It was scary in its own way, that resemblance. But I still couldn't call it ugly. It was cute in its own way, but I knew that its exterior was so totally different to the cold evil heart that lay within. This was no cute little puppy dog. It was a monster of great power and I wanted to get as far away from it as possible.

"Looks like you lucked out," I laughed at it.

I could hear Grekon, the old guy right behind me now. I wasn't going to take any more chances. I reached out with my hand and tried to grasp the ball.

I felt a rush as my hand drew close to it. As before, the heat seemed to disappear and my body was overcome with a coolness I could easily associate with a beautiful spring day. It happened so quickly it was like a shock to my system. I don't think we were supposed to jump at it so quickly. My head felt a little light as I finally made non-contact with the ball. I still couldn't touch it, though I could.

My body shook as a bolt of energy passed right through it and I found myself frozen to the spot. I could still see One getting closer, though I could no longer hear anything. He looked very angry.

Slowly, bit by bit, my body began to disappear into the ball. It was still unnerving even the second, if not the third or fourth, though I couldn't remember exactly how many times I had actually done this, time round, to find yourself left with only your mind. I felt so vulnerable, especially with these two bad guys coming straight at me. But soon enough, it wouldn't be a concern of mine any longer.

Finally, I felt myself being sucked in. One moment I was in the hellhole where One lived, the next I was in that dreaded tunnel of light.

Colours flashed all around me. Blues, reds, greens. I was flying down this light tunnel. Then it struck me. Light tunnel. Flying fast. Light. Speed. Light-Speed. Maybe that was what it was. Maybe, just maybe, we were travelling at light speed, allowing us to cross some kind of dimensional barrier. Maybe travelling faster than light doesn't make you go faster, but makes you go sideways, through the very essence of reality into a totally different reality but the exact same time. Time still occurred here and there. In my reality and the one I had just left.

I don't know. It's only a theory.

The flashes disappeared, once more to be replaced by images. But the images I saw this time were familiar to me. More natural than the swords and castles and junk I had seen last time through. I saw sofas, houses, office buildings. Things I knew from my world, but there were faces too. The owner of the deli down the road from my apartment, friends I go to Uni with, family and relations. Everything was so familiar and not once did I see that horrible scarred face, then again, I didn't see Bob's face either.

I had to admit I was glad I never ran into that mean looking dude, but Bob… I was going to miss him. We had some good adventures together. I wanted to smile in memory, but I couldn't. I didn't have a mouth still. So I let my mind wander again over what had happened over the past number of hours.

How long had it been? It felt like half a day at least. And with me being knocked out all that time, I was sure it was even longer than it felt. Wow.

Well, I was lucky I didn't have a lecture this morning, or I would be screwed. It would be what, Tuesday, now. Hmm. Good. I don't have any lectures today or tomorrow. I could just see it now. Me, lying in bed, safe and sound in my own apartment, with no worries about that One character or the old dude, Grekon I think his name was. Sleeping, reading, watching the television. Peace and quite. Rest and relaxation. That's the life I want to live for the next couple of days. No worries.

Most of those thoughts flew from my mind when I felt my "self" jarring to a halt.

Almost there. I was almost home. Safe and sound in my lounge room.

I was relieved when I saw the colour begin to split, forming another gateway. I could hardly wait to get away from all this nonsense.

But when I looked through the portal, I didn't see my home. It was only small, granted, but it was not my home. It was somewhere else, totally.

In a number of short moments I could finally make out some more detail and I was not impressed.

There in front of me was what appeared to be the backs to a lot of heads. Each sat on either side of an aisle. At the end of the aisle was what could only be called a windscreen. There was no denying it. I knew where I was headed and I was far from impressed.

Who ever was in charge of this blasted tunnel transporter thingy was a real pain in the neck. It's bad enough they chose me to travel between worlds in the first place, but now they have to go and dump me back home on a bloody bus.

I hate public transport! How could they do this to me?

Sure enough, I felt my mind's body being pulled toward the gateway. The sensation was the same, being dragged through a pool of goo. I wanted to swim through it, but still didn't have any limbs so it was a waste of thought.

You couldn't imagine how relieved I was, though, when I finally passed through the rip and watched my body piece itself back together. But it was different. Something was different. Not the make up or anything. Something was just different from how I was when I touched the ball back in the other reality.

Then I noticed it. My cords. I was still wearing them. But it wasn't that. They were no longer ripped. And my knees. There was no pain. The bandages were still there, I could feel them, but the pain had totally gone. It was as if everything had repaired itself.

Oh this was going to be one glorious day or two of relaxation. No pain, no worries. All I had to do now was find out which bus I was on and how to get back home.

No one had noticed my arrival. Shows how much people really pay attention to one another whilst on public transport. They always seem to enter a world of their own, keeping to themselves and not wanting to disturb anyone else. That was, of course, if they weren't pain in the arse school kids who never shut up and think the world of themselves when, in fact, they are just a bunch of obnoxious twits that have no idea about decency, intelligence or respect.

But they learn. Well, they usually do. I know my school friends did. Not that they were really my friends. They were in the same year, but I didn't hang with them because they were just like the kids I described and I hated that. So I avoided them. Oh well, no loss on my part I don't think. Yeah right.

Anyway, I was back in my reality and boy was I happy. I knew I had a dumb looking grin on my face but I didn't care. Neither did anyone else.

Looking out the window, I recognised where I was. This was the bus I could catch to go out to Uni. But it was going the other way, into the city. That was a relief. Meant it wouldn't be a problem at all to get home. Heck, I could do some shopping first.

Hang on... Where was Sarah? Don't tell me that who ever was in charge of the light tunnel chose to split us up, yet again.

I looked around. There was no sign of her.

Obviously they had.

All I could hope now was that she would get home alright. I could then give her a call, or she me and make sure we were both okay.

R

When I got home, I went straight to the answering machine. The little light was flashing. Usually it isn't, that's why I normally just leave it, never really bothering to check it. The only people I get calls from are my parents or rellies. But as far as I could remember, there was no momentous family occasion, so I could only assume it was Sarah.

I pressed the stop button and rewound the tape. Yes I still had an old archaic tape run answering machine. I thought it was quaint. It clicked to a halt shortly after and the play light lit up. I hit the appropriate button and waited a few moments.

Following a beep -someone hanging up- I heard a familiar voice.

"Scott? You there?"

Pause.

"Well, it's me, Sarah. I was just wondering if you got home okay. Give us a call as soon as you can. Okay?"

She paused again.

"Bye."

Yet another pause. But she didn't hang up.

"Scott?"

The machine beeped out.

I picked up the phone and quickly dialled in her number, stuck my finger on the cut off button and dialled again. I was never good at fast dialling and I often found myself hitting the wrong button as I had just done.

The line began to ring. Once. Twice. Five times. No answer. I waited for another eight. Still no answer.

Maybe she was in the shower or something. She didn't have an answering machine so I couldn't leave a message.

I kept holding the line until the connection broke into an engaged signal.

I put down the receiver.

Maybe she was out shopping. Eating, relaxing, I don't know.

I went into my room and looked around. Nothing had been touched. Just the same as it was when I had left last night. My bed lay unmade and everything. But I didn't care. I was home and I was happy.

I went over to my bed and jumped onto it. Landing face down, I turned onto my back and tried to make myself comfortable.

I just lay there. Not closing my eyes. Wondering. Wondering about everything that had happened over the last... I looked at my watch. Nineteen hours. A long time. I must have been over there for, what, about sixteen and a bit hours. Hmm.

It didn't feel that long. Maybe because I was unconscious for a lot of it. Who knows? But it was exciting. Problem was what did it all mean? I mean, sure, maybe it was just a freak occurrence. Maybe both Sarah and I were fortunate enough to be dragged across dimensions twice in one day just by chance. I still couldn't remember much about my first visit there, but this second one was much clearer in my memory. I was sure I wouldn't forget it in a hurry.

But who could I talk about it to? Sarah, sure, but she'll grow tired of it. There would only be so far we could discuss it without ever knowing what the real point of it all was. It could have just been a freak occurrence like you read about in those wacky newspapers. Maybe that stuff did happen. Then again, maybe it didn't. But this did. I knew it did. Sarah did too. But no one else would believe it. Why would they? It's way too weird for anyone to believe let alone care about.

So it was our little secret.

But I couldn't help wondering... Why? Why her? Why me? Why everything?

I don't mean the point to life, but surely there was something behind the two of us having such freaky experiences.

Oh, I don't know.

I closed my eyes, to try and sleep, I guess. But they found themselves falling open again. I wasn't tired. I was both excited, yet, mellow. Hard to explain I guess. I just wanted to lie there doing nothing but thinking.

That was until I heard a knock at the door.

I pulled myself off the bed.

"Who is it?"

"Sarah! You did make it home!"

"Sounds that way, doesn't it," I joked with her. She sounded all excited.

I opened the door for her.

She was standing on the door step dressed in a pair of black combat pants, like those I had gone over in.

Damn. I would never see them again. At least I still had my wallet.

Over that she was wearing a black t-shirt with a grey jumper tied around her waist. She looked good, fresh and clean. Her hair was damp. Another shower. Her eyes were bright and her smile was huge.

She dumped a plastic bag on the ground beside her and grabbed me, hugging me.

I hugged her back and couldn't help smiling.

"Good to see you're okay," I told her.

She pulled away, "You too."

Picking up the bag, she came into my apartment.

I shut the door behind her and locked it, "What's that?"

"Your clothes."

She offered them to me and I took them, looking in the bag. On top was my jumper, totally clean and mended. Obviously the trip back had been as good for her as it was to me. I was glad for my new clothes.

I went back into my room and dumped the bag beside my cupboard.

"Take a seat, I'm just getting changed," I called.

I liked the clothes, but I wasn't going to stay in them for the rest of the day. They were too good. I didn't want to risk damaging them, catching them on something or spilling something on them. I'm like that I guess. Fussy. But not vain.

A smile came to my face when I thought about that.

Vain. Not me. Oh, well.

The smile faded quickly. We hadn't done anything. We had been there, hoping we could help Bob and Narelle and everyone else, but we hadn't done squat. One was still in control. They would still be suffering there.

Great, now I was in a bad mood.

I took off my new clothes and hung the shirt and the pants in the cupboard. The t-shirt I folded and put into my drawer. Pulling out a pair of black jeans, another black t-shirt and a black jumper, I pulled them all on and wrapped the jumper around my waist. I knew I would look a lot like Sarah, but she was copying my fashion anyway. Another scary thought.

Tying my boots up, I heard a knock on my bedroom door.

"Yup?"

"Do you want a drink of something?"

"Sure. Tea, thanks."

"Great."

When I was dressed, I went into the kitchen. She was prepping the sugar, milk and tea whilst the kettle was just starting to boil.

"So what happened to you? Where did you end up?"

She scooped the sugar into the two cups she had laid out as she answered, "Coming back, you mean? The park just down the road from my place. Quite handy actually. Not far to walk."

"Good for some," I joked.

"Why? Where were you?"

"On a bus."

She looked at me and laughed, "A bus? You really do pick them."

"Pick them? Like I had a choice!"

Winking at me, she turned her attention back to the drinks, "I know, I was joking."

I decided to go and sit down in the lounge. When I walked in I noticed that the cups we had dropped last night had gone, but the stain remained.

"Thanks for picking up the mugs."

"Not a problem. I wasn't sure what you wanted me to put on the carpet so I was going to leave it for you."

"I think mum has some stuff I could borrow."

I ran my hand through the spillage. It was slightly, and I mean slightly, damp. Oh well, small price to pay for a bit of excitement.

I sat back down on the couch, listening to Sarah make the drinks and when she finally brought them in, I took mine gratefully as she sat down on one of the other chairs.

There was a bit of silence. I don't think either of us knew what to say. I know I was feeling rather uncomfortable. Not just with the silence, but with everything. It was weird. We had shared this experience but had nothing to say about it. Not that it was absolutely necessary to talk about it. I mean, hell, we had lives to live. We may as well get on and live them.

I took a sip of my tea.

"Nice. Thanks."

She smiled at me over her cup as she was blowing on it, to cool it down.

S

That night, after she had left, I found I was rather restless. Anxious. I don't know. Something. I just wanted to get out and do something. There wasn't much I could do. It was a Tuesday night. Nothing but the movies, but I just wasn't in the mood to be sitting down.

I got up, grabbed my keys, my wallet and went outside, locking the door behind me.

It was a nice night. The sky was mostly clear, with only a few clouds hovering above. Every so often they would cross in front of the moon, casting a little darkness into what could already be considered a dark night. I liked the night. The moon. The stars. Two of the most beautiful things in nature and they were both seen at the same time. Night. Everything looked so surreal and beautiful. A silvery hue covered the world. The road, the trees. The moon wasn't quite full but it was near enough. When the clouds wisped past it, it too looked beautiful, supernatural, even.

But even the beauty of the night wasn't enough. I felt so, I don't know, bored. I wanted to do something. But not without reason. It wasn't boredom, no. I know it isn't. It's something else. Like I have to do something rather than wanting.

It could be my failure on the other side catching up to me. Who knows? I would get over it. But right now, the walk was nice and it would at least help to clear my mind.

I walked for half an hour. But I didn't want to go back. Not yet. Something. Something still to be done.

Weird. Walking past a park, I noted how much it looked like snow covered it. I was almost convinced it was snow. A white blanket covered all the grass, but not a drop had touched the trees or the surrounding road. Maybe it had fallen or melted. But why would snow be so localised? It was a neat square of white glistening in the moonlight.

Another freak occurrence?

I ran over to the park and dipped my finger into the 'snow', excited at the prospect of another weird adventure. But when I drew it out again, it was moist and cold, but its texture was all wrong. It was sand. They had covered the grass with sand, perhaps to help it grow.

Laughing to myself I walked on.

It was a cool night. Not cold, but cool. A gentle breeze, the temperature was around fifteen degrees Celsius. Nice. I unwrapped my jumper from my waist and pulled it on. Cut out a bit of the chill that was present, preventing the chances of getting pneumonia.

115

God damn it! Everything felt so slow. So down right boring. So empty. There was something missing. Not just the excitement, but, oh, I don't know! I don't know.

I felt like that was all that was running through my head. Those three words.

Lifting my arms like aeroplane wings, I began to spin around like a child repeating over and over, "I don't know. I don't know."

I liked to do that. Not say those words, but spin like that. Even having my arms out and pretending I am a plane, it sort of brings me back to something. Something safe perhaps. Again, I don't know. It just felt comfortable, though I knew it looked stupid. But, hey, there was no one around. Or so I thought.

"Happy to be home, are we?"

I very nearly jumped out of my skin. For one thing, it was the shock that someone was there. For another, the person knew I had been away. But it sounded like no one I knew.

I dropped my arms quickly and looked about.

Standing in the middle of the park, right in the middle of the 'snow' was a largish man. A fair distance away. But he had sounded so close. Like he was standing next to me.

I took a step toward him, "I'm sorry. Do I know you?"

He didn't move.

"Oh yes. You know me. And I know you."

Another step. He was a big guy; there was no way I wanted to get too close.

"Well, you have me at a loss. I'm sorry."

"No need to apologise. It happens to the best of us. You see, some of us change. Some stay the same."

An old song ran through my head, "Something is lost, something is found. They will keep on speaking her name. Some things change, some stay the same."

I wasn't sure about the lyrics, but I liked the song. I like most of those slow, sentimental songs. This one was especially good due to the name. Hymn to Her. How beautiful sounding and poignant in meaning.

I tried to clear it out of my mind. It wasn't relevant as far as I could tell.

"Do you mind me asking your name?"

"No. Not at all. Though, I do feel it will be of no use to you."

I waited. He did not say his name.

"Well?"

"Come now, forget about it. Go back to your spinning."

This guy was weird. And, okay, sure, familiar. Everything seemed familiar.

I took another step forward and decided to be a bit more persistent.

"Who are you?"

"A friend."

He didn't seem like any friend I knew. He didn't seem like any friend I would want to know.

There was something about him though, I knew him. He was from There. That other place, but I didn't know who he was, or why he was here. I thought it best to ask him that considering he was avoiding my 'Who' question.

"Why do you think?"

Then I knew it. I remembered who he was. Not entirely, but I knew who he worked for. Why he was here was only a quick jump to what One had told me earlier. He was here to take control. This was one of One's minions and how he had gotten here, I hadn't the faintest. But if he was here, by Christ, this world could be in serious trouble.

Sure, we've got plenty of weapons and nuclear, biological devices to fight with, but this guy had more. The memory of the sweltering heat of One's room had me think that even the Global Warming that was over the news would be more helpful than a hindrance to that evil beast. That guy was magical, manipulative and pure evil. And, unfortunately, there are enough people with the same goals in mind in my reality to allow him to at least find some footing, leverage or power to take even a small amount of control and from then on, it would be so easy for him. A little manipulation here and there and soon enough, the world would be his.

That's the pessimistic view of the situation anyway. The other way to look at it would be that the world would pull together with the thoughts of peace, love and joy and conquer him.

You decide which sounds most probable. I know I already have an idea.

I couldn't let that happen. I had to find out how this stranger had gotten here and how to get him back to where he had come from.

This guy began to shake his head, letting out a little laugh.

"You know you won't be able to do that, don't you?"

He was reading my mind? Geez! Was there anything these freaks couldn't do?

"You don't even know how you did it. How could you possibly think you could send us back?"

Us? My God! There were more than just him. That was not good. Oop, got to clear my mind. Then again, my mental babble might just drive him insane.

"It just might do that."

"Why can't you just go home and look after your own world? Leave ours alone?"

"Come now, that's very selfish of you."

"Selfish," now here was a hypocrite and I hated hypocrites, "You're a fine one to talk about selfish!"

117

"Don't think you can even comprehend why we're doing what we are."

"Oh, right! You have justification for taking control of whole civilisations?"

He shrugged, "Yes. Of course."

"I'd like to hear that."

"I'm sure you would. But that's not why I am here."

"And why would you be here, may I ask?"

"To finish something I started yesterday."

"Hmm?"

"Oh, don't break my heart. Don't tell me you've forgotten the mirrors already. Nor the thrill of the hunt you allowed me yesterday morning when you escaped."

The hunt? I didn't remember the hunt. But that was in the morning. That weird episode I couldn't remember. But the mirrors. The mirrors? What about them?

Then it struck me.

No. It couldn't be.

The old guy? What was his name, Grekon?

"Grekon?"

"Ahh, now you're catching on," He sounded so smug.

"But... You're..."

"Not old? No. As I said, some things change, some stay the same. Just like that song."

Damn! This guy. Just like my clothes had mended as had my wounds. Like Sarah's were cleaned. This guy had somehow gotten, well, young. Bigger, stronger. Younger.

"Now," He started moving toward me, "Are you ready to die?"

"Wait!"

I had to try something. He would walk all over me now if we tried fighting, "How did you get through?"

"The same way you and your friend did. The same way One did. The same way the rest of his minions will. You forget there is life after you're gone. Once you had left our world, there was still us, time and that little glowing ball of yours. It hung around for a while. Long enough for both myself and The One to make the transition to this world of yours. Now we are here, and amongst other things, The One wants revenge! And quite frankly, so do I!"

Ooooooooooooooooooooooooh Bugger.

He was walking toward me. He was in no hurry. He knew he had the power here. I knew I was totally screwed. I started moving backward. Not taking my eye off of him. Back along my 'snow' to the road, never once looking away. He was getting closer. I couldn't keep going like this. He would catch me, no doubt about it.

So I did the only thing I could think of. I spun on my heels and I ran.

I was the fastest runner in my Tae Kwon Do class. Not at school when I was in the sports carnivals sadly enough, but once I started Tae Kwon Do, I pushed myself. Got faster. I was no weakling when it came to running. Now it was all I had to save me from certain death. I may not be fit, or be able to run very far, but the more I tried in escaping, the better the chance I had of surviving.

He was not going to catch me and I was determined not only to believe that, but to make it true.

I ran as fast as I could push myself, bolting. Head down, muscles taut. I sprung off one leg onto the other, pushing me forward. My body on such an odd angle, but my momentum keeping me moving forward and stopping me from falling flat on my face.

I could hear him behind me. He was still a fair distance. Heck, I had a head start. But his foot falls were loud and heavy. Not a very agile person.

I kept mainly to the side of the road, that way I would avoid trees hanging over the sidewalk and anything else that could get in my way. It just meant I had to be careful of any dangerous pot holes that had formed or broken away at the edge of the tar.

That wasn't going to be too hard. With the moon giving off the amount of light it was, I was able to see pretty clearly. But that meant that the old guy would also be able to see me.

No. Not the old guy. Young Grekon. Damn it all! How the hell did he get so young and virile? Why hadn't the same happened to me, at least on the way over to his world? I remained the same puny little idiot I am now. Maybe I was one of those things that stayed the same. But that didn't mean I was useless. I knew that. I had almost beaten this guy before and I was going to do it again. If it hadn't been for me being so cocky, I probably would have been fine. But I've learnt from that mistake and it won't happen again.

There was a side road coming up. I thought it may be a good idea to take it, rather than running along the one road in a straight line. If he wanted, he could start firing something at me as he had before.

Problem was if he was a telepath as well, I had no chance of escaping.

I sent out a thought to him, you know, focusing on a sentence and trying to force it out of your mind.

"You are so going to lose."

There was no response.

I tried again, "A piece of crap like you, you couldn't even take over an ant colony let alone this world."

Again, nothing.

Maybe I was wrong. Maybe he wasn't a telepath. Just a lucky guesser. Or maybe I was just a bad receptor, or he had limited range. Who knows? I wasn't going to start questioning his abilities right now. I would have to wait until I got a better idea of whom, or what this guy really is.

I took the turn to the left. This street was darker as the foliage from the trees lining the street blocked much of the light. That made my navigation a little harder, but I would endure that.

Taking a quick glance over my shoulder, I saw he had rounded the corner after me. He was still a fair distance behind me and didn't seem to be catching. That was a relief. But I had to find some way out of this mess. I couldn't keep running all night; otherwise the stitch I could feel forming in my gut would take over and virtually cripple me.

I wasn't used to pushing myself so much. This certainly gave me the incentive to get back into shape.

Another road to the left. I could run in circles all night, or chance a trick shot.

I turned into the road. More light, but still plenty of shadows to disappear into.

I jumped onto the sidewalk, behind a tree that had been jutting out. That meant I couldn't see him, but that went both ways. But now I was shrouded in darkness.

There was a fence beside me. Not too high if I chose to jump over it, but the front garden consisted of mainly grass. Not something I could hide in.

There would only be a couple of moments before he rounded the corner. I could see the next garden by now, it was full of trees, plenty of hiding spaces. Bush like. If I could manage that, I would be in the clear for a moment or two, at least so I could catch my breath.

I decided to go for it. Once I reached the new property, I ran to the fence and using my hand for support and leverage, I pushed myself over and down into the shadows. From here, I kept low and moved quickly into the shrubs. I tried my best to keep quiet, but there was only so much you could do when moving fast.

Finally, I managed to find a little niche among some trees that I thought would be a good place to hide for a while. Moving into it, I quickly settled down, but keeping my body squatted, ready to jump up if needs be. I also did my best not to think. If anything I tried to think of things someone in the house might be thinking like 'I hate ironing,' or 'How could he miss that goal'.

Fortunately with my choice of colours, it would be very hard for him to spot me in the darkness. The only thing that would really stand out would be my face. So, I ducked my head down and covered it with my arms. Pulling my hands into the sleeves, I effectively concealed myself in the night. I did, however, keep a slit open between my arms so I could peer out, and kept my ears open for any indication that he was coming.

Footsteps on the pavement. They were getting closer.

My muscles tightened instinctively, ready to spring, slowing my breathing just in case I would give my position away. That was hard work considering how pooped I was. I could feel the tightness in my gut. It hurt still, but was slowly ebbing away. It got me to thinking how much further could I go? Not far at all from the way I was feeling. My legs were sore from the effort; my stitch was bound to come back with a vengeance if I had to take up running again. I was virtually knackered for now. But I had to remain ready for any possibilities.

A couple of seconds passed, his foot steps got closer, but after that, they started to get distant. That was until they began to halter. He was stopping. I tried peering out of the bushes.

Sure enough, he was standing in the middle of the road about fifteen meters away, right in the light. It was easy to see him, but impossible to know what he was thinking or planning to do next.

He looked around. The other side of the road, this side. Searching the trees and bushes. He obviously had an idea what I had done. It was just a case of whether or not he knew which way I had gone. Grekon looked again to the other side of the street. It looked like he had decided. The garden over there, from what I could see, appeared to be similar to the one I was hiding in. He started moving toward it and I knew it was now my turn to get out of here.

Once he had disappeared into the darkness on the other side of the road, I got to my feet, not all the way up but staying low and crouched. It was now going to have to be slow going. Staying to the shadows and going as slowly as need be to stop making too much noise.

I made my way out of my hiding spot and circled around the tree so I put it between myself and the road. It should add a little cover.

There was a fence dividing this garden and the grass one I had passed earlier. If I could jump over that, I could circle the house next door and get back onto the other road, effectively back tracking. That way I would be able to escape rather successfully, I think.

It was worth a try at least. I moved slowly toward the fence. It was about shoulder height. Awkward height for a dividing fence. Usually they were either above head height or waist height. Oh well, it would only take a bit more effort to get over.

Reaching it, I looked across the road. I couldn't see much, but with my eyes adjusting to the dark, I could make out his shadow roaming among the trees like some great ape. That analogy wasn't far off. From what I had seen earlier, he was a big man. I don't know how, but if he were to get hold of me, I was sure he would be able to crush my wrist with one small squeeze of his hand. I would just have to make sure he never catches me.

Back to my task at hand, I grabbed the top of the fence. It was sturdy enough and thick enough to put my feet on if I needed to stop for support, which I'm sure I would need to.

I pulled up with my hands and kicked my leg over. It was going to be awkward, but, hooking that leg, I was able to pull the rest of my body up until I was sitting straddled over the top.

Now, getting down was going to be fun. I swung my other leg over so I was sitting facing the grass yard. Now it was going to be a case of corkscrewing myself around as I jumped off, so I would be able to use my hands to push me away from the wall. Otherwise, knowing my luck, I would wind up scraping my back against the fence.

Normally I wouldn't do things like this. I'm usually very safety conscious, not to mention the fact I hate the idea of sneaking around on people's property. It was trespassing and invasion of privacy. Besides if I damage anything of value, I'd be kicking myself for weeks. But my main worry was hurting myself when jumping over things. But now, I should be okay. Besides, I've felt enough pain lately to be able to deal with whatever I could encounter in someone's front yard.

I did what I was planning; using both my body and my arms as leverage to push me away from the wall. It wasn't the most gracious of movements or the best of landings, but once my feet found ground, I was off again. I bolted across the lawn and found the side of the house.

I nearly tripped over a step I hadn't seen, but that wasn't going to be a worry for much longer.

A light flicked on, damn bright if you ask me, from the wall of the house. I stumbled briefly as I tried to adjust my eyes to the light. What I hadn't noticed was the damn security light on the house. One of those that sense motion. I had just triggered it. Bugger!

That totally blew my escape plan. I didn't know how long it would take for Grekon to notice the light if he hadn't already, but I was going to have to make the most of my head start again.

I took off at my full speed. I could already feel my stitch coming back, but I pressed on.

No sound came from behind me. He wasn't chasing me. Maybe he hadn't noticed, or the light scared him off. I don't know. But as far as I was concerned, as long as he wasn't chasing me, I was safe.

I saw the fence that sided with the road I had run down earlier. It was an easy jump. Once over, I headed back onto the side of the road and promptly tripped over.

It wasn't a pot hole or anything I had hit. It was the mere shock of seeing this gigantic figure standing in the middle of the road just meters away. It was Grekon, obviously. As for how he had gotten in front of me, I wasn't sure. All I could tell you was falling on road tarmac, or whatever you want to call it, certainly is not a cushion job. It hurt. I could feel some grazes coming along as my hands skidded across the ground. Maybe if I was lucky, they would be more bruises than real cuts. Who knows?

Once I had stopped, I looked up at Grekon.

He was standing, silhouetted by the light from down the other end of the street. I couldn't see his face, but I could tell he was standing with his arms crossed, which gave me the impression he was smiling at me. Patronising me.

I was not happy.

I slowly got back up onto my feet. There was no point running now. I was too tired. My stitch was throbbing in my gut and my muscles ached.

Pain is always such a bloody nuisance! It always gets in the way, stopping you from doing one thing or another. Even a paper cut can prevent you from scrubbing your hands clean after a dirty day's work in the garden. It had stopped me before and yet again. Pain, not the paper cut.

Now I was going to have to face this guy head on. Unless, of course, I could have another of those miracles, like bringing Bob or Sarah along to over come this bad guy, or even that teleport thingy to take me back to the other reality. Heck, even that would be better than this, I think.

But it wasn't likely. Instead, I decided to just stop. Stop running away. Stop delaying the inevitable. So, I sat down. Right there and then, on the side of the road. The curb was far from comfy, but it would do.

His head tilted to the side, as if he was confused by my action. I would have thought he would have learnt by now I was not always going to do what was expected of me. If not, he wasn't very bright.

There was a flash of light at the other end of the road. It caught my attention, but disappeared for a second. I wasn't sure if it had been there or not. But when it returned, I knew I had seen it, that there was a light. He hadn't noticed it. Why would he, it was behind him.

There was also a distant noise, like a rumbling.

Great. Now I choose to sit down and give up. There was a car coming, maybe they could have helped. Ah, what's the use? I would have just gotten someone else involved, possibly, no, probably putting them in danger. I didn't want that. So, I decided to remain sitting. Keeping my thoughts silent or to the point.

"So, what are you planning to do with me?"

Simple question. I tried to keep it devoid of any emotional inflections. I wanted to sound as neutral and carefree as I could about the whole situation. I wasn't going to give him the satisfaction of my fear. Maybe that sounded stupid, but I'm very much an emotional value person. I think I can read the value of specific emotions in people. Like some people just need to be depressed all the time. It keeps them happy in their own weird way. Others like to be happy. Me, I like a range of emotions. I put a lot of emphasis on emotions when I get right down to it. They play a huge part in out lives, and the funny thing is, it is rare to feel the same exact emotion more than once in your life.

I mean, say you're at a really cool party with your best of friends, celebrating a really important birthday, say. And you have the best of times and you never want to forget any of it. That feeling, the one created by that whole night is something you will never be able to grasp again.

It's a volume of happiness that, although you may be just as happy somewhere else, you will never be able to hold onto or find again.

Once it passes it has gone. No longer will it hold the sentimental, the tangible or other parts that make it up. Do you know what I mean? Sorry if this is confusing you, but the way I see it, emotion is made up of the minute. But not just the time, but everything that is there at that time. The good, the bad, the people around you, those that aren't, the place, the time of day, the everything. Everything in that moment is a part of that emotion and once it changes, once one thing moves away from that, it has changed, gone, lost forever, never to be touched again. Oh, you may well come close, but it won't be the same. And you can look back on it. You can get shivers down your spine or all over your body thinking of how happy you were at that moment. You may try to recreate the feeling in your mind or try to express it to someone else. But in doing so, it's just a cheap copy. It won't be there. It won't be real.

And that's one thing I hate. That inability to hold onto that emotion, that experience. Once it's gone, it has gone for good. It becomes a conversation piece, a thought process, but no longer the emotion that affected you so deeply or so wonderfully. But the same goes for the smaller emotions. The negative ones too. They are all gone once they have gone. I just wish we could record them, that we could put them on disc or something and put them in a library. And every time we wanted to feel that emotion again, all we would have to do is go into the library and say, "Oh, I want to feel scared today like I did when…" or, "I want to be really happy today," or, "I want to be non-plussed like I was last week when my rellies came over and I sat in my room veging out."

Then we could put in the disc and live that experience, feel that emotion all over again.

But we can't. They are lost to us. But that doesn't mean we can't think back on it. Or feel good about the fact we have experienced what we have, the good and the bad moments. They all make up a part of our lives and that has to be a good thing because that's what makes us who we are. And even if we find no consolation in that, we can always think about how happy or sad or scared or whatever we may be in the future, how it will affect our lives one day again. Maybe not in the same way as before, but in a different way. A new way. New experiences, new emotions. New everything. And that's our lives. That's what we should be looking forward to. And even now, knowing I will probably not have a future for much longer, I can still look forward to what I may have or may have had. But not just that, I can hold onto what I am feeling now. So it isn't something happy and wonderful, but it is still unique and wonderful in its own way and I'm grateful for that. So I'm about to die, I can live with that. As long as I can feel something when I do. Maybe I will get to experience it all again. You know what people say about your whole life flashing before your eyes before you die.

But this guy, he's different to me. He gets more joy out of his emotions when he knows his victims are scared out of their brains. Well I was, but I wasn't going to show him and I knew that would annoy him. Why? Because I knew that is the kind of person he is. He likes to see people suffering. So, I may suffer, but I won't show fear. He would have to learn to live with that. Live with the fact that this experience for him will not be as good as it could have been had I been showing how truly scared I was. But no way was I going to do that. Stuff him!

The rumbling of the car was getting louder, but he still hadn't noticed it. Instead he was considering what he could do to me. I could tell because he didn't say anything for a moment, making me wonder if he had heard the car, but when he spoke, I knew he hadn't.

"Oh, I don't know. Dismember you. Disembowel you. Decapitate? Dissect. So many wonderful 'D' words I could use. What do you prefer?"

Hmm. Good question. I thought about it for a moment, hoping I could come up with a witty retort involving a 'D' word. Not a one. But I had something else.

"How about 'Don't give a care about and thus lets me go'. How does that sound?"

He let out a little chuckle. He liked my attempt at humour, but he wasn't going to follow through with it. I could hardly blame him with the psychotic mind he must be carrying.

The car had gotten really loud really quickly. The lights were also a lot brighter. They must have been speeding. But when he started to turn around to find out what was going on, it was too late. For him, I mean.

As he turned, I saw the car reaching the corner. I could also see its indicator. They were definitely speeding. There was a squeal of brakes and tyres as the car turned into the street.

This was going to be good.

T

Grekon obviously had no idea what was going on. He had never seen a car before as far as I knew and to have this thing with two bright head lights bearing down on you... I would be packing myself even knowing what a car was. But he just stood there. Maybe he couldn't see that between those two headlights, that did give a distinct impression that the vehicle was actually two different objects, rather than one solid body. Maybe even an impression that these were two glowing fireballs coming straight for him. They were going to miss him as far as he was concerned, but from what I knew of my reality and of automobile accidents, this was going to be a doozey.

There was another screech of tyres as the driver must have seen Grekon.

In any other situation I would have been freaking out. This guy was totally in the wrong. He shouldn't have been speeding. He should have slowed down considerably to turn the corner. Grekon could have been a kid playing in the street or something and in this same situation, the kid wouldn't have stood a chance of survival. I think that thought made me cringe rather than what actually happened.

There was a loud thump and I looked away. I couldn't honestly watch a cold blooded murder of anyone, I didn't care who it was. Real or not, evil or not. It wasn't who I was. But there was little I could do about it, not that I was sure if I would do anything or not even if I could once the accident was over.

I heard Grekon let out what sounded like a scream. It was more in horror than in pain. I didn't blame him. It would have been a frightening experience, not to mention painful, but he obviously wasn't registering the pain. Which I found weird considering every bone in his body should have been shattered as far as I could tell. Then again I wasn't a doctor or physics scientist able to tell what effect a car going at 'X' speed would have on an individual 'Y' that was stupid enough to stand in the middle of the street.

Obviously, unfortunately for me, not bad enough.

Grekon landed with another loud thud. It was horrible to think about. He didn't move. He was either unconscious or dead, I wasn't sure. But the way his scream was cut off when he landed, it sent shivers down my spine.

The car screeched to a stop. It mustn't have been going too fast, but I would still have thought it fast enough to kill a man if it had hit one. But then again, Grekon was no ordinary man. That left me feeling a little jumpy. More so than the horrible images that flashed through my mind of real human beings being hit by cars – like in the infomercials telling you not to speed. It ran over in my mind a couple of times, but I had to shake it clear. This was my only chance of getting out of here.

I jumped to my feet and got ready to start running when I heard a car door opening. The driver had decided to get out of their car from what I could tell.

"Oh God! No! No! No! No! No!"

He kept repeating it. Obviously both shocked and stuck on one vocabulary word. The driver was not going to be in a good position if Grekon woke up to find him standing over his body. The evil bugger would probably kill him without a second thought.

Now, even though this guy had broken the law, which I was sure he would probably learn from this experience and never do again, I couldn't let him be killed because of my inaction.

Yeah, right, now I get a hero complex.

I stopped myself from turning tail and quickly turned back to the sight of the accident. The car had a rather hefty dent in the front, but it didn't look like it would have done much damage to the engine. It looked to be a rather sturdy vehicle actually. The guy who was driving it was kind of the same. Tall, well built. He did, however, have a funny dress sense. His flare-like pants were dark, as were his dress shoes and in this light all I could tell was that there was a floral design on his button up shirt that looked almost foppish. It was like he had stepped out of a hippy version of the English Restoration period.

This guy had a really weird dress sense, but he had long dark and really curly hair, which I thought was cool. I always wanted curly hair and found myself rather envious of any bloke that had managed to grow it and still look good. It was hard to say that this guy had succeeded, but that really wasn't my concern.

He had already started moving around to the front of his car. I had to stop him before he got too close to Grekon, or before the jerk woke up, if he was going to, that was.

"Hey! Stop! Don't get too close to him!"

The guy jumped and stopped, looking over at me, "What?"

He had a funny accent. More of a nasal pinch or tendency than an accent, but it sounded different.

I walked toward him, so I would place myself between him and Grekon, "Take my word for it. He's better off being left alone."

He wasn't buying. In fact, from the look in his eyes, I could tell this guy thought I was a complete and utter loony, "What are you talking about? He could be dead! He might need a hospital!"

He started to move toward the prone body again, but I shoved my hand against his chest. He knocked it away but I stayed firm in my position. So what, he was a big guy, but I had to keep him safe and if that meant letting him walk over me as I tried to do so, so be it. At least I would have tried.

I raised my voice a little, trying to sound authoritarian, "Listen to me! Leave him be! You're better off not getting involved!"

"But that's a hit and run!"

He went to walk around me, but I stepped to the side, blocking him off.

"I don't think that will matter very much to the police. This guy... Look. Just get back into your car and get the hell out of here."

He took a step toward me, to try and frighten me out of his way, but there wasn't much conviction to it. He was a couple of years older than me and a number of inches taller, but even with him looking down on me in every respect, the driver still wasn't sure of himself.

"Trust me. Go."

I lowered my voice for that. To try and sound more soothing, friendly.

"But... he's hurt," although he wasn't so determined, he wasn't going to give up. Even though if it were me, I would take every opportunity to get away if I had broken the law. He was still a concerned individual, determined to find out if this guy was okay.

I was about to speak again, but the words caught in my throat. I didn't know what to say. He wouldn't believe me if I told the truth. There was nothing I could use to back me up, or explain why he had to leave. He wouldn't believe I was a police man or anything. Sure, I had the upper hand now, but my lack of words or even an idea what to say was fast making me lose it.

He hadn't, however, made any further attempt to get past me. That was good, because there was no way I could have stopped him if he wanted to be forceful. But, heck, then it would be his own fault if something happened.

I really didn't think it was wise hanging around. Once Grekon woke up, he would be after me for sure. I didn't want to be any where near this vicinity when that happened.

So, I tried a different tactic.

"Fine. If you want to help him, do it. Don't say I didn't warn you. But I am out of here."

I started to hurry off until he spoke after me, "You're just going to leave him here? How can you do that?"

I turned back to him, "Because he isn't what he appears to be."

"What the hell is that supposed to mean?"

I took a couple of steps toward him again, I was getting annoyed, "Look, why can't you just listen to me. I suggest you get back in your car and get out of here!"

I heard Grekon moan. It wouldn't be long before he got up. Sure, I wasn't sure if he was immortal, indestructible or what, but I knew he wasn't human. I was only guessing the car wouldn't have caused any

128

major injuries this new version of Grekon couldn't withstand. I wasn't going to play on my chances.

"He's waking up."

No duh, I thought, "Then I suggest you get out of here."

I was beginning to sound like a broken record. How many more times would I have to tell him? Sure, this is a huge moral dilemma for the guy, but if I had someone as adamant as myself telling me to piss off, well, hmm… I probably wouldn't listen to me.

I couldn't leave him here. But he wasn't going to leave on his own. What could I do?

There was a low growl. Yes, a growl. It was as if Grekon's moan had just turned into a growl. Great. A werewolfian creature?

"Oh, Scott," the way he said it, it was like a sing-song approach. Like in a horror movie with an adult chasing after a kid with a huge axe, trying to ease the kid out of hiding by sounding so sweet and innocent. It scared me half to death to hear Grekon say it. He was definitely getting better with every passing second.

This guy with the dark hair was looking at me, confused. I think he was surprised by Grekon speaking that way. It would certainly make the most caring and worrisome of bystanders wonder what the heck was going on.

The body began to move, he was trying to push himself up. The two of us left standing began to back away. I think the message had finally gotten across.

"Scott? You're still here," his head flicked up, revealing his face. But it was his eyes I saw. His eyes were glowing again as they had in the mirror room. Glowing with an evil fire and they were fixed right on me. The rest of his face was shadowed and dark. But these eyes, it was impossible to ignore them. It was just so… well… not human!

"Holy crap," it wasn't me that said that. I think the other guy had just realised Grekon was not human, or even if he was, only remotely. And there was no doubting the fact that this thing was pure evil.

Grekon didn't stop watching me as he slowly got to his feet. Once he was up, I was sure I would have no chance of surviving.

No where to run, nothing to protect me now. Except…

The car. I moved over to the other guy. He was getting close to the driver's side door of his car.

"Umm, think you could give me a lift?"

"Yeah," he whispered it. I don't think his throat was giving him much more than that. Grekon looked freaky as all hell.

I reached around through the driver's doorway and unlocked the back door. Once done, I yanked open the rear door and jumped in. The owner of the car hopped in just as I did so, but I wasn't sure if it was going to be too late or not. Grekon was on his feet and boy were his eyes on fire.

"Can we get out of here?"

129

The engine turned over without a hitch. The car was still warm and, as I suspected, the engine hadn't been damaged by the collision.

Both our doors slammed shut simultaneously, but my attention was focused on the big guy that was coming toward us.

I could see his face now in the headlights. And I knew I had seen this guy before. Not just Grekon, but this younger version. No longer did he have the cuts on his face that he had received from the shattering mirror. They had healed, from the teleportation I guessed. But not cleanly. His whole face was covered in a number of dark and really ugly looking scars, adding to the severity of his already evil appearance. But this was the face I had seen in the light tunnel, the one I couldn't remember seeing on the other side. This is that second, evil face that kept repeating itself along with Bob's as I sped without a body along my trip last night.

I was now, more than ever, determined to get the hell out of here.

I heard the gears of the car grind as the driver tried to force the car into reverse. He tried again and it eased in quite simply.

It was now a case of getting away.

The guy slammed his foot on the accelerator; I could hear the clunk as he did so. Once we started to move I felt the car jerk backward, sending me flying forward. Fortunately I was able to dodge the front seat, but I nearly head butted the driver as he was looking over his shoulder to see where he was reversing to.

He dodged his head out of the way and I felt the car begin to turn slightly. Correcting the angle as I looked back through the windscreen at Grekon, we were soon heading back the right way from the evil man. He was just standing there, getting further away as the car reversed, granted, but he hadn't moved a muscle.

No, wait. I was wrong. He had. His mouth. He had opened his mouth, and I had no doubt about what was going to come out of it. I could see it already. A bright orange fire burning within him. If it were the old Grekon, I wouldn't have a problem. His fire breath didn't last very long and didn't seem that strong, but this is the new and improved version. I had no idea what he could do.

"Watch out," I called to the driver.

"What?"

He was panicking, trying to get as far away from Grekon as he could from the looks of it, but he didn't have eyes in the back of his head, nor any idea about what this guy could do.

There was a bright flash of light that nearly blinded me, but once it had gone, I could see what had happened.

There was a huge fireball coming straight at us. When I say huge I mean about the size of a basketball. Huge for something that came out of a mouth, not huge for a truck.

It was going to hit us if we didn't move. It was travelling faster than we were and I was sure this car would definitely not like to be hit by that thing. For all I knew the petrol would blow and us with it.

I lurched forward into the front and grabbed the steering wheel. I accidentally elbowed my driver on the side of the head as I did so. He fell off to the side, but his hands still held the wheel.

I didn't let that phase me. Neither of us could have afforded to let anything get in my way right now.

I took hold of the wheel and spun it to the left. It was very difficult to do, spinning a steering wheel, I mean. The wheels were obviously not going to turn so easily, but I kept pushing it around. I could feel the vehicle turning, but I had no idea where we were headed. All I could do was hope there wasn't a tree in the way.

The fireball just missed the edge of the windscreen which I thought was a good thing, but when it hit the road beside us, I knew I was wrong to have thought so.

There was a bone-jarring explosion, but thank god for suspension, huh? I felt the car lurch into the air, the right side pushed higher by the explosion than the left, but by no means enough to flip the vehicle. A wash of flame swept over the left side of the car and there was a sound of metal screeching from the driver's side of the car, where the ball had exploded. I could only imagine it to have been something scraping against us.

We kept going backwards, even through the air, but our trajectory had changed a little.

When the car landed, the rear right wheel hit first followed, on a rather weird angle, by the left rear, then the right front and then the other.

As we continued backward, the front tyre hit the curb and we started to bounce again.

I had no idea where the hell we were headed, so I decided to turn the wheel back the other way, to get us back on the road.

We mounted the curb briefly before falling back onto flat road. I got a little winded as the driver's seat hit me in the gut as we bounced.

"Damn!"

My driver was still conscious, but I don't think he was quite with it, maybe a combination of my elbow and all the strange stuff that was happening.

Once we reached flat road, I turned the wheel slightly and looked quickly over my shoulder. From what I could tell, we were just about near the corner. I looked back to the front just in time to see my dear old Grekon let loose with his mouth again. This time it wasn't a ball of fire, but a stream, as it had been in the mirror maze. But this didn't go in a straight line. It flayed out in a wide band, hitting the edges of trees and bushes along the road as it spread. It came rolling toward us, but going the speed we were, it was obvious we weren't going to escape it.

It seemed to crawl up the bonnet toward the windscreen. Covering it in mere seconds. Fortunately the windows were up otherwise we would have been fried. It totally enveloped the car, but there was still no explosion.

I pushed the wheel to the right and subsequently felt the car lurch in the appropriate direction. The way we ended up facing down this road would take us back to the park I had been at initially. But from there to where? I had no where to go. I didn't know if this guy knew where I lived or not. It hadn't been hard for him to find me, so I was sure it would be just as easy for him to find my apartment.

"Clutch," I yelled.

I grabbed onto the gear stick and jerked it into second for a better start, rather than a crawl.

"Floor it!"

I yelled it right in the guy's ear, but he did exactly what I told him to do.

The car was still enveloped with fire, and I wasn't sure how much more it could take. It was getting rather warm inside, sweat had beaded my forehead, so I could just imagine how the outside was going.

Grekon sure had a long breath for this one.

The wheels screeched below the car and I found myself being pulled backward by the momentum. Fortunately, my grip on the steering wheel kept me from falling backward.

I watched as the fire seemed to dissipate from the windscreen, knowing full well that we were leaving the radius of Grekon's fire breath. It wasn't long before we were all the way out.

I took a quick look to the side rear view mirrors and was quite shocked to see that the plastic that had encased them had melted. I couldn't see a thing out of the now covered mirrors. That was annoying because now I had no idea what Grekon was doing.

"Can you take the wheel?"

"Yeah," he replied, sounding a bit better.

I waited for him to take full control before sitting back in my seat. From here, I turned around and looked out the back window.

He was no where to be seen. That was only a small comfort. It wasn't entirely a good thing. It didn't mean he had given up, nor did it mean Grekon had decided to leave off for the moment. Either way, I only had to look forward to seeing him again.

I let out a deep sigh, allowing myself to fall down in my seat, coming to face front.

My driver was looking in the rear view mirror every few seconds. I wasn't sure if he was looking at me or looking out for Grekon.

I didn't know what to say.

"Sorry about that," it was all I could think of.

"Who was that guy?"

I shook my head and looked out the side window, "You wouldn t believe me."

"After all that? Try me."

He asked for it, "He's from an alternate reality."

"How do you mean?"

"Well, there's this tunnel, this transport thing that takes you from here, our reality, to this way out place of which I have no idea where it is. All I know is it isn't Earth. But in this place there was a big guy called One. He had, like, taken control of everything. Forcing people into slavery to do his bidding and make him more powerful. Decadent and evil bastard. But, this guy, the one you just drove over, Grekon is his name; he's this One's second in command. I had a run in with him this afternoon which I came out of the worse for wear, but I found my way back here and, unfortunately, so did One and Grekon. But he's changed. He seems to be heaps stronger here than he was there. He has these wicked powers and I don't know how far they go. But he is one dangerous mother!"

I wasn't sure if he was believing it or not, but frankly, I didn't care. It was nice to vent.

"So what is he doing here?"

"He wants to take over this world, like he did his own."

"Sounds a bit far-fetched."

I knew he wouldn't believe it.

"I mean, with all our military and stuff, there is no way he could do it, right?"

"Think of it this way, Grekon is a dangerous lunatic. One is possibly a thousand times worse. Even when he speaks, you can feel his power."

"So they could do it?"

I nodded, "If they really wanted to."

We drove in silence for a bit. I wasn't sure where he was going. I wasn't too worried.

I decided to change seats. It's weird being the back seat passenger.

"Mind if I come up front?"

"No, go ahead."

It was an awkward move, but I managed it rather simply. Once I had settled, I put on my seat belt.

I decided it was also time for introductions, "Scott."

"Huh?"

"My name is Scott."

He looked over to me, "Morrissey."

That's a rather weird name. More of a surname, I thought. Oh, well. No need to be rude or picky.

"Nice to meet you. You certainly came at a most opportune time, back there."

"I can imagine."

I could only smile. I wasn't sure if he could. But that was rather presumptuous of me. Again, who was I to judge whether this guy had an imagination or not. He had to, the way he was dressed. I actually thought his dress sense was rather cool. But I didn't say so; he probably heard it a lot. As for what he thought of me, the supposed defender of Earth, who knows? I am certainly not what you would expect and I am pretty sure just looking at me I do not inspire confidence.

"So. Where to?"

"Good question."

I really had no idea. I could go to Sarah's, but the chances that he would go there were high. Then again, if Sarah was there, that meant that was all the more reason to go.

"Would you mind dropping me off at a friend's place?"

"Not at all."

I gave him the directions and he said he knew where to go.

"I am so sorry about your car," I didn't know what it looked like on the outside, but I had a feeling it was pretty bad, either scoured by the fire or damaged by the fireball. There was also the dent on the front.

"Hey, not a problem. I can claim it on insurance. It's a business car."

"What do you do?"

"My folks own a restaurant. Dad just added a delivery service. Since I have my license, Dad thought it would be a good idea to help him out. So, I was just heading home after my last drop."

That bought me back to thinking about his really dangerous driving before he hit Grekon. He had certainly changed his style. He was slowing down quite considerably before turning corners for one.

"Good to see you've learnt your lesson, though."

"What?"

"Your driving."

"Yeah. I was being a muppet. Not thinking about the consequences."

I let out a little laugh, he was feeling quite down about it actually, "Just don't do it again, otherwise it might be some kid you hit and not some inter-dimensional overlord."

He laughed at that a little, too.

It took us about ten minutes to reach Sarah's place. He pulled into the parking lot and I told him where to park in the visitor's bay.

"Wanna come up?"

It was the least I could do in return for him saving my life and ruining his car. Hell, Sarah would probably like him anyway.

He looked at his watch briefly and then nodded, "Sure."

When we got out of the car we both had a look at the car. It wasn't too bad, all things considered. The front was a little blackened and very dented. Anything that wasn't metal, or was flammable had either melted or just burnt away. Fortunately the tyres had escaped that fate. The driver's side doors were pock-marked with a number of blackened dents where the fireball had exploded. But in all, it wasn't much of a wreck. That was if you weren't going to have to pay for it of course. Otherwise, it would still be one large headache.

I explained who Sarah was as we went up the stairs. Basically, she's an old school friend, she went through the same dimensional trip as me, and she likes football, movies and romantic evenings by candle light. You know; all the basics.

Her's was the third door on the right on the third floor. Nice place. Better than mine. Then again, she was a bit better off than me financially. Her parents had helped her put the down payment on the joint, now she was paying off the mortgage and if she ever needed help, her folks would always be willing to lend a hand. Maybe that's what I should have done, bought the place rather than rent it. Ah, well.

The door was still attached to its hinges and there were no strange sounds coming from inside which was comforting, so I knocked on the door.

"Who is it?"

"Scott."

I wasn't sure she was going to like my little bit of news. She had obviously had a run in with Grekon herself back in the other reality and she hated the guy. If she found out he was here, she'd flip her lid, to put it lightly.

"Hey, what's up?"

I heard her fiddling with the locks on her door. I didn't answer her until she had the door open.

She stood smiling at me until she noticed I had brought a friend. She knew most of my friends so she would of course wonder who he was I didn't wait for her to ask.

"Grekon. That's what's up," I moved in and indicated for Morrissey to follow, which he did. She moved aside for us, her smile replaced by a look of vague confusion.

"Grekon? Why, what's happened?"

She shut the door and locked it behind us, "He's here. He came through after us. But he wasn't alone. From the sounds of it, One is here too."

Her eyes widened, "No. Are you sure?"

"Of course I'm sure. If you don't believe me, have a look at Morrissey's car. It's in bay three."

That was my subtle way of introducing Morrissey, you may have noticed.

"Your car, what's wrong with it?"

She seemed to be full of questions now.

"Just a few dents and scorch marks is all. I don't think he was trying very hard when he started breathing fire at us," Okay, I was being a little sarcastic. Also I was stopping Morrissey from getting a word in, which was rude. Besides, I could already tell he had eyes for Sarah. It wasn't a love at first sight thing. Nothing like that. But he was showing interest, just from his body language and eyes and everything. Subtle, but noticeable. Then again, I could just be reading something into it. I usually do, so why wouldn't I be now.

Anyway, Sarah told us to go through to her living room. I liked the idea. Get off my feet and try and calm down a little. I was still sore from all my running, but I was also a little shaken by it all. Can you blame me? A near death experience or three like that can get your heart beating like it would burst from your body. It had calmed down a little since, though.

"He just appeared in the park. One moment he wasn't there, no one was there. The next, bang. He was standing right in the middle. I had no idea who he was 'cause he looked so different. But it didn't take long through a little questioning to find out it was him. Then I just bolted. There was no way I'd hang around with that guy coming after me. He is huge, like an ox or something. Damn scary. Anyway, I nearly managed to escape if it wasn't for those damn sensor lights, but he caught me. That was when Morrissey, here, sped around the corner and knocked him for six. But, as I said, he is heaps bigger and heaps stronger. It didn't take long for him to get up again. Then we made a run for it."

"He actually blew fire out of his mouth," Morrissey explained to Sarah.

"Doesn't surprise me. The guy is a demon of some sort," Morrissey seemed a little taken aback by her casual dismissal of such a miraculous feat.

"I'd just like to know what the hell we're going to do," I was getting annoyed. I thought we were going to be free of these freaks once we got back. I can't believe that they came through as well.

At least we know it wasn't a dream.

She shrugged, "Not much we can do."

Great! I knew she was right, but I wasn't going to accept that. We couldn't just let them try and take over the world without alerting anyone. But who could we tell? No one would believe it. They wouldn't even know where to find them. We didn't even know where to find them. Then I had an idea.

"But they know where to find us."

The other two looked at me, confused. I realised I had just spoken out the second part of my thought process, leaving them a little in the dark as to what I was talking about, though what I said sort of spoke for itself.

"So?"

I stood up and walked to the glass sliding door that led onto the balcony. I didn't open it, just stood there for a moment before turning back to face them. Being dramatic you see.

"So, if we can get them to come to us. If I let them take me back to their hideaway, then we may have a chance."

Sarah had to find the logical flaw, however, "But how are we supposed to find out where you are?"

"Good point."

"Then why let them take you. Why can't you take them?"

Now Morrissey had an idea. Thinking about it, not a bad one either.

"Yes, that's an idea, but how do we do that?"

"Well, if you get that guy we ran into to turn up, you might be able to coax him into getting the other one to turn up."

I looked over at Sarah and saw she was already looking at me expectantly, "Well?"

"Sounds good to me. But what do we do when we have them?"

Something changed in Sarah's eyes. But it extended from there. They seemed to widen quite a bit, but then the rest of her face dropped, like she had just been doped or something.

"Sarah? What's wrong?"

She started to nod. Only slightly, like her head was convulsing. I looked over at Morrissey; he was looking at her as well. This was certainly no way to make a first impression, Sarah, was all I could think.

I looked back at her. She had stopped nodding and her face had taken on an expression resembling something more, well, normal.

"Get away from the door," she whispered it. I nearly couldn't understand what she said. It was so quiet.

But that didn't concern me any longer. A cold flush went through my body. Something was very wrong.

Ever so slowly, I began to walk away from the door, turning slowly as I did so.

The first thing I saw was the black sky of the night, dotted with those stars I like so much. But when I finally made it around to be able to see pretty much everything in the window, I realised what had gotten Sarah so riled.

There, shining brightly in the moonlight and hovering three floors above the ground was Morrissey's car.

U

It was only moving slowly, but I could see the car was rotating in mid air.

I continued to back away from the window coming to stand between Sarah and Morrissey, both of which had stood up.

All three of us jumped as the headlights flicked on, flooding the room with its high beams. We couldn't keep staring into that sort of barrage of light, so we all shaded our eyes.

"Umm, guys. I really think we should get out of here," I thought it was a very good suggestion on my behalf.

We began to file our way out of the lounge room toward the front door, moving quickly. Sarah started to unlock the door for us when we heard him. Grekon.

"Where do you think you're running to? You can't escape us. You can't escape your fates."

She kept working at the locks. She wasn't going to let him get to her. I was with her on that one. But Morrissey, he was looking a little pale. He hadn't expected anything like this, I was sure. But this was only the beginning, only simple stuff. Maybe he should try being catapulted to another reality where you encounter talking paintings, robed Amazon women and other weird and wonderful things, of which I was sure I only briefly touched on in my short stay.

I took hold of his upper arm, trying to be calming and reassuring.

"Don't let him get to you. He's mostly talk."

He looked at me, "Mostly?"

"The rest we learn to deal with. Look at us. The two of us survived him before," I wasn't going to say that the only way we did that was by a pure miracle of timing with that ball of light.

Sarah got the rest of the door unlocked and yanked it open. It was then like a pile on as we all tried to push our way out of the apartment. As to where we would go now? Like all the other times before, God only knew.

She stayed behind to lock up her place again, while we headed for the stairs. It would only take us a minute or so to get to the ground floor if we hurried, so we waited for Sarah to catch up once we got to them.

When we did finally reach the bottom, we ran straight for the car park. But we had no car to get into. It was still hovering above us, headlights beaming into Sarah's lounge room. With it just hanging up there, no doubt by Grekon's powers, I was not going to chance walking under it. Knowing him, he would simply let it go so it could fall on us, squashing the three of us to death. Instead, we made a wide birthing below the car, keeping a watchful eye on it.

"You insolent creatures! Think you can run away! Think you can destroy me! You are all wrong!"

I had no idea where he was. I couldn't see him. There was no general direction from which his voice came. It simply was. Like it was put into my head. Telepathy again? I still wasn't sure.

As we made it to the driveway out of the parking lot, the car began to move again. Only slowly, but surely. It was rotating toward us, its headlights still burning away. Rotating on two axis. I watched in only what I could describe as awe. How was he doing this? How did he have so much power? Why hadn't he used it before? Was he growing in power the longer he stayed? What was he? And, more importantly, where was he?

"I suggest you two turn and run. Get out of here now!"

That was me.

"You must be joking!"

"No. I'm deadly serious. That car is going to come after us, you can count on it. Now, I think Grekon is a bit more pissed off with me; otherwise he wouldn't have come after me first. Don't you think? So, if you two just run for it now, and I stay here, I have a good feeling you'll have a better chance of getting away."

"But what about you?"

"Forget about me! I can handle myself."

I knew they were both looking at me. But I could also imagine what Sarah looked like. She wouldn't want to leave me. Her face would say that much, even if she never did. We were good friends. But she had to go.

"Go!"

They started to move off slowly. The car was now facing us directly. I wasn't at all surprised when it started coming after us.

"Run!"

I hadn't stopped moving. I was backing up slowly. But they had to run. They had to get away, even if they split up. That would make it so much harder for Grekon to get us.

They had started running. I could hear their footsteps pattering along the pavement. Now it was just me, the car and the invisible Grekon.

The vehicle was gaining speed as it came. It wasn't going tremendously fast yet, but by the time it would reach me, it would probably be going at over eighty kilometres an hour. Pretty fast for a flying car.

I continued moving backward, admittedly speeding up.

Hell, I didn't want to be hit by a car, let alone have one drop out of the sky on me.

This was not going to be fun.

It was only going to be a matter of seconds before it reached me. Of course, time goes so slowly when you're scared out of your wits.

But I had a plan.

I always do. Even if it isn't a good one, I still have a plan.

Isn't it funny how, in even the worst situations, your mind can continue to function and come up with some ideas. Granted some are just ridiculous but others do have a lot of credit to be owed. I wasn't sure where the one I had right now stood, but it was all I had.

It was getting so close. The headlights were blinding, but I forced myself to look toward them. If I didn't I would lose my timing and blow my chances. But that just wouldn't do, now, would it?

Geez, what an idiot I am. To go about sacrificing myself for my friends. Is that valiant or just plain stupid? Of course, it has to be the first. But sometimes I think the latter option plays a big part in a lot of my thinking. Sure, I'm not the brightest of people. I'm not even the nicest. I can be the biggest prick in the world when I want to be and, as you know, I am so self-centred and opinionated it isn't funny, but that's me. I'm sure you're all pretty much the same. But, again, that isn't my concern right now. I'm the one standing here waiting to be flattened by a burnt up, dented car that's flying through the air with high beams on.

Now that's what I hate. People that use high beams when they don't need to. On a night with a full moon, or with street lights on the whole way down the street, people still insist on using the high beam. Even going around corners and over inclines, which it says in the little book you get when you're learning how to drive, that you should not do on any occasion. But do they listen? Of course not! People can be so inconsiderate. And I for one think that this Grekon fellow is one inconsiderate, obnoxious son of a bitch!

Who gave him the right to scare the daylights out of innocent people? If you can call me innocent, though I like to think I am. Sure, I've done some really bad things in my time, but this guy, he's just evil. And what's worse is that he is evil for the sake of being evil. Couldn't he just lighten up? Geez! Him and his boss. They both need an attitude adjustment, and if I make it out of this, I am sure as hell going to do my best to give it them.

The car was almost on me. It was zooming through the air like nobody's business and was soon to squash me. But it was time for me to act.

I prepped my legs, though they were still tired. And squatted down a little over them. I made a mental count down in my head, though I had no idea if it would even be accurate or not. Most likely not. But when those headlights were even with my head, I just went.

I did exactly as I did against those magpies. I pushed myself forward and down. But this time I made sure I wasn't going to slide. If I did, I would be totally scratched to death on the pavement.

I felt a rush of air as the car zipped over head. It was close. I could almost feel it as it passed. But once I hit the ground, I covered my head with my arms and prayed to god that would offer me enough protection.

Okay, I'm not religious. I take the Lord's name in vain a lot. I blaspheme; I do all sorts of terrible things. I don't really know if I believe in him or not. If there was some sort of proof, fine, I would consider it. But as there is nothing, I still find myself in that gap between believing and not believing. I don't believe it is so simple to put your faith into something that just isn't there to you. Not something you can't see, hear, touch or anything like that. I mean, sure he, or she, may be watching over us, making sure we do what's right or whatever. But right now, after all that has happened, I just can't see where he has anything to do with it, and if he did, I don't know what kind of sick humour he has.

But I pray. Just in the off chance God might exist. Not often. Usually in my times of need, hoping there is at least one chance for things to be made right. But no matter what the outcome, I still can't believe if he is there or not. So I say I'm agnostic. Don't hold it against me. Just accept that that is my view. Everyone should be free to that.

So I was praying silently in my head, "Please, help me."

There was a tremendous explosion behind me. I could just imagine the car as its nose, followed by its body and everything else made contact with the ground, crumpling forward to become like a slinky or something else totally squashed from back to front. If you know what I mean?

If not, well, just imagine the subsequent explosion. I knew it was going to be ringing in my ears for a while to come. But it wasn't just the noise. Heat seared up my legs, not causing any damage or setting my pants on fire or anything, but it was damn hot, like standing way too close to a fire. That's what this was like. Funny thing that, considering I was mere metres from the explosion.

After the initial explosion, there were a number of smaller ones followed by the tinkling of metal and glass on pavement. I could only imagine this as debris falling to the ground again. Obviously that was what it was. Duh!

But what a rush it was.

Life was never this exciting. I wasn't happy it had taken on such a dangerous curve, but it was so exciting now I felt the adrenaline pumping through my body. It was so cool.

As for what Morrissey was going to do about his car now, well, that would depend on how far his insurance covered it. For sure it was a total right off now.

I was safe. I had come out on top, yet again.

Or so I thought.

I lifted my head as I started to get up and what did I see? Well it certainly wasn't no purple people eater staring at me.

Two large black boots. Those and the lower half of a pair of black jeans. It was all I could see. Frankly it was more than I wanted to see. I knew who they belonged to and I just didn't want to see him. I wanted him to go away. I was starting to get tired of him. Keep the excitement but get rid of him. He was just so damn annoying. And the way he likes to taunt you, geez, I've never known a bigger sadistic prick in my life.

"Can't you just go away?"

"You'd like that wouldn't you?"

I knew it was a rhetorical question, but as I pushed myself up and onto my knees so I could actually look at him in his dark clothing; by this I mean a black trench coat and black everything else; I just had to answer him.

"Yes! I would like that! Why the hell can't you just do it? You are really beginning to piss me off!"

He was totally taken aback by my tone of voice. I really was angry with this guy.

"It isn't about being scared anymore! I'm sick of being scared of you! So what, you can breathe fire, survive car crashes, even throw the damn things through the air! But I don't care! To me, you're just another annoying prick in this world, and believe me, there are enough of them around to make me wonder if defeating you would be worth it. Go ahead! Take over this world. It's full of a bunch of stubborn self obsessed arse wipes, just like you! I'm sure you'd get on with them just fine! So, be my guest! Kill me, kill everybody. It'll probably do this world a huge favour, the way it's heading with the environmental problems we have. Oh but you wouldn't know about those would you? You and your unrealistic reality as your home. Geez, what kind of a freak show was that anyway? I mean, you just made things so weird and wonderful, but us, we have to work to do that. We have to deal with the problems of this planet, not turn them into something else. We don't have your kind of magic. We have polluted water; we have to deal with it. You, I saw your polluted water and it was doing nothing at all to the lake into which it was flowing. I don't know how you do that, but it sure as hell doesn't happen like that here. So if you want this planet and want to keep it, you're going to have to work at it! Now, you have a look at that and see if you think it is worth it or not! Okay?"

I was so livid! Now that's a word you don't hear every day, but I was! This arsehole of a guy! Why the hell couldn't he just go away?

There was silence. Apart from the flames crackling off the car and the odd creak of metal as it settled, there was nothing. No sound.

I looked into his face. There was something… His eyes weren't on fire anymore. They were actually normal. They were looking right at me. Not through me like I was some kind of dirt or stain. But at me.

And his face, well, it no longer looked so severe. Sure, the scars didn't give it the most friendly of faces, but it didn't hold that expression of menace anymore. It was as if he was thinking. That he was thinking about what I had said.

Maybe he was. I couldn't be sure, but I knew something had gotten to him. There was none of that menace. Just a face. And his eyes. Blue they were. I could see by the firelight. Nice blue eyes and he was looking straight into mine. Neither of us blinked. We just stared. Him thinking about what I had said and me thinking about if that was what he was actually thinking about and if not, what the hell was he thinking about?

Neither of us spoke, nor blinked, nor moved. Not for over a minute. We just sat and stood there until he finally made the first move.

I could see in his eyes that he had made some sort of decision.

"Hmm."

It was all he said as he turned and began to walk away. I kept my eyes glued to him. Watching until he had disappeared into the darkness.

No trace of him was left.

I let out the breath I had been holding all that time, letting my body crumple. It was so tight with tension, but letting it go, I let my head hang and my shoulders slump.

Had I really gotten through to him?

It was all I could think. Had I touched him with what I said?

I couldn't know. Maybe he just went off to think about it some more. Maybe he would be back some day to finish us off when we least expected it. I didn't know.

All I knew was that for now, he was gone.

I had to leave quite quickly afterwards. There was no way I could hang around and explain it all to the police. But I only went up to Sarah's apartment. I could hear the sirens and when I looked out the window, I could also see the large crowd of people that had started to gather around the wreckage. The Fire Department put out the fire, making sure the wreckage was safe for the police to examine.

I didn't want a part of it. I just wanted to forget about it all right now. I certainly didn't need the hassle. That was why I came up here. I knew where Sarah kept her key, but through courtesy we never used them to get into each other's place. We would always knock first. But she wasn't home. I didn't know where she was. Probably out with Morrissey looking for cover. I didn't blame them. I told them to run. I just hoped they were safe.

Well, Grekon was gone, so I guess they were. But I wouldn't know until they decided to come back, whenever that was. I was happy for the time by myself, though. Time to think things through. I was sort of doing that when I went for the walk, but it didn't quite end up the way I had expected. Now, I had the happenings of the past few minutes running over in my head. Actually, the entire hour.

I opened the slider door and walked out onto the balcony. The wind was still blowing. It was nice. I leant on the railing and surveyed the crowd below. They wouldn't have the foggiest of ideas what happened. I smiled at that. Not that they were naive, but how I was the only one that knew. That was my little secret. A part of me no one else had. I liked that feeling. Sure, they wouldn't care about that, but my knowing that I was just that little bit different was a comforting thought.

Why? I guess because what I told Grekon was running through my head. Was this world really full of arrogant power hungry people? Or the same arrogant people but on a different scale, just rude and uncaring. How would I know? I knew a lot of people, but not enough to make such a huge generalisation. But it is the impression you get when you hear about everything that takes place on this planet. I'm hardly an exception to those that cause it problems.

Fine, so I'm not a Greenie, not so concerned with the environment. What gets me more is the notion of war. The fact that people can die without doing anything at all to cause it. And even worse, not being able to do anything to stop it. They have no choice. It's just those brain dead fools that run the countries that cause the problems, but let's not forget those small terrorist groups that do the bombing and stuff though. They're probably worse. How can they be so selfish, so stupid?

They ask for freedom, equality or whatever else, yet they are so willing to deny people just like themselves the greatest right to live. What kind of monsters do we breed on this planet?

I shook my head. I didn't want to know. There were enough problems of my own to worry about right now. Now, the fate of the world possibly lay in my hands. That's a big and egotistical notion, but for all I knew, it was true.

One was still out there and if he had increased in power as Grekon had, well, we were probably screwed.

There was a fresh gust of wind. I lifted my face to take it head on. It was in exhilarating feeling. A sense of freedom. I let out a small laugh. It felt good, like a release. In a sense, I was free. Free of that other place. Free of Grekon, though the worry of his return still remained. Free of the responsibility of explaining what happened with the car.

I closed my eyes and took in a deep breath of air and promptly started coughing. It tasted awful. It seemed to stick in my throat forcing me to try and cough it back up. I opened my eyes and couldn't believe it.

V

No longer was I standing on the balcony. It was amazing, I had somehow been teleported from the balcony to here, where ever that is. I hadn't felt it. Not one small thing. There was still a breeze on my face, but it now consisted of that acrid stuff that had caught in my throat. There was also something in front of me that took the place of the railing. But on inspection, it was just a low dividing wall. Brick, as the railing had been, but it wasn't the railing I had been standing behind seconds before.

I now stood in the middle of a warehouse. Not the same as the others I had found myself in over the last day or so. This was different. Multi-layered. I was standing on the second story, looking out over the dark and dusty ground floor.

I glanced around. Almost everything was shrouded in darkness. There were some sky lights in the roof, but very little got through them as they were obviously streaked with dirt, not to mention the fact it was night. I could make out the outline of the main sliding door entrance at the other end of the room.

But when I looked down at what I was standing on I nearly freaked. They were boards. Thin boards that were positioned so haphazardly, it would be easy to get your toes caught in one of the gaps. I could also see down into the darkness below, not that that made much difference. I couldn't see anything excepting where a few streams of light from above cut through. But the boards were so thin, so old. I was almost too scared to move my feet for fear of the damn things breaking. Fortunately my fear of heights wouldn't be a problem with that as there was this railing in front of me. I was fine as long as I had something to hold onto.

"I don't know what you did to rid me of my colleague. He was faithful enough before. But now he is gone," The voice came from below. Below and behind me, further back in the darkness.

"No matter. I have you now."

If that was the case, then why hadn't he simply transported me to here in the first place? What had stopped him from doing that rather than sending Grekon on after me? I really did not get this guy's way of thinking.

"I suppose he informed you of my goals. My destiny. And, of course, yours."

"He may have mentioned something. I can't really remember," I lied. Maybe I could play dumb. Didn't know what it would get me if I did, but, hey, it would at least be an experience to remember, if I survived.

"Ha! You amuse me if nothing else. Maybe I should make you my jester."

Jester? What was this guy? When did he come from? The middle ages? Weirdo.

"Yeah, why not? I'm sure I'd do a good job at that one."

"I'm afraid, my dear little Pissant, you will be doing very little of anything."

I heard something from below. I knew he was moving about down there, but I wasn't sure where. I kept my eyes open, searching the darkness and watching those small spaces where light did exist.

"Whatever."

"Whatever? You don't sound too concerned at your imminent departure."

I saw him. It, rather. It was still black and sleek. Smooth too as the light reflected off whatever it was that passed through the light. It was almost directly below me. Not that helped me in any way. I had nothing to kill it with.

"Why? I mean, why do you want to kill me? What have I done?"

"Annoyed me."

It moved its head into the light. More specifically its eye. The way the light lay across his face, it looked as though he had been scarred from forehead to chin by light, with his eye directly in the way.

It was still green. Not burning so much now, but regarding me. Staring at me. Very unnerving.

Its face had changed somewhat. It was no longer cute. It was as if the teleporting over to my reality had hardened his features, making them sharper, more vicious. If you asked me, I already thought those teeth of his were vicious enough. I didn't particularly want to see them now. It was as if the teleporting had improved these two megalomaniacs. Both Grekon and One seemed different, more threatening. I don't know why, but it had worked.

"Annoyed you? Fair enough," sure I was trying to sound tougher than I was. I had nothing else to do, so I may as well pass it having fun, playing the big shot. It wasn't working on him, though. Come to mention it, it wasn't working on me either. It didn't instil me with confidence. I just wanted to get out of here.

It smiled. I saw the light gleam off its teeth. I was right. They were a horrendous visage. They were just fangs, the whole way round, still with its canines being way over sized and razor sharp. One chomp of those things and I was sure it could cut straight through a lead wall two foot thick.

"You are taking this pretty well. I don't admire you for it. I pity you. I pity your whole species. Weak. Repulsive. Futile."

"But annoying. You can't forget that."

"Yes. Annoying," Yep, he did sound pretty annoyed with me. Maybe if I kept pushing, he'd really get annoyed. Yeah, great idea. Then he can gut me with those razor sharp teeth. No thanks. Maybe I should be trying a different tact. Maybe being friendlier, more cooperative. Hell, he had just lost his side-kick; maybe if I tried hard enough I could take his place. Not that I wanted to, but I would be more able to do something to get rid of him if I did. That just wasn't a likely outcome. But it was worth a try. What did I have to lose?

"Sorry. Just being facetious. Anyway, you were saying?"

It began to move again, not back into the shadows but out from underneath my balcony. He was coming out into the open of the warehouse where I would get a really good look at how terrifying he really was. I wasn't sure if that was his intention, but it was what was going to happen. I was already scared of this guy, seeing how evil looking and terrifying he had become on transit would probably nearly take me over the edge. So, I prepared myself.

When he began to emerge, I saw his head first of course. It seemed to sway from side to side ever so gracefully. Its face, from what I could remember, had become more squashed, pug-ish even, but I couldn't see it from above, not yet anyway. Two large horns curled out from just above its forehead and between its now pointed ears. They rose up before curling away and down. Their points: tusk-like as they sat just below his jaw line. It looked more demonic now than before. I wonder if it knew this.

It seemed to move slowly, but the muscles rippling along its hairless back told me it was far from weak.

Its neck was long with a bunch of skin gathered up along it into a series of folds. I didn't know why, but it was interesting. Its shoulder blades stuck out more than normal shoulder blades would. It was as if two large bones had formed and spiked out of its back, but they curved at such an angle to point straight ahead and about a foot past his shoulders as He walked. Evil looking spikes, they were, and I was sure they would do a mean shish kebab. It's back held that muscular v-shape and all the way down its spine was a long line of small spikes, miniature versions of those further up its back, but just as painful looking. It had surprisingly narrow hips, but growing out of its backside was that tail. Long and slithery. Horrid looking thing. Smooth and pointed, swaying back and forth along with its body as it moved out into my view.

The way it walked reminded me very much of a Komodo Dragon. Lizard-like in its slow slithery movements. Its body was huge. Not just muscle wise, but long and broad. In his entirety, One would have had to have been at least eighteen feet long, so it had grown in size as well as developing those horrid protrusions. It was a damn scary looking creature to me and I hadn't even seen its face yet.

When it got clear of the balcony on which I stood, it started to turn around, but rather than doing it in a large circular walk, it pushed itself up off of its front legs and put its weight onto its tail. Now it stood as tall as I had thought it was before. I had to look up to see its head.

It turned at a casual pace and glared at me with its horrible green eyes. Now I was scared.

Not only was it a big mother, but it was able to stand and walk on two legs as well as four. On careful inspection, I could see he had hands, just like a human, though his fingers ended with rather sharp looking claws. This was truly a creature out of some nightmare or horror flick.

But its face, my God, its face was gruesome.

Its teeth could no longer be contained behind its lips. The lower two canines rose upward along its cheeks, the larger upper teeth reached far below its chin.

The hard brow line it had before had somehow reformed on a v-like angle rising up toward its ears and down to its nose which now looked very demonic. No longer dog-like nor human; it just was. Two grossly flared nostrils. And the eyes. Those green, glaring eyes were so hard, so penetrating as they stared at me. He didn't blink. He just seemed to stare straight through me.

His body, I now noted, wasn't just a tough hide-like skin. It appeared to be some sort of plating, not metallic, but a natural kind of armour. An exo-skeleton that looked rather like leather.

When he spoke next, his voice carried the same power it had back in his own reality. I could feel the force behind his words. It was weird because when he was below me, when I could barely see him and he had that one single eye looking at me, I felt nothing, just scared. Now, when his words came, it was as if he was trying to blow me away, to crush me with each syllable.

"Soon, you will mean nothing to me. You will be little more than a memory."

I had to force myself to speak, "Why soon? Why not now?"

"Because I still need you."

Need me? But why? What could I do for him? What could I do that he could not?

"Need me for what?"

He smiled at me, but it looked more like a teeth baring sneer, "In a matter of minutes, another of your portals will be opening. Once it has come, I will have no more need of you. You will die."

"Another of my portals?"

"Yes."

My portals? What did he mean my portals?

It seemed that talking to him didn't answer any of my questions; it just brought new ones to light.

"My portals?"

"Yes."

"How are they 'my' portals?"

I really wanted to know that.

He leant over, bringing his face close to mine, but still past arms reach. My arms, anyway. I could feel myself trembling. I was damn scared. Now he was so close, I could see every line in his face, every curve in his teeth. Daunting would be the most understated description I could give it.

"You, but not only you. Your friend and a score of others of your kind create these portals. I don't know how and on encountering your friends, neither do they. As I said, I wish to study you. I will take you back with me. I will take some of your friends along also. Some will stay alive so I can better grasp their abilities, but you will die. You are a trouble-maker and I don't want any more of your meddling. I will study each and every one of you to find out how you make these portals."

That still left so many questions like, "How do you know one is coming soon?"

He stood up again to his full height, "Cycles. On the one cycle, it comes twice. One after sixteen hours, the other after eight. I have been watching these cycles of not only yourself but your friends. It is the same with all of your kind. They only started recently. Some a week ago, others a couple of days ago, and you and that female friend of yours began your journeys yesterday on synchronised times. Now, you will both return and I with you. I can then dispose of your life force and use you at my discretion to finally learn how I can bring my minions over to help me conquer this wasteland you call a reality."

Now I understood. Well, a little more than I used to. I still didn't know how these teleporting globes were created in the first place, but I knew now what the hell had been going on. But where were these other people, these other travellers?

At least I would be seeing Sarah soon enough, the problem was that she would be on the other side, only to become a slave of One. I couldn't have that. I couldn't let that happen. Fine, kill me, but not her.

If only I knew how to stop these damn teleporting things. Damn it!

"Only seconds, now."

Great. Why didn't he just start a count down? I was helpless. Screwed. If some kind of miracle didn't happen soon, I would be dead as well.

There was silence. Nothing moved. There was just me, him and his big smile. Now he was rude.

The funny thing was, and this only just occurred to me, he couldn't get back without me. He had to have me near for him to get back, so he could use my globe to return home.

Well, I say stuff that if he thinks he is going to win that easily!

I don't think he was ready for what I did. I remember him looking startled when I began to move.

I pushed off from the balcony and spun on my heels, hard work on wooden planks especially if they aren't secure or well placed. But I managed it. Once I was facing the other way, I just ran. I ran as fast as I could, dodging the gaps and the nooks where my feet could get caught.

I nearly leapt out of my skin when he finally reacted. It wasn't with words, but with a roar.

I was sure that people would have heard it for miles away. It sent a horrible shiver all the way through my body. I wasn't sure if it was because of its concussive force or whether it was just so god damn loud.

It was a full, open mouth yell, but with his bestial manner and everything else about him, I associated it so much with a roar of total anger and surprise. It lasted only a couple of seconds but it echoed through the building for at lest twenty times that afterwards.

Like a turtle, I ducked my head into my shoulders and just bolted. I doubt if and when he caught me, he would hesitate to do something horrible to me. So, I would just have to prevent him from catching me.

I didn't look back. I didn't want to. I could just imagine his flaming green eyes and his wide toothy sneer. If I looked back now, I would freeze in absolute terror. But right now, that was what I was using to motivate myself. I was running the fastest and hardest I ever had in my life. My legs just whirled beneath me, my breathing became hard and short. And I wanted to scream so much, it was welling up inside of me. But I used it to push me even further.

This thing would not get me! It would not! I would not let it! And I was going to out run it and get away from it before it could use Sarah or me or any of those other people as guinea pigs! I would not let that happen!

I ran. And ran. I couldn't see where I was going, though my eyes were quickly adjusting to the darkness. I had no idea how far back this warehouse went, but the way I was feeling, I would run straight through the back wall and keep running through the sky. He was not going to catch me! He will not catch me and that was final!

There was another roar, louder than the first and much closer. I didn't know where One was, but he was close. Moving faster than me. He had added size and strength as a bonus over me and he was using it. But this roar. When it came, I felt my own scream come leaping out of its container. I couldn't help myself! I was so worked up and scared out of my wits, it just came. I opened my mouth and I screamed and I couldn't help thinking how well it harmonised with his roar. But it was no laughing matter. I screamed so hard, all my pent up energy and tension just flew from within me in this single scream!

It died before his roar did. There was a reason other than loss of breath for that.

The wood in front of me, the very ground I was heading toward splintered upwards, showering me in wood and debris. I put on my brakes immediately, stopping myself and almost flying head first toward this eruption. But up through the wood came a massive black hand. I

150

knew it was him, but it was bigger. Much bigger than before. Three times the size at least. He had grown even more. This big black arm with a clenched fist at the end stood there in the middle of the flying wood and dust like an unmoving monolith.

And there was no way I was going to hang around for the rest of it to come.

I turned around and with just as much enthusiasm, power and sheer terror I ran in the opposite direction.

This time, however, I didn't make any compensation for what covered the floor, not to mention the unevenness of it all. I literally began to spin on my heel and found myself floundering as I fell sideways onto the floor. When I opened my eyes again almost immediately after, I saw him. I saw his eye just below me staring at me. It burned with so much rage. But there was no way I was going to feel any sort of sympathy for that bastard! If I had as much power as him, I would show him how pissed off I would be and in that puny little mind of his, there would be no room for anger or any other emotion because he would be so overcome with fear he would be doomed to be a mindless zombie for the rest of his life for the sheer terror I would cause him! I was so pissed off! More than I was with Grekon! This was way beyond a joke and there was no way in hell he was going to beat me. Not this time, not ever! I was going to kick his butt so far out of this reality and every other reality; he was just not going to exist anymore, anywhere!

But I didn't have that power. I didn't have anything. All I had were my hands and feet and my mind. And right now they amounted to very little. But I was going to use them to the best of their potential. They, like me were not going to give up

I pushed myself onto my feet again and I ran. I didn't care what he was doing this time. He could roar as much as he liked, but I would not give in! He could destroy this whole floor and I would never succumb to him! This was more than just me or my life or my pride! This was Sarah! This was all those other people jumping back and forth between realities. This was Bob and Narelle and Tom and all the people in his reality not to mention mine! This was about everything and everyone!

But most of all this was for the principal of the matter! This guy had no morals, no consideration no anything and a person like that, or a monster like that has no place in any reality as far as I was concerned and if he brought this down to being just me and him then he was going to have to suffer the consequences of his decision! He should have picked some other fool to mess with

It seemed to take me less time to reach the balcony on the way back, I don't know why, but once I was there, I didn't stop. I did something I normally wouldn't have the guts to do, let alone think I would ever survive. But on this occasion, it didn't matter if I survived. If I died, then there would be no portal for him to use me with. But if I made it I would be on the same level as him, more vulnerable. But it was the only way out I could see and I was sure as hell going to make it.

I apologise for saying 'hell' so much, but as God is my witness, I was not going to let him win! I told you I got all religious when I got into trouble. So please excuse me for my language, but I damn well think it is excusable on this occasion!

I grabbed onto the balcony with my left hand and kicked my legs up high, using my momentum as leverage as well. Once I let go of that balcony, I swear I was flying. I felt I would never touch the ground again.

How little did I know that I was right.

Out of nowhere, right in front of me, there was a flash of light. And I swore.

W

I had lost. I knew it once I saw the light. And I sure as hell knew it when I finally made contact with it and found my body and my very soul being sucked into this glowing ball of light.

I had failed. I had failed Sarah and I had failed everyone.

Even as I sped down that light tunnel and even though I knew I had no body, I felt my gut wrench. It hurt. Not physically, but deep inside. Way beyond a mere tangible pain, this was truly gut wrenching. I had failed everyone and I had tried so hard to stop it, to get away. But I failed. I could just imagine the tears welling in my eyes. But there weren't any. Not really. Nor was there a gut.

But I felt it. And I saw it. It came out in the tunnel. The colours weren't the usual bright reds, greens and unnameable ones. They were there but mixed among them were greys and blacks. Flashing and mixing with the other colours. They were all there. Every colour, light and dark, real and unreal. Right in front of me, so familiar to me and in more than one way, too. This tunnel was more than just a tunnel. It had been my pathway to excitement and danger and my pathway home to what I thought would be safety and loving friends and relations. Now, it was to be my pathway to death and failure.

I watched as the images came flashing by again. There were those castles and swords again. And Bob. Bob was there, smiling a friendly little smile which I couldn't help but feel a deep down sense of happiness derived from that smile. Then came the realisation that soon enough, because of me, he would probably never smile again if One had his way.

More images. Narelle, also beaming in a glorious white dress. It looked like a wedding gown of some sort. It was as if she was looking directly at me, smiling at me and all. And then there was Tom. Ugly big Tom. So friendly. And he was looking at me too I was sure of it. Although I couldn't tell with that horrid face of his, his eyes were lit up. Not just in his naive little childish way, but in a happy, smiley way. He was smiling. The guard at the gate, some of the people I had seen in the street on the way to the castle and those I had seen in the portraits along that corridor with Narelle. They all flashed past me, but they were all looking at me. And they were all smiling at me. But they knew. It was as if I knew that they knew that I had failed. But they weren't angry with me. No! They weren't angry at me and there was something else.

In their smiles, in their eyes. Reassurance. That was what it was. They were there, not just as images, but they were there with me. A part of me.

Sure this must sound all idealistic and ridiculous, but if I wasn't seeing it with my own soul and feeling it, I wouldn't believe it either. But they were. They were reassuring me that I had not failed. Not yet at least. But they were there for me. I had their support. I had not failed yet and I would not!

I didn't know that for sure, but I wanted it to be true. I would not fail yet. I still had a chance to over come him. Once I arrived, I would be there first. I would show him who was boss. But not only that! I would show him that people like him are not wanted and will not be tolerated by people like me, Bob, Sarah and everyone else!

You wouldn't believe what a relief that was. The sense that I was not alone. It was almost overwhelming. It certainly made getting a grip on myself a lot easier. I knew that was what I needed to do. Get a grip. I couldn't afford to face him thinking irrationally, not if I was going to make a stupid mistake as I had when I had turned around back in the warehouse. Another slip like that and I could be dead. I started to ease my temper down, to try and gain some sense of peace. It didn't take me long knowing I had all those people behind me.

When I felt my Self jar to a halt, I waited calmly for the rip to open. I knew it would happen soon and I waited. I would not panic. I would take this logically and intelligently. Well as logically and intelligently as was possible for me.

What I saw beyond this rip was unlike anything I had seen before. It was black and white as it had been on the previous occasions, but this was no warehouse or bus or anything like that. All I could see was what looked to be flying pieces of rock mixed within a background of black. It didn't look the most welcoming of places. But I had no choice but to go through the rift. It was where I was dragged by whatever force was propelling me along the light tunnel.

The sensation of passing through the rip was similar, but once I had made it out the other side, I felt totally weird. But that was the least of my concerns for I found myself standing in the middle of one of those floating pieces of rock. It was more like a platform that hovered in the one spot, though there were those that moved about as I could clearly see by looking in any direction. Floating pieces of debris, stone, dirt. Some flat, others just your average stone shape.

There were walls, however. Not many, but I could see them. Blood red and glowing, which was often the case in this reality. They were very much rocky substances with large jagged edges jutting out here and there. As for where they came from below and disappeared to above, I could not say. Firstly there was no way I was going to look over the edge of this platform. What if I fell? And what if there was no bottom to this cavern. I would be totally stuffed. Besides, looking down would only make me feel sick and I would lose any sense of control I had regained back in the light tunnel.

But that was what One wanted. That was why I was here. He had brought me here, just as he had brought me to those warehouses. I don't know how I knew that, but it was just coincidental that every time I arrived, it was a place I would be easy prey for him. So, if he wasn't causing the teleporting, he was definitely controlling where we arrived. But how? How could he possibly do that without either knowing how we teleported or if we actually were? I mean, what happens if we decide not to touch the glowing ball of light, though I didn't have a choice last time as it appeared right in front of me. Would it suck us in or would we just not be teleported? There were so many unanswered questions but that was because no one seemed to know any of those answers I am looking for.

All of a sudden, I wasn't alone. It had only been a number of seconds since I arrived. Time I should have spent working out what the hell to do, but wasted on trying to get my bearings and thinking about all that crap.

He had come through, but I didn't know where. I couldn't see him. That wasn't to say I couldn't hear him, however. He was below me. I knew that. It sounded as if he was scrabbling on the rock.

Looking at the average size of the platforms, however, it seemed highly probable that he hadn't shrunken down to a more manageable size and had passed through as the giant I had been threatened by in my reality. But the size of these rocks, the average diameter of each was about five foot. He would have had no chance of staying on.

The scrabbling disappeared and all that was left was silence. Nothing made a noise. All I could hear was my breathing, though that wasn't too loud.

I looked around for somewhere to go, somewhere to jump to safety, even a way out of this horrid place. I wasn't too impressed with the idea of standing around on floating rocks in the middle of some endless pit of darkness for the eight or sixteen hour stay I had ahead of me.

Fortunately, there were a number of platforms within jumping distance; some would mean jumping down a level as I could just see their edges beyond the edge of my own rock. One I would probably be able to jump up and grab the side of, hopefully pulling myself up if I was strong enough, though I didn't like my chances. And what if these platforms didn't adjust to your weight. What if they tilted with every little weight transferral?

I decided to test that idea. I stepped outwards; putting my legs apart and slowly tested my theory by moving my weight between my two legs. Steady as a rock, which seemed logical, though it was flying.

Other than those two platforms, I was stuck between leaping a huge gap to reach one or jump onto one that would pass by sooner or later.

So none of my options were comforting. The safest took me downward toward One, where ever he was. So what can I do?

"Very appropriate, don't you think?"

It was One, of course. I wasn't sure exactly what he was talking about, but I was guessing he was referring to my fear of heights. Knowledge that must have been given to him by Grekon. Even if that wasn't the case, I wasn't going to answer him. If I did I would give away my position. As far as I knew, he had just as much of an idea of where I was than I did of him. Probably me more so than him as I had heard his arrival. Right now, this was a stale mate. Until one of us made a move, we would be stuck in this place for ages.

Thing is, where was Sarah? And were there going to be any other people who travelled back and forth turning up now or later.

Hang on. This was obviously my cycle. That was why he chose me. He wanted to come back on my cycle, which was the same as Sarah's, but that meant the others wouldn't be here yet. Or maybe they were, but not anywhere nearby. Not very comforting.

I really have to get away from this pathetic idea that anything about this place or my predicament would be comforting. It was more likely to be horrifying or debilitating. That was why I had to keep a calm disposition. And I was going to do that. For all I know, those people that turned up in the light tunnel may be watching me now, unable to help me, but watching none the less to see what the fate of their reality will be. A bit far-fetched, but what have I already learnt about this place? Nothing is impossible.

And that was it. The people here believe that. They live by that. One, Bob, Narelle, Grekon. They all have their special powers because of the lack of confines to logic and reality in this place. So they may not be totally omnipotent in this reality, One and Grekon sure seemed that way back in mine.

That could mean a number of different things. Firstly, Bob and Narelle might be more powerful than they give themselves credit for. Secondly, One may have considerably less power here due to the confines of his own imagination in this reality, making him less than God-like and reverting him back to his natural form.

But the sounds from below didn't sound like that had been the case. So maybe my idea is totally screwed. I don't know. But the implications of it all are enormous.

"I thought you would like it. I was hoping for some constructive criticism and some feedback on what you're feeling right now."

Oh, he was going to try and play the fear card, flush me out by making me terrified of where I was. But I had no need to be. This place wasn't real. Like the landscape around that lake wasn't real. Just a wall. An illusion. This would have to be an illusion too. A very convincing illusion, granted, but still an illusion. Besides, I wasn't scared of him. I was angry. I was tired of being scared of everything. It was time to stand up for myself and the people of this reality and my own. I couldn't let fear stand in my way. I had people supporting me, so I know that whatever happens, they will still be here. But what about him?

Who does he have if things go wrong, or even if they go right? He has no real support. He has little minions he has mind controlled to do his

156

bidding. That is far from real support. I have friends to help me. He has zombies.

Then again, a person like him wouldn't care about friends. He'd probably mind control or sell out on his friends than actually rely on their support.

But he didn't have me. Not yet. He didn't have me scared and I have a feeling, like Grekon, he is very much one for enjoying people's fear. I was not going to give him that satisfaction. He was just going to have to try another card.

"Not answering me, Scott? What's the matter? Fear got your tongue?"

What an egotistical prick. I was right. This guy was far from omnipotent. He thinks he knows everything, but he knows diddley squat. He lacked empathy, courtesy, morals and everything else. But if he wanted to feel that way, wanted to think I was feeling that way, then I would let him.

I could hear him moving below. There was a soft thud. Distant, but noticeable. It sounded like he was trying to make his way along other platforms, looking for me. He had no idea where I was, whether I was up or down.

But if I stayed here, it would just be ridiculous. I would be running away from everything, my responsibilities, a conclusion to the fates of both of these realities. I couldn't do that. I couldn't just leave it all hanging. It had to come to a head sooner or later and it was going to be now or never. Or until one of the other travellers made it across.

I decided now would be as good a time as ever.

"You know, for a supposedly powerful being, you are pretty useless when it comes to people."

"Ah, so you can speak."

"Of course I can. I just didn't think your words deserved a response."

"Or was I right? Had fear knocked the breath out of you?"

"What an obvious and pathetic question. Of course it hadn't. I was just biding my time," I was quite serious when I said that, both in meaning and in delivery. It was going to have to be a level headed conversation from now on. I couldn't risk losing my head over anything.

"A bit harsh in your judgement, are you not?"

"No. Just honest. I find you and your behaviour rather crude and ridiculous. And in all honesty, sad and pitiful."

That got him. The anger in his voice was evident with the snarl that preceded his words, "And I have no interest in what you think. You will soon be dead and I will have no need to worry about you any more."

"You have to find me first and once you've done that, you're going to have a hard time killing me. You're too weak. You've already lost your mind, don't try and lose your life as well. Wasteful. That's all you are. You had so many opportunities to kill me but you wasted them all."

I was just being pretentious. I was allowed to be. Besides, he was.

"You must have me mistaken for some one else. Don't think that you could ever possibly defeat me. You are nothing; a helpless creature. You are nothing compared to me and what I control."

"What you control? You could easily and rightfully be called the King of Sweet F All! Jack Shit would be even more appropriate. Hell, you've got your head stuck so far up your own backside all you can see is the glory of your own faeces, which frankly, I've had enough of your throwing it around. It's about time you found out what you really are and what you mean to the people you think worship you."

His roar was loud. I could almost feel the shock waves from it. I was really getting him riled.

And beside that, he was getting closer. I could hear him scrabbling along rocks and jumping from one platform to another. He must have been getting desperate to get to me. I could just imagine what kind of things he had in mind for me when he killed me. If he killed me. Which he won't.

"Wow, you really have a temper, or was that just flatulence. Something in there isn't healthy if you're that heavy winded."

"You insolent gnat! You do not talk to me this way!"

"Oh, don't I? I don't see you doing anything to stop me."

That was where I made my mistake.

I felt something grab onto me. His big black fingers, not as large as they had been when he was back in the warehouse, but big enough, closed around me, pinning my arms and body in the one spot. I didn't realise he was so close to me. I certainly didn't expect him to be within reaching distance.

I didn't have time to jump or react. He had a firm grasp on me before I knew what was happening. Now, I knew I was in a very difficult position, but I had a few theories up my sleeve I still wanted to try out regarding this place and all of its wacky traits.

Once he had a firm grip, I felt myself lifted off the platform. His head soon rose above the edge of where I was previously standing, his other arm swung up to give him a hold on my rock. I knew now he was standing on the platform below, the one I could have jumped onto if I wanted to.

Well, I couldn't now. I was stuck. But I wasn't without options. It seemed he was going to blow yet another opportunity to kill me.

"Who is the weak one now? Who is the one with the power?"

"Well, it certainly wouldn't be you."

"What?"

He seemed genuinely puzzled.

"So what? You have me in your grasp. So you can crush me with one small squeeze of your hand. Fine. I dare you. Do it. Kill me now. But I wonder. Where is Sarah? Where is my friend who was supposed to have come with me?"

He didn't answer.

"She didn't come through did she? She didn't enter the teleport, or perhaps it didn't open for her."

"Or perhaps I have her somewhere else."

Oh bugger! I didn't think of that.

"And what then? What are your plans for her? If you think she's going to let you run tests, you're sadly mistaken. She doesn't like doctors at the best of times; she's not going to let you with your grubby little paws get within one kilometre of her."

"She has no choice in the matter."

"No? I wouldn't put it past her to have a few things up her sleeve. Besides, she isn't alone here. She has friends here as I do. Friends who don't succumb to you, that would so all in their power to depose you. She will not suffer by yours or anyone else's hand."

"You do not scare me with your idle threats."

"Nor you me."

A look, perhaps a shadow, passed over his face, "You aren't afraid?"

"Frankly, no. I'm just annoyed. I could be sitting home watching television right now, not that there is anything on, but I have a life to live," as I said those words I realised how true they were. I do have a life to live and I haven't been making the most of it. I wanted excitement and now I had it. It would be up to me to keep that excitement going when I got back home again. It was amazing how that simple thought was enough to spur me onward, "and as far as I'm concerned, you aren't a part of it. So why don't you just put me down and piss off."

"I will kill you; that is what I will do!"

Despite the fact his fingers began to tighten slowly, squeezing me, I smiled at him. I didn't know why, but I thought it would be appropriate, especially if what I was about to do would work or not. I was hoping it would, but I had no way of telling.

"I don't think so," I said simply.

With that, I concentrated really hard. This was just a guess, but I focused all my thought and everything else on the concept of my growth. You know, like wishing really hard that you would grow another foot or so. Well, that was what I was trying to do, but more like another fifteen feet or so. I concentrated so hard, I could feel my forehead furrow with strain as I actually willed myself to grow.

He was looking at me as if I was some kind of freak, "What are you doing?"

"Just you wait and see."

But nothing was happening. I was still the same size. Nothing had changed despite all my efforts and willing. Now that was embarrassing. Unless...

"Bob? Mind giving me an extra fifteen feet or so?"

"Who are you talking to?"

"A friend of mine."

"There is no one here."

He was right. Bob hadn't heard me. I was hoping the idea that they were all watching was an accurate one. I was hoping they could see and hear everything that was going on and that Bob, with his ability to adapt and change people's appearance, that he could perhaps make me grow, or seem to grow another fifteen feet. But it wasn't to work like that.

"Just die."

"Wait!"

"What?"

Plan A was scrapped. I had to try something else and what sprang to mind had to be worth a try, even if he didn't grant me it.

I bent down my head and opened my mouth really wide. Sure, his skin looked tough and he was about five times my size, but I was sure that my biting him would either hurt or distract him. I know mozzies that can be distracting when they bite and they are less than one hundredth of my size.

I chomped down really hard on his finger. At first it didn't give, but I felt my teeth sink in. It was a gross experience. I have only bitten someone once before enough to cause blood to start flowing, but I couldn't remember the sensation. But this, this was gross. I felt his blood start to weep into my mouth all warm and wet. I quickly withdrew my mouth as I heard him yell. It wasn't a roar. Just a yell. It had hurt him obviously, but not as much as I had annoyed him earlier. I spat the blood out of my mouth, noting its dark hue. More like black than red. I continued to spit my mouth clean as his fingers relaxed and I managed to weasel an arm free and proceeded to bring my elbow down hard on one of his knuckles.

That was when I felt his fingers start to close in on me. He was squeezing his hand.

The pressure against my ribs grew, not to mention the rest of my body, but with my ribs being compressed, it was getting harder to breath. He could probably have squeezed really tight, really fast and snapped my body, but One obviously wanted mine to be a slow death.

I kept hammering at his knuckle. It wasn't working very well, so I took another bite.

Again, I felt his blood start to weep into my mouth.

That set him off a little more. He began to shake me, back and forth and up and down, like he was trying to shake me free. He had at least stopped squeezing me, but he hadn't let go. I guess what he was trying to do was disorient me or make me feel sick, stopping me from trying to attack.

Everything became a blur as his hand shook really fast. I felt my head flop loosely around, no matter how much I tried to keep it firm and supported. I was worrying it would snap off my neck and I'd be dead with out him ever realising it. Perhaps that would be good for me. A quick death, rather than the slow one he had planned.

I held on to his fingers with my free hand and hoped to God he wouldn't let go and let me go flying through this huge cavern either landing head first on one of the floating rocks or forever falling to my doom, but never making it to the bottom.

He kept it up for only a few seconds, but it was enough to make me feel rather woozy and sick. I was about to throw up, but I knew that wouldn't be a good idea. I was never very good with roller coasters, and this was like the worst you could ever hope to be on. I had no real idea if I would come out of it alive or not. Fortunately, I did. As for what he had planned to do next, I didn't have a clue.

"Hey!"

"Huh," that was both One and I. Someone else was here. I tried to stop my head from swimming and the world from moving, but even through my grogginess, I could tell it was Bob.

X

He was standing on the platform I had the choice of leaping to. Stupid me for not trying earlier. Or was it? If I had, I would simply have been closer to the thing.

"Pick on someone your own size!"

With those words, I felt a really peculiar sensation rip through my body and I knew at once, Bob had heard my call. They could hear what was going on. Bob had come to help and he was granting me exactly what I had asked for.

Every fibre in my body began to burn. Not like in the hot sense of the word, but it was a similar sensation. Like I had worked my muscles too much. I still couldn't see things perfectly as everything was still moving at funny angles, but I could see as well as feel that One's fingers were no longer as big as they were before. But that was the wrong summation. It was me who was no longer as big as I was before. I was growing. It wasn't long before One could no longer hold me. He had been doing his best to squeeze the life out of me when he finally realised what was happening, but whatever magic was doing this was also fighting against him.

I felt my feet touch the ground, but as I watched, I saw the rock I was standing on get further and further away. I could now see One where he stood on his platform. I could see so much more below me. Everything seemed so small as I continued to grow. I don't know how big I was when I stopped, but I knew I was about One's size now.

It was hard work doing the balancing act on the rock. I was worried I would slip over the edge or something, but my feet didn't fit too badly on the rock and I didn't have an annoying tail to worry about.

It took me a moment to adjust, but once I had I turned to look at Bob who was smiling proudly at his handy work. He was standing on one of the rock platforms adjacent to mine.

What One did next, I didn't even see it coming. One moment Bob was standing on the platform all proud and defiant toward One and his evil ways. The next, He was flying backwards toward nothingness.

It took a moment to register the fact that One had just backhanded my friend. And with his exceptional size, I knew it was more than just a pushing blow. I wouldn't have been surprised if many of Bob's bones had been broken or shattered under so much force.

But I couldn't let him fall. I wasn't even sure if he had survived the blow, but I couldn't let him fall. If he was alive, he would keep falling and falling. I couldn't let that happen!

I could already see a path I could run along, hopping these dreadful rock platforms that had become like stepping stones. I was about to start

162

chasing after him when he vanished. There was a flash of light and Bob just wasn't there any more. I could only hope that he had teleported away as he had when he fell down that pit this morning. Then again, it could be their transition to the other side. If they believed in heaven and hell and all that, maybe what I had just seen was how they died. They vanished from reality without a trace. Maybe that was what had happened. I didn't know. It could have been anything. But he was hurt, or dead. One had done it to him. One had caused pain in another life, some one who was generous, trying to find a way to free his people from the tyranny that had just knocked him for six!

That was it!

I looked down at the prick that stood below me. He had a smug little smile on his face as He looked back at me.

It was time that someone wiped that look from his face.

I pulled back my leg and lashed out with it at his horned, devil-like face. It connected square with his nose.

I don't think he even saw it coming.

One reeled back in pain and grabbed at his snout with his hands, managing to stay standing despite the pain.

I got down on my knees and grabbed the back of his head. It was easily within reach. Immediately I felt his hands grasp my wrists, revealing his bloody wet face. I had hurt him pretty bad with my kick. Perhaps broken his nose, but I had broken the skin as well.

He tried to pull me downward, but I wasn't going to let him. Instead, I yanked at his head. Not up as he had obviously prepared for, but forward, toward me.

The rock I was kneeling on shook quite profusely when One's face made contact with it. It had to have hurt, especially hitting his probably broken nose again.

The hands loosened and I pulled my own arms free. This was going to be a difficult fight with us on different levels, but I was determined to win. This guy had caused too much pain and I wasn't going to let him cause any more.

He didn't take as long to recover this time. Instead, One lashed out with his claws. I felt his heavy hand make contact to the side of my knee, but following that, I felt four sharp stabs of pain simultaneously as he drove his nails into the lower part of my thigh. He didn't draw them out, however. He had a hold of me, wrapping his thumb around my knee and holding me in place with his claws.

I yelled with pain, but used it also to my advantage. I lashed out at his head again with a punch. He moved his head to the side, but I managed to lip him on the ear.

He glared up at me with his big green eyes and smiled.

I could see it in his eyes what he planned next.

He jerked his arm backwards and I felt my leg go flying forward, dragging me to the edge of my rock, but that wasn't what hurt. I felt his claws ripping through more of my flesh. He was literally dragging his nails through my muscle and tendon as he pulled me toward him. I let out another howl of pain. It hurt like hell! He was going to rip me to shreds or kill me with the pain, which ever came first, I don't think he cared.

I lunged at the hand that had a hold of my leg and with both of my arms I tried to pry him off. But this guy was proportionally stronger than me. Me with my weak little frame and him with his muscles. We were the same height, but by no means the same strength.

So I did the only thing I think I could. I held his hand and my leg in place, trying to prevent him from doing any more damage. With my other leg, I swung it around so I ended up sitting half on my backside and the other, on my wounded leg. I pulled back with my spare leg and was about to kick at his face again when his other hand lashed out and grabbed my foot!

Damn it!

Fine! He wanted to play dirty? So will I!

I knew it was going to hurt like hell, but it was the only option I had left open to me.

I pushed myself up off my backside with my hands and used my wounded leg, my body and my arms to propel myself forward, over the side of my platform and straight at the bastard that had a hold of me.

There was a horrible tearing sensation in my thigh. I could feel One's claws ripping through it some more. As for how much or how badly, I wasn't sure and I didn't want to know. It hurt, but I was determined to use that pain to help me.

I saw his face coming at me. But not just his face. Those horns of his were going to be one hell of a problem if I wasn't careful.

I reached out for them with my hands and was lucky enough to grab onto them. I don't think One was ready for that because he yelled with surprise. The rest of my body continued forward and downward. I landed smack into One, knocking him off balance. His claws disappeared from my leg and my foot, but I had no idea what he was doing with them.

The next thing I know, we were toppling backward. Well, he was and I was falling on top of him. The problem was that I was about to land on his face and his head wasn't going to land on anything. We were going to keep falling down this massive chasm.

Had I just killed the two of us in my haste?

He was falling off his platform.

I found myself over taking the rest of his body, but with my hold on his horns, I was taking his head with me.

I could see the fear in his eyes. I don't think he would have ever felt that emotion in his life, but it was so clear on his face now. It was amazing to see. Such a strong and arrogant creature, his eyes no longer alight with pride and arrogance, but replaced with such a look of sheer terror.

But I didn't care. Now I was the arrogant one. This guy was going down, and if that meant I went with him, so be it! I pulled myself closer to his face so I could look straight into his eyes.

"You're dead."

I don't know if he heard me as we tumbled over the edge of the platform. I didn't care. I think he got the message.

Or so I thought.

Something flashed in his eyes. The fear seemed to dissolve instantaneously. I felt his arms wrap around my back and pull me toward him, but two could play at that game.

With him pulling me toward him, it was easy for me to wrap my legs around him. Well, one leg anyway. The other was hurting like crazy and I couldn't properly draw it around him and even if I could, I wasn't going to be able to squeeze. The muscles had to be shredded

The other leg, however, was perfectly fine. I hooked myself onto him and squeezed it as I tight as I could. He retaliated by squeezing me toward him. I used my arms and my hold on his horns to lever me away, to push against his pull. But I was losing the battle. So I tried something different. He wasn't going to stop fighting, no matter if we were going to fall or not. He wanted to see me dead. But that just wasn't going to happen.

I let go of one of his horns and felt the pull of his arms begin to take its toll on my remaining arm, but I still had time to act.

I made my hand into a fist and lifting it up, I brought it crashing back down on the side of his head, hitting him square on his ear. I knew that was going to hurt.

His grip on me faltered and I pushed away from him with my arm. Once I was free of his grip, I let go of his horns and grabbed at his arms. I missed the first couple of times as they were flailing out of control, or he was dodging me, I wasn't sure. But once I found a hold, I pulled them together and tried to hold them there with my own hands. I knew it wouldn't hold for long. He was too strong, but I had to make the most of the delay I had caused.

Looking around, I could see so many rock platforms passing by us. We weren't moving particularly fast, but even the idea of trying to grab onto one of them seemed like a bone jarring experience. It would hurt to say the least, but if it meant surviving, I had to try. Beside I was already in agony, what harm could a little more do?

Releasing my leg hold on him, I moved my legs around and up, until I was squatting on his stomach. It was difficult to say the least with him flailing about with his arms, trying to break free from my grasp. He was definitely straining my hands, but he hadn't succeeded in escaping my hold.

That done, I now had a means of propulsion away from his body. It was going to be damn risky, but it was also going to be the difference between life and death.

I looked past One's body to see if I could see any more platforms coming my way. There were a couple, one really soon and one in the distance. I decided to wait and give a better preparation on the second one.

It came speeding toward us. I tightened my grip on One's hands, but it was getting difficult to keep them together. His constant moving of them was making me lose balance, so I pulled back on them, like a brake in a steam train. I pushed against his stomach with my legs and pulled really hard on his arms.

That was until I saw it coming up. My platform. I had to be ready when it came.

I steadied my feet again, subconsciously counting down the seconds until it came. I had to time it right. Not perfectly, but right. If I missed by being to early, I still had a chance of grabbing onto the other side. If I was too late, however, I would have missed the rock and my chance of saving myself.

It was coming. I did my best to ignore One as he squirmed. I don't know if he knew what I was doing, but that wasn't going to bother me. Soon I would be safe and away from him. And he will be dead or forever falling into darkness.

It was time.

I pushed off with my legs and let go of One's hands at the same time, making like a frog and leaping toward salvation. It was zooming up pretty quickly and it was going to hurt when I made contact.

It came sooner than I anticipated. I landed, forearms first on the top of the rock, jarring them and definitely making them prime candidates for bruises. My legs continued downward and past the side of the rock, however and nearly dragged me back into the fall. I grabbed at the opposite edge of this new platform. When my hands made contact I felt the secure rock beneath my fingers. I knew I was safe. I had left him behind. One was doomed to fall forever.

Blood was pumping through my ears. I could hear it now that the air had stopped rushing past. It was more like a rumbling, but I didn't mind. I lay flat on the rock and took a number of deep breaths.

I was safe.

Reality was free.

One had been defeated.

I had only been lying on the rock for a few moments before the noise in my ears started to die down. My heart beat was returning to normal. I was calming down after an exhilarating free fall. Not my most ideal rides, but one I would never forget. But there was something else now, in my ears. I could hear something else. An internal sound. I know that sounds weird, but it was. It wasn't from anywhere in this cavern. It came from within me. You know how you cover your ears and listen to yourself talk. You can hear yourself on the inside. That was what this sounded like. But it was so faint. I strained to hear it. It was difficult to make out for a few moments, but it was getting louder. It was weird. Before I knew what it was, I felt a little disturbed.

Something wasn't right. When it became clearer to me what it was, I knew I was wrong. I was dreadfully wrong. This whole bloody time!

One was doomed. As far as I knew, he was falling to his death below me.

What was in my head was laughter. Laughing in my head, just as Grekon had spoken to me earlier. In my head.

But it wasn't One who was laughing. It couldn't be! Something was way wrong here and I wanted to know what the hell it was. There was more to this… this whole experience. More than just One. I was sure of it.

I felt like everyone was laughing at me. As if I had just fallen for a huge cosmic joke that everyone but me knew.

"What the hell is going on?"

I mouthed it more than said it. I was really getting annoyed. What the hell was I supposed to do?

I sat up.

The laughing in my head continued. Getting louder and louder.

"What!"

Louder. Like it was becoming the same as my thoughts. Merging with them, tainting them. It was getting hard to think clearly. It was starting to drown it all out. I didn't know what the hell was going on! It was more than annoying. It was scary. I didn't know where this laughter was coming from, whose it was or anything. But I wanted it gone. Out of my head. I wanted it out of my head and I wanted out of here. It was getting so loud!

So loud. I couldn't think properly. I was having to shout my thoughts over my head. So loud I felt my head would soon burst. Just loud laughter. Nothing else. Nothing else but laughter and it was really starting to hurt. More than my leg hurt. More than when I cut open my knees. This was hurting from within. Within my head and my mind. Just laughing getting louder and louder still!

"Get out of my head!"

But it wouldn't listen. I grabbed at my ears, trying to block it out, but it was coming from inside. How can you block something on the inside out? It hurt!

What the hell was going on? I just wanted to scream! I wanted to scream and let all the laughter flow out of me. But it wasn't my laughing.

I didn't feel the laugh. It was there and it wasn't nice. It wasn't a nice laugh and I didn't like what they were feeling. It was an evil laugh and it was inside my head! So loud!

"Get out! I'm sick and tired of this! Get out of my head! Get out! Let me out of here! I want out of here! Narelle! Tom! Anyone! I want the hell out of here! This is not a joke anymore! Let me out! Get out! OUT!"

No one was listening. I yelled it so loud. No one heard me. I couldn't even here me! It was so loud! Laughing! Loud! Get out! Not listening! Not! Get out! No!

"Aaargh!"

Y

I awoke on the same rock platform floating through air. I was no longer as big as I was before. I was my normal height. I didn't care. I pushed myself up. It was difficult with my leg being the way it was. But there was surprisingly little blood. Every part of me ached. Everything seemed to throb with pain and I felt so weak.

When I was on my feet again, I looked around, watching, listening.

The laughing was gone. Everything was gone except me, the rock I was standing on and the air.

There were no other platforms. No walls. Just me and the blackness to keep me company. But I could still see. There was light coming from somewhere, but no where I could distinguish. I was alone.

"Hello?"

My word echoed through the nothingness that was there. Bouncing of the very air.

No matter where I turned, there was nothing. Not a sign of anything or anyone.

"Where are your friends now?"

It was him.

One.

Again, in my head, but no where around me. His voice was so calm, almost soothing. Gone was the anger and ferocity he had always spoken with, as if he were calming an unsettled dog.

"You tell me."

I was too weak to come up with anything witty or stupid.

"Gone. You are alone now," not hostile, just stating facts.

"I know."

"So what will you do now?"

Good question, but too deep. I wasn't in the mood to think about it right now.

"I don't know."

"You haven't won. You can't win."

"I don't care. I just want to go home."

"I'm afraid I can't let you do that."

"Why?"

"I need you here."

"I don't care."

Silence.

"Where are you?" I asked the air.

"I am here."

"Where?"

"Everywhere."

169

"I don't believe you."

"So?"

"Show yourself."

Silence. Nothing stirred.

"Why do you want me?"

"I need you."

"Why?"

"To help me take control."

"Of my home?"

Silence.

Finally, he spoke, "Yes."

"Goodbye."

"What?"

With that, I closed my eyes and walked toward the edge of my platform. I had to drag my injured leg a little but I thought that made the effort all the more real. I had nothing else to do. He had me trapped. I could do nothing. He would use me. Doing nothing was giving up. Failing.

I had already failed this world. I would not fail mine as well.

I would not fail. Not again. Not anymore.

He had no idea what I was doing until I took that final step off the side of the platform.

I didn't want to be here anymore. I didn't want to be anyone's toy, anyone's pawn. But staying here, that was what I was. I would not do that.

I would not give up.

I let the nothingness embrace me, as if I was falling onto the softest of beds. The most comfortable array of pillows. I let it take me, hold me, cradle me as I fell.

"No!"

He was screaming for me. But he could do nothing for me. He could not touch me, control me. I was not his and I never will be. I knew that now.

The air blew past me; it cooled me. I felt so fresh and revived. So free. Free of troubles. Free from evil. Yet at home. At peace. Nothing could touch me now.

And I kept falling. Air blowing past me. Thoughts no longer racing through my mind. My worries left up at the rock. I was calm, collected and happy.

Just falling.

I closed my eyes to allow the sensation envelope me for a moment. I thought of far away places, of my home and my family. I dreamt of warm beaches and cool forests. I dreamt of a beautiful English Moor. So many images drifted in and out of my mind, running like movie reels on the backs of my eyelids.

When I opened them again, I was standing in the middle of a lush green field not unlike the English Moor I had thought of. The lawn looked freshly mown. Trees surrounded this place on all sides and the sun, held high in the deep blue sky gave cover from above.

Everything was clean. Everything was peaceful. But I was not alone.

One was here. He stood only meters away. He looked lost and confused as he glanced around his new surroundings. I had brought him here. This was my place. This was my illusion. No more darkness. No more rocks. No more evil.

This was my ground and here I had control.

"Welcome."

"Where are we?"

"This is mine."

"But... How?"

The realisation struck me. I understood now.

"The same way as you. I couldn't see why if you could do it, why shouldn't I be able to? This reality is so flexible. I made it into what I wanted it to be just as you had made it what you wanted it to be. I tried before, but I was trying too hard, like frantically swatting at a fly, when all it takes is one patient and quick blow. It's quite simple really. Now you are in my reality."

He was scared. Very scared.

"Why?"

"I was tired. Have you ever felt so tired of something, you just finally decide to make a change? I was tired of behaving the way I was. Taking everything as a joke and chancing everything. It was time to take a stand and do what needed to be done. So I did. And here we are."

"What do you want from me?"

"Leave this place. Leave the people of this place alone. They don't want you. You can make your own way of life. But it doesn't need to be with them. If you really want to take control, take control of yourself, your emotions and obsessions. Create a little pocket somewhere to look at how you live. At who you are. If you want real power, learn from who you are and change yourself. Things can be so much easier, so much better if you learn to get along, to cohabit with everyone else. Not to take control of them. That is a lonely life. Don't be such a misery guts. No one likes that either.

"I don't want to fight you. I'm in no mood for it. I just want you to realise that the way you're heading now, it's ridiculous. It'll get you no where. You'll always find adversity. Always find hardship. There is always a better way to live than that. Maybe you should look into it. But until you do, stay away from me, my reality and the people in this one. We don't want anything to do with you and if you decide not to heed my words, I will be back and there is no way in hell I'll be happy about it. So... behave."

To highlight my point, with a quick thought, six sharp rocky spikes erupted out of the ground in a circle pointing toward him. I didn't move. I simply watched him, watched for his reaction, not completely knowing what to expect.

All he did was nod. He had listened to my words. He had thought about it and he had decided.

He raised his head to look at me, his eyes no longer burning green. They were just green. A natural green.

"Okay."

With that, his body began to shimmer, shake and then twist. It was as if someone had stuck a stick in him and begun to stir. His body began to swirl and shrink and rap in on itself until it was no bigger than a basketball. Then a tennis ball. And he vanished. Not a trace of him. I was left alone on my field.

I couldn't help smiling. I had won, for now at least. But it wasn't that. The smile, I mean. I was relieved. It was over. No more running. No more fear. No more pain. For anyone. Now I could go home and relax.

I stood in that field, my head hung, but far from feeling down for minutes. The sun beating down on my neck, the breeze blowing; cooling me down. Everything was wonderful. Everything felt great.

"Are you ready?"

I didn't have to look up. I knew it was Narelle.

"What about Bob?"

"I'm fine. Our power goes a bit further than just clothes, you know."

I looked up and felt the smile on my face broaden. I couldn't help it.

Narelle, Bob, Tom and a few other people stood around in a group a few meters away. They all looked happy. Bob wore his cool tight clothing. Narelle wore the same wedding gown I had seen her in in the tunnel.

"Getting married?"

"Being the King and all, I have certain responsibilities to uphold," Bob explained.

Narelle elbowed him, "We have been planning it for years. I had just gotten attached to the dress."

I just nodded.

"We really appreciate everything, Scott."

"It was nothing, Narelle. Just don't let it happen again."

It was far from tense, but the words weren't coming easily. Like it was hard to say the inevitable good byes. I would miss them. But before I left, I had one more question.

"So, how did you do it? How did you bring me over?"

Bob and Narelle looked at each other and at some of the people surrounding them. Bob answered.

"Some of us have more, well, detailed abilities. We have them to thank for bringing you and your friends. But we needed some help from your side. Maybe you're not as ordinary as you think."

I just nodded.

"Well, I'm ready."

"Thank you again, Scott. If there is ever anything we can do to thank you, don't be afraid to call."

"Call?"

"You'll know," both Narelle and Bob said it together.

With that, two of the individuals that flanked the King and his bride to be started to weave their hands in a series of intricate movements. I knew what was to come next.

The globe of light didn't take long to appear. But before I reached into it to make my final journey through that light tunnel, I had to say it.

"This time, can you just take me home?"

Both of them smiled and nodded.

"Goodbye."

With that, I reached out and touched the glowing ball.

The ride home was very much the same as the others. The flashes, the colours. The images, again, were those of my friends and family. I was going home, where I belonged. And when that rip opened for me to return, I could see they had done as I had asked. It was my lounge room. I was home.

Z

Friday night. Nothing on television. I had been home for two nights without a jump, or any weird occurrence. I had explained it all to Sarah and Morrissey, who now seemed to have grown an attachment for one another, which was predictable. They seemed each other's type, not to be rude or anything. So they were out.

What was left for me to do? Well, I sure as hell wasn't going to mope around the house waiting to be bitten by a bug. I was sick of sitting around home doing bugger all. That was what I usually did. No social life, not fun, no excitement. But that was going to change. It was time to add some spice to my life. It was time to start living!

I looked at my watch. It was six o'clock. Almost time to leave. Had to be there by half past.

I hadn't stopped thinking about what had happened over the last few days. It had already sunk in and settled in the core of my being. An adventure like that wasn't something you could just walk away from, shrug it off, dust your shoulders and say, "Right, what's for breakfast."

I had figured out what had happened at the end though. How I had managed to turn the tables on One?

From the first moment I had gotten there, I had been faced by weird and wacky creatures and situations. Each one seemingly pulled out of a nightmare or fear of my own. The thought of drowning in that sludge filled dungeon. Walking forever in a never ending tunnel. The Australian magpies chasing me. And then there were the heights. The bridge we had to cross, the floating platforms. Each of those things had been something I'd never have even thought of facing. And I did. When I jumped off that platform I had come to an acceptance. Within myself, of myself and I confronted my ultimate fear.

And somehow, just somehow, I was able to turn that back on One. To manipulate the world to represent what One feared the most. His kingdom gone. His servants deserted him. And his power was useless against me. One was now locked in a world created by his own fears, much like the one I had just escaped.

Okay, it is a load of bollocks, but maybe it was true. One could hope.

Anyway, it was time to give a friend a call.

"Yo! Bob! Do you wanna come over and play?"

Laughing. Not inside my head, this time. It came from absolutely no where at first. Then the ball appeared. That shiny, glowing ball. And in a matter of seconds, Bob and Narelle were standing in my lounge room.

"Howdy!" I almost yelped in a mix of anticipation and delight to see them again.

We skipped all the rest of the formal hellos and things. I was actually in a hurry.

"You ready?"

"Are you sure I look okay?"

That was Narelle. Worried that the gorgeous black dress she had conjured up for herself was inadequate.

"You look stunning!"

"I told you," Bob said. Obviously they'd been through this earlier.

"So, who's the lucky girl then?"

"Geez, you're quick off the mark, Narelle."

"Just curious who won my little Cutie over," She smiled.

She was still calling me Cutie. Who was I to complain?

"A friend from uni. I've been meaning to ask her out for ages, but I never found the time." I wanted to add: "or the confidence."

Both Bob and Narelle seemed to have read my mind anyway as they both nodded, tiny smirks appearing on their faces.

Who was I to try and lie to royalty? I checked my pockets for my wallet and my keys. Finding them in place I asked my guests from the other reality, "Well, where shall we go?"

Bob wrapped his arm around my shoulders and gave me a sly wink, "You're going to love it."

Narelle wriggled her own arm around my waste from the other side, "Shh. Now that, my big nosed boy, is a surprise."

www.ingramcontent.com/pod-product-compliance
Lightning Source LLC
Chambersburg PA
CBHW050744250626
47155CB00005B/1920